THROUGH A MIRROR, DARKLY

KEVIN LUCIA

PROOFREAD BY:
LEX JONES, LINZI OSBURN, AND
HASSE CHACON

Crystal Lake Publishing
www.CrystalLakePub.com

FOR THE LATE CHARLES L. GRANT:

Thank you for your gift of quiet shadows, which still linger with us, like the caress of a long-past autumn breeze.

Copyright acknowledgements

And I Watered It, With Tears was originally published in serial format in Lamplight Magazine, 2012-2013.

PRAISE FOR KEVIN LUCIA

"*Literate and stylish, yet fast-paced and accessible,* Through a Mirror, Darkly *is a thoroughly engrossing read. Kevin Lucia is a major new voice in the horror genre.*"
Jonathan Janz, acclaimed author of
The Nightmare Girl* and *House of Skin

"*Kevin Lucia writes my favorite kind of horror, the kind not enough folks are writing anymore. The scares in* Through A Mirror Darkly *(and there is no shortage of them), are of the subtle breed, the sort you don't see coming until they're already upon you and you realize it's too late to catch a breath. Charles L. Grant excelled with this type of creeping, insidious terror. So too, does Lucia, and if this collection is any indication, we're going to be enjoying his wonderfully quiet horror for decades to come.*"
Kealan Patrick Burke, Bram Stoker Award®-winning author of The Turtle Boy and Kin

"Through a Mirror, Darkly *serves as Kevin Lucia's early-warning system to the horror filed; I'm approaching fast, and I will fall on your heads like a curse from Heaven . . . and oh, yes—it's too late to take shelter. Brace yourselves, folks, with this collection, Lucia will subtract a pound of flesh and then some from your nervous system.*"
Gary A. Braunbeck, Bram Stoker Award®-winner of To Each Their Darkness, Destinations Unknown, and the forthcoming A Cracked and Broken Path

"The Time has come," the Walrus said,
"to talk of many things."

—*Through the Looking Glass,* and
What Alice Found There
Lewis Carroll

"The Thing, they whisper, wears a silken mask
Of yellow, whose queer folds appear to hide
A face not of this earth, though none dares ask
just what those features are, which bulge inside."

—H. P. Lovecraft

ARCANE DELIGHTS

Main Street
Clifton Heights
September 15th, Friday

IT'S TWO IN the afternoon when Cassie Tillman emerges from the store's back room, wiping her hands and saying, "That's it, boss. Sorted through all the recent donations except the box on your desk. Anything else? If not, I'm calling it quits. Got the graveyard shift at the Home tonight and the evening shift at The 'Lark tomorrow."

I look up from sorting tax-deduction forms at the front counter and smile. *Boss.* Cassie's only worked here for two weeks, but she's already tossing around 'boss' casually. Hell, she acts as if *she*'s in charge, half the time.

Which, of course, is one of the reasons I hired her on the spot when she inquired about my 'Help Wanted' sign a month ago. Her confidence radiates from her like ambient energy. She's at ease in her own skin, content to be herself, uncaring of what others think of her . . . yet, she has class. She's polite, friendly and respectful. Maybe a little sarcastic, but she toes the line. She takes the initiative quickly but smoothly. Since she started I've never once felt as if she's stepped on my toes. She's smart, capable and hardworking, savvy to boot . . . and she knows it. But, she doesn't feel the need to rub anyone's nose in it.

If she wasn't already working two other part-time jobs

3

in addition to *this* part-time gig, I'd have offered her a full-time position as assistant manager. I've danced around the topic a few times, wondering why she works three part-time jobs instead of settling into one full-time job with benefits. Her only answer has been a smiling, cryptic: "Naw. I get bored easy." I haven't pressed the matter, figuring I'd rather have her part-time than not at all.

Don't know how she manages it. She does excellent work at all three jobs. Here at Arcane Delights; at The Skylark Diner she's one of the most reliable waitresses, and Dad liked her best as he languished in the grip of Alzheimer's at the Webb County Assisted Living Home before passing away four months ago.

I've often wondered if she wanted to work here because of her close relationship with Dad (as his nurse), drawn by the chance of helping revive his passion. This is all speculation, however. I've never asked her and we've never spoken much of Dad's last days.

I shake my head, smiling wider. "You've been here since ten, helping me reorganize the shelves and sort through donations. Tonight, you'll work the overnight shift at the Home, and tomorrow night wait tables all evening at The Skylark. How the *hell* do you do it?"

She sticks her hands into her pockets, shrugs and grins. With her skater-cut black hair, those dimples, sparkling green eyes and crystal nose-stud, she doesn't look a day over sixteen, though I know she's twenty-four. "What can I say? I eat my Wheaties and my spinach, boss. Plenty of Vitamin D, too."

"You've got a full-time job here, whenever you want," I try again, knowing my offer is futile. "Say the word."

She smile-winces. "Nooo. Full-time job in one place? Told ya already. I get bored easy."

"All right then. Have it your way. Door's always open."
I glance at the tax-deduction forms various book donors
have sent the past few days. "So where'd this last batch of
donations come from?"

"Let's see. Bassler Memorial Library sent over a box of
discards," she says, quickly becoming all-business, "mostly
teen paperback novels from the eighties. All in good shape,
but stamped BASSLER LIBRARY on the leafs, with the
sign-out-cards still pasted in the back. I put those in the
twenty-five cent bin like you said."

"Cool. What was in those UPS boxes dropped off this
morning?"

"A donation from the used bookstore in Binghamton
that closed. Paperbacks Plus? A whole collection of Leisure
Horror paperbacks. Keene, Kenyon, Braunbeck, Ketchum,
Sangiovanni . . . big catch, all brand new copies. How'd you
work *that*?"

I shrug, sorting out the tax forms for Bassler Library
and Paperbacks Plus. "I've known the manager for a while.
Used to go there a lot when I attended Binghamton
University. She was one of the first people I called for
advice when I decided to reopen this place, so when she
learned *her* store owner was dropping the ax, she called
and promised to send me her best stuff. So, great donation,
sucky circumstances."

Cassie snorts. "No doubt."

"What about those two small FedEx boxes?"

"Most recent novels from Samhain Horror."

"Awesome. Those books I bought at the Webb County
Library sale last week?"

"Sorted into general and mystery fiction. Struck the
mother lode with all those Mary Higgins Clark novels."

"We cater to all tastes, miss. Unless you like Twilight,

5

50 Shades of Gray or James Patterson. Folks want drivel, they can drive to Utica."

"Hey. I actually liked Twilight. It wasn't *all* bad."

I offer a smirk of my own. "Right. And James Patterson actually still *writes* all his own novels."

Cassie grins. "You're a literary snob. Aren't you?"

I wave her off, playing the game. "And you my dear are like the rest of your poor, deprived generation: You lack *taste*, Cassie. *Taste*."

"*Oh*." She tilts her head and cocks an eyebrow. "*Taste*. That explains all those trashy Mills & Boon books you have in the Romance section."

I affect a stern expression and point at her. "*Those* are British *first editions*, young whelp. And also Martha Wilkins's favorites, from what I understand. Martha Wilkins, wife of Bob Wilkins, owner of Dooley's Ice Cream and Subs, *and* chairman of the Town Board. Friends in high places, you see."

Cassie crosses her arms. "Ah. And I imagine those Mills & Boon novels take Martha Wilkins to *high* places, indeed."

"*Thanks*. Gonna need brain-bleach to get rid of *that* image."

Cassie chuckles and takes a half-bow. "My pleasure."

I sigh, doing my best to repress images of Martha Wilkins (all three-hundred pounds of her) *enjoying* the latest Mills & Boon novel, say *Midnight in the Desert*, *Midnight in the Summer*, or, predictably, *Midnight in the Harem*. "All right, then. You're free. Nothing coming until Monday morning. Got a shipment of comic books due. The York Book Emporium from Pennsylvania is sending us some of their overstock."

"Cool. Oh, and hey—like I said. There's a box on your desk. Didn't touch it. Thought maybe you'd set it aside special or something."

I frown, confused. "Wait. *What* box?"

Cassie smiles as she waves over her shoulder to the back room, obviously assuming I'm playing the role of distracted-but-well-meaning-shop-owner again. "There's a cardboard box sitting on your desk. I peeked inside. Some old books and other things, like diaries or journals or something, so I left them. Figured you wanted to sort those yourself."

"Huh. Sure you didn't move one of the library sale boxes onto the desk to make room, and then . . . "

" . . . forgot?" Cassie raises an eyebrow. "Really?"

I shrug, feeling sheepish without knowing why, especially since *I'm* Cassie's boss and she works *for* me, not the other way around. "It happens," I offer lamely.

"To you maybe. Not to me. At least, not this time. I only touched the boxes you told me to. Didn't move anything except for those."

I straighten, curious, maybe a little disconcerted.
because that's how it started for Dad
wasn't it?

"Honestly, Cassie, no playing around. When I came in this morning there wasn't a box on the desk." I smile to let her know I'm not offended. "I'll admit my brain slips a few gears now and then . . . "
like Dad's did
before
" . . . but this isn't one of those times. There *wasn't* a box there this morning."

Part of what makes Cassie so unique (and such a good employee) is she knows when things are serious. Seeing my expression, she quits her teasing and glances over her shoulder into the back room, her expression thoughtful. "Huh. Weird. Where'd it come from, then?"

"Anyone stop in while I was on lunch?"

She shakes her head. "Nope. No one I saw, anyway, unless they snuck in during one of my smoke breaks and was the quietest, quickest person ever. And invisible, too. Besides, I'm certain that box has been there since I started at ten. First thing I saw."

"And it's got . . . What? Journals in it? Diaries, or something?"

Cassie shrugs. "Didn't look too close, honestly."

"Hmm. Curiouser and curiouser."

I rub my mouth and tap my nose with a forefinger, thinking. Cassie's a good, hard, honest worker. If she says there's a mystery box sitting on my desk, there is. Me, on the other hand? I'm easily distracted, forgetful, absent-minded, and a step short of addled on my best days.

a lot like Dad

before

So it's possible I received a box of donations at closing yesterday, put them on my desk and forgot. More likely, anyway, than Cassie being wrong, or even more improbably, lying. Soon as I see this mystery box, I'll probably remember exactly where it came from and feel every inch the fool for forgetting.

I smile and wave Cassie off. "Y'know, it's probably a donation that slipped my mind. I'll take care of it. You scram and enjoy your weekend. See you Monday morning?"

She smiles and offers me a jaunty two-fingered salute on her way to the door. "Bright and early, boss."

The door opens, jingling the bell hanging from the door-frame, ushering Cassie into a sunny September afternoon on Main Street. The door closes with another jingle and a click, leaving me in a soft, velvet quiet. I try to resume sorting those tax-deduction forms, but the lure of curiosity (and maybe a touch of unease) proves too much. I lay the paperwork aside and go to investigate this mystery box I don't remember.

The ten years my father owned Arcane Delights (which he started after retiring from All Saints High, ironically the same institution I've recently left), the back room was a study in organized chaos. Homemade shelves set into the walls overflowing with surplus stock, trade-ins, duplicate copies and donations. Stacks of books, comics and magazines ringed the floor in haphazard but strangely symmetrical patterns. Books and comics always littered the big metal desk Dad hardly ever used.

Quite simply, it looked like a "book bomb" detonated. Oddly, while the place appeared cluttered as hell its disorganization also appeared dignified in its own way. It was the store-room embodiment of the slightly clueless but highly learned man my father used to be in life . . . before Alzheimer's took it all away.

Standing in the doorway, gazing at the barely organized chaos of Arcane Delight's back room under *my* watch, I'm proud to say it appears much the same as it used to. After months of fumigating, renovating, ditching old books left to decay after Dad closed his doors, Arcane Delights is almost ready for business.

What started the decay—what I've spent the better part of my summer cleaning and repairing—was one of the worst rainstorms the Adirondacks has seen in recent years. Main Street, Barstow Road and many of the side streets flooded, ruining many homes and businesses. Several stores on Main Street in particular suffered significant water damage, and Arcane Delights was one of them. The back room's ceiling leaked terribly, slowly soaking hundreds of books over the course of the storm, which lasted nearly two days.

Unfortunately Dad never caught on until it was too late, several days after. How did he miss the smell of damp, rotting books? Quite simply, he'd apparently descended much further into his Alzheimer's than any of us suspected. For a whole week after the storm he'd probably opened in the morning, discovered the damage in the back room (drawn there by the faint smell of damp rot), frantically made plans to clean the mess before it ruined the whole store . . .

And then he'd calmly and coolly shut the back room door, locked it, forgot about it, and went on with his business. He'd closed the store (never once going out back), went home, then rediscovered the mess anew the next day only to repeat the whole damn cycle.

This must have gone on until late Friday evening, when I couldn't get him on the phone at home (Mom had passed away a few years before). I called one of his neighbors and asked them to check on him, and if they found the house empty (which they did) to call me back. I then checked the store, where I did indeed find him.

Lying on the floor of the back room.

Curled into a ball. His pants soiled, sobbing uncontrollably while he clutched piles of ruined books to his chest.

He was admitted to the Home the next day, where he wandered through an ever thickening haze of Alzheimer's until he passed away last Spring. For the most part—with the exception of the occasional bursts of unfocused senile rage—his time at the Home was peaceful, if muddled.

THROUGH A MIRROR, DARKLY

To be horribly blunt: He got off lucky. My wife's grandmother has drifted on Alzheimer's vague seas for the past fifteen years at the Veteran's Home in Old Forge. She no longer recognizes anyone, spends every day asleep and can barely feed herself, but her vitals remain steady. Despite numerous close calls, she shows no signs of passing on any time soon.

There but for the grace of God, for sure and for certain.

After his admission to the Home, we emptied the store's back room, filling a dumpster with water-swollen novels, dissolving magazines and comic books. We removed the ruined shelving, ripped up the carpet, did our best to dry things with industrial-strength fans, then locked the place, leaving all the books on the main shelves as they were.

My sister lives downstate near New York City. Though she's a librarian and loves books as much as me, her husband owns a business and they have two little ones to take care of. She'd been in no position to move here and take over a ruined bookstore. At the time *I* was still content (or so I'd desperately lied to myself every single day) teaching high school English to teenagers who mostly didn't give two farts about Hawthorne, Poe, or even Stephen King.

So the store remained closed and forgotten until Dad passed away this past Spring and his will left me everything, declaring *me* the owner of Arcane Delights. By then, I'd hit a threshold for my tolerance of high school education. Dad's will provided us the start-up funds. My wife approved, hoping a break from teaching might make me a little less grumpy (it has). For my part I was ready to trade teaching teenagers who still didn't give two farts for running a small bookstore on a shoe-string budget (and hopefully fitting in some of my own writing somewhere, too).

Looking around, I feel content. Fulfilled. The backroom of Arcane Delights is once again in disorganized splendor. The shelves are stuffed full with donations from various sources and careful purchases (staying within our modest budget) from book distributors. Things are *right* again, and . . .

There, sure enough, is Cassie's mystery box. Sitting plain as day on the big metal desk in the middle of the back room. Cassie's right. Somehow, I must've overlooked it this morning.

It's an ordinary cardboard box. Not mysterious at all. Somehow, when arranging the boxes I wanted Cassie to sort, I must've set it on the desk and then forgot it.

Except a part of me is sure: When I opened the store this morning, that box *wasn't* there.

Approaching it, I briefly wonder if Cassie's having me on. In the short time she's worked here she hasn't proven herself a prankster by any means, but like I've already said: The girl is brimming with confidence. If we'd known each other longer, I wouldn't put it past her . . .

But not this early in the work relationship, I don't think. Thing is, I *can't* make myself believe I left this box here and clean forgot about it.

Of course it occurs to me as I begin sorting through the box's contents: Maybe this is how it started for Dad. A missed car payment here. *How could I have forgotten?* A skipped dentist's appointment there. *Blast if I didn't see that on the calendar last night.* Car keys mislaid, cell phone missing . . . how many small things "slipped his mind" before the end?

But I'm only thirty-five, right? Too young for Alzheimer's or dementia, or to show symptoms.

Aren't I?

Like I always do when my mind skitters around such

thoughts, I veer away, giving them a wide berth, focusing instead on whatever else is at hand. *Anything* else at hand.

Like Dad must've done in the early stages, I'm sure.

Sorting through Cassie's mystery box on my desk, I see she's right. There are several black-leather journals inside. On closer inspection, they appear rather plain. One could buy them in any bookstore. We have a nice selection of them, actually.

Along with the journals are some musty cloth-bound editions of classic literary texts. You know the kind. Books which appear antique and valuable but aren't. Here's a damp, musty-smelling copy of *Benito Cereno*, next to a collection of Shakespeare's plays. Also, several classic editions of Hemingway's novels.

Now here's something interesting. A diary. Upon opening it, a name scrawled on the inside cover grabs my attention: "Jebediah Bassler." Of Bassler House? Bassler Road, and Bassler Memorial Library? *This* is interesting, to say the least.

But flipping through it I find mostly passages written in what appears to be Latin or some other language, maybe some sort of cipher. I've got a friend who's a Linguistics expert doing grant work through Webb County Community College. I close the diary or whatever it is and set it aside, thinking it's right up his alley.

I return my attention to one of the black leather-bound journals, picking it up, running my fingers along its pebbly exterior, wondering where this box came from. Maybe from the York Book Emporium? They deal in oddities like these. Maybe they sent this box ahead of the comics and I overlooked it?

Not likely.

unless you simply received the box, then forgot

Of course, early onset Alzheimer's is rare, accounting for only 5 to 10% of all cases. However, in familial cases, when the Alzheimer's is inherited, the odds raise to 13-20%. Still long odds. I'm forgetful because I'm forgetful, not necessarily because I'm predisposed to Alzheimer's. Even so.

Even so.

However, a quick glance at the box's open flaps assures me it wasn't shipped here. No labels, no addresses, no remnants of shipping tape. Only a plain, ordinary cardboard box with a bunch of old books, a diary or something, and some black leather-bound journals inside.

Curiouser and curiouser.

I open the journal and begin flipping through it, noting pages filled with neat handwriting. Cursive, but easy to read. Wondering what's written inside—and presumably, what's written in the others—I stop on a random page, focus on one paragraph in particular, and a familiar name pops up . . .

Greene's Metal Salvage.

I frown and tap the paragraph, reading a few lines of what appears to be a narrative detailing someone's workday at Greene's Metal Salvage, recognizable as *our* Greene's Metal Salvage, which is on the other side of town by the lumber mill near Black Creek Bridge. Scanning the page further, I catch a reference to "Mr. Jingo's County Fair."

Our Jingo's County Fair? The one which comes every August?

Intrigued, I flip ahead several pages, seeing references to Henry's Drive-In, The Skylark Diner, Yellow Cab, Paddy's Place, The Commons Trailer Park on Bassler Road . . .

I close the journal and again examine its plain, black

leather-bound cover. Stories about Clifton Heights? *Real* stories? Or someone trying their hand at fiction?

Either possibility fascinates me. Especially because I'm ready to begin a classic rite of passage for all small-town authors: the ubiquitous "coming of age novel which is a thinly veiled account of the author's childhood." Whomever this journal belongs to, it's not lost on me how much inspiration these stories could provide, possibly kick-starting my own childhood recollections.

I glance at the clock on the wall. It's only two-thirty in the afternoon. Things are put away enough for now. The Grand Reopening of Arcane Delights is still a week off. I don't have any more shipments coming in until those comics Monday morning. Abby and the kids are spending the day at Raedeker Park Zoo with some other mothers and their kids, I've got a few hours to kill, and something of an enigma on my hands. Which, suddenly, I feel compelled to investigate. I'm intellectually curious in a way I haven't been for quite a while. Also?

Maybe a little . . . nervous.

Frightened?

Which is silly. Whatever is written in here is harmless, surely. That's what I tell myself, anyway, as I take a seat and kick up my feet next to Cassie's Mystery Box.

It's a journal filled with stories.

What's there to fear?

SUFFER THE CHILDREN COME UNTO ME

1.

HE SHIELDS HIS eyes with his careworn Bible as
he approaches a sandstone hovel on the village's
outskirts. The sun's rays are bouncing off the hovel's tin
roof, casting a harsh glare that stings his eyes. He pushes
on however, despite the sun and the cold unease souring
his guts.

He wants to run away. He knows he *should*, on some
primal level. But he can't. He's come here so many times,
and no matter how hard he tries not to, he knows he'll
come here again.

Because this is where everything changed.

This is where he learned True Evil exists. It's also where
his faith was exposed for a *lie*.

As he approaches the hovel's rectangular entrance, a
darkness oozes toward him like a viscous black slime. Cold
air wafts from the doorway, rippling across his skin,
smelling of death and rotting things.

He steps closer, muttering prayers which sound like
meaningless gibberish, clutching his rosary tight. He hears
the screams. The thrashing body. He hears profanities and
an incomprehensible tongue . . .

go fuck yourself priest!

I know you're out there!

*don't fuck with me, you goddamn ph'nglui mglw'nafh
wgah'nagl fhtagn . . . hastur!*

He tells himself again to run away, to flee . . .

But as always, he steps through the hovel's entrance, into the darkness . . .

And screams.

———— ∞ ————

Monday, 3:00 AM
April 17th, 2007

Father Bill Ward stood before the bathroom sink, holding his trembling hands under the cold water rushing from the tap. He closed his eyes, breathed, and splashed water against his face.

The icy shock awakened him completely. He brushed back his hair, opened his eyes and gazed into the mirror. A haunted face stared back. The shadows under his eyes and the pallor of his skin spoke of how little sleep he'd been getting. His face looked much thinner than a year ago, when he'd first returned from Afghanistan. No surprise, because he hadn't been eating well. Not hungry most days, which was ironic. During his tour he'd wished every day for good, solid American food instead of MREs, but now that he *was* home? He could barely stomach rice or toast, let alone a full meal.

Because his nightmares wouldn't go away.

They didn't come every night, but they troubled his sleep often enough, waking him around 2 or 3 AM. Usually, he was unable to fall back asleep for fear of slipping into another nightmare.

This morning, however, weariness tugged at his mind. Maybe for once he *could* return to sleep. His eyelids fluttered, fatigue sweeping over him . . .

priest!

where's your faith?

damn you!

Father Ward shivered, eyes snapping open. He turned off the sink's faucet and glanced at the clock on the bathroom wall. 3:15. Might as well get ready for school. Have some toast, a cup of coffee and attend to his morning devotions, which felt emptier by the day. He hadn't lost faith in the power of prayer . . . but he was beginning to wonder if anyone was listening to *his*, anymore.

He turned from the mirror to get dressed, ignoring the whisper threatening to drag him to hell.

Because he was already there.

Father Ward sat before his Bible and missal, feeling hollow and frustrated. Today's reading dealt with the importance of charity and a giving heart. A worthy message, it still felt prescribed and detached from the real world.

He grunted, flipped the missal closed and glanced at his watch. 4:15. If he left now and took the back way (to avoid construction on Main Street) he could get to All Saints early. Stacks of essays were waiting on his desk. Also, there was a faculty meeting after school tonight, and his monthly counseling session with Father Thomas. Given his nightmare this morning, he didn't think he should miss that.

He stood from the small table in his kitchen to gather his things.

5:00 AM

Maybe it was the morning's cloying dark, but Father Ward couldn't suppress a slight shiver when he saw it at the intersection of Hollow and Beartown Road.

A school bus.

Idling at the corner.

Its exterior lights blazing in the early morning dark. But the bus was pitch black inside. As he drove past, he couldn't see anyone sitting behind the wheel.

It was only five in the morning.

Awfully early for school buses.

However, a logical explanation surely existed. Maybe the driver lived in the Heights and drove his bus home last night. Now he needed to start earlier than usual. Admittedly, Father Ward hadn't driven to school this way before. Maybe a bus always sat here this time of morning.

He didn't *think* it was an All Saints bus. Most of those didn't leave school until six thirty. However, many of the back roads in the Heights were narrow and slow-going. Maybe those drivers left earlier in order to arrive at school on time.

All these explanations sounded logical. They didn't, however, blunt the vague dread shifting in his belly. Still, he brushed his unease aside. He didn't have the energy to ponder such mysteries this morning.

But curiosity continued to nibble at the edges of his thoughts all the way to school.

———— ⚬⚬ ————

All Saints
5:30

Father Ward's shoes squeaked on tile along the partially lit hall leading to his classroom. At his door, he withdrew his keys, savoring their jingle in the morning silence.

He enjoyed arriving at school early. He'd enjoyed everything about teaching at All Saints. It had been a fine year. He'd nothing but good memories of working with his students, getting to know them, watching them grow and mature. Good, pleasant memories, memories which almost eclipsed *other* memories . . .

The key half-turned.

He stopped and closed his eyes, gripping the cool brass knob. He breathed deep, pushing away the dark thoughts.

He'd become a *good* teacher. God had given him a new purpose here at All Saints. What happened in Afghanistan wasn't his fault. He was only human. He couldn't predict the future. He couldn't have foreseen what happened when . . .

Where's your faith, priest? WHERE?

It wasn't his fault.

DAMN YOU! BE DAMNED AND KNOW I DAMNED YOU!

One more deep breath. Father Ward turned the key and the knob, opening the door. He entered his classroom, hoping he could forget Afghanistan for now, trying to tell himself what happened hadn't been his fault, and only partially succeeding.

6:00 AM

Father Ward was through half a dozen essays when he heard it: the faint squeak of a large vehicle braking, the distant rumble of its idling engine. His classroom was located in the rear of the high school wing. His windows faced the bus parking lot. It sounded as if the noise was coming from there.

He glanced at the wall clock, which read six. Bus drivers wouldn't show for another thirty minutes, along with the custodians. He should be the only one on campus.

A faint sense of unease, like he'd felt this morning when passing that odd bus, returned. He stood from his desk and walked toward the windows.

He heard another squeak.

A high pneumatic hissing.

The rumbling pulled away. By the time he drew the blinds aside and peered into the parking lot, red taillights were slipping out the school's front entrance and down the road.

Father Ward stood and stared for several seconds. On the other side of the parking lot, the elementary wing's sidewalks were empty. Far as he could see, the high school's sidewalks were empty, too, except where the sidewalk rounded to the school's front entrance . . .

A shadow flickered.

Father Ward closed his eyes and rubbed the bridge of his nose. Tired. With the dark slowly brightening to pale dawn, his exhausted eyes had imagined the shadow. That's all.

Even so, he stood there for several minutes. Watching the sidewalk where it bent around the corner, searching for movement or shadows.

He saw nothing.

12:15 PM

Father Ward noticed the new student in his 6th period Catechism class as he took attendance. His class was working on the daily opening exercise explicating a Bible passage he'd written on the white board. In the back row next to the door hunched a slight figure with a scraggly head of hair, hands clasped on his desk.

Father Ward re-checked the class roster on his computer. It showed the usual twenty students, no additions. He frowned, stood and approached the boy.

"Excuse me," he said, "I don't have you on my attendance register. Are you new?"

The boy looked up.

Dark eyes met Father Ward's gaze. A creeping unease filled him as the new student stared at him with a blank expression.

"His name's Maurice, Father Ward. Maurice Leck. Moe for short. He's shadowing me today, visiting All Saints. Might transfer here next year."

Father Ward glanced at the speaker, sitting next to "Moe." Bobby Mavis' parents Eileen and Lee had been no account white trash who'd also run a bargain-rate meth operation from their trailer in the Commons Trailer Park. One day while Bobby was in school, their ramshackle little meth lab exploded. The incident caused enough of a stir to warrant a brief mention on the national news.

In a macabre way, many folks viewed the explosion as a blessing. The Department of Social Services hounded Bobby's parents for years with no success, citing multiple incidents of parental neglect. Despite teachers and counselors' best efforts, it appeared likely Bobby would follow his parents' misbegotten path. The explosion was viewed as much as Providence as it was clumsiness. Free from his parents, Bobby became a ward of the state and was placed in the Boys of Faith Residence Home, located in a stately old Colonial on Clarke Street. Father Ward himself worked the summers there during his seminary years.

All Saints headmaster Father Thomas served on its Board of Directors. Soon after his placement, Bobby Mavis began attending All Saints Elementary. A bright, happy boy, Bobby flourished, a true testament to the good work being done at Boys of Faith.

Father Ward offered what he hoped was a friendly smile. "I see." Back at Maurice. "Do you attend Clifton Heights, then? Or maybe Webb High or Old Forge?"

The boy's wooden face remained expressionless, his gaze distant. "I'm home-schooled," Moe said, "and my father wants more structure in my education."

Father Ward nodded. "Excellent. I hope your father will find the structure you need here. How long will you be shadowing us?"

Maurice blinked and spoke what sounded like a pre-recorded script. "Only today. He'll make a decision by the end of the week."

"Well then. I hope your experience proves fruitful."

Maurice nodded stiffly, staring at him, but he said nothing more. Father Ward nodded back, feeling uneasy and yes, why not admit it?

A little afraid.

Which was foolish. Surely he was only spooked by this morning's nightmare. Surely *that* was the source of his unease. There was nothing to fear from this boy.

Surely.

However, returning to his desk to gather the day's lesson, he didn't like turning his back on the new student. Not one little bit.

3:15 PM

Before heading to the library for the faculty meeting, Father Ward slipped through the main office to the guidance counselor's wing to ask after Maurice Leck.

Usually he received an email from guidance when a prospective student was shadowing his class. He hadn't this time, although he knew the entire school's population was split among only two guidance counselors, making their days hectic. However, it was hardly a crisis. Shadows appeared unannounced in his classes often.

Regardless, after his Catechism class he hadn't been able to shake the sense of cool disdain he'd seen in Maurice's eyes. Much as he hated to admit it, something about the boy bothered him. A twinge in his gut, nothing more . . . but his years of religious service in the military taught him to take such twinges seriously.

He stopped at Elizabeth Hull's office and knocked on the door-frame. Elizabeth, a petite woman with shoulder-length blond hair, glanced up from her computer and smiled. "Father Ward. What's up?"

He leaned against the door-frame. "Got a question. Had a student shadowing Bobby Mavis in my Catechism class today. Didn't get an email."

Elizabeth grimaced. "Sorry. Been getting ready for Advanced Placement tests next week and things have been crazy around here. Totally slipped my mind. Realized it around lunch today." Elizabeth offered him an apologetic grin. "You're not the only one, don't worry. I totally dropped the ball."

Father Ward waved. "No problem. Just curious. He acted . . . oddly."

Elizabeth wrinkled her nose while she clicked her computer's mouse. "Yeah, his situation *is* unusual. His father arranged the visit over the phone but we didn't have our usual introductory face-to-face meeting because he lives out of town—downstate, somewhere—and Maurice is staying with an aunt over in Inlet. So his father called, I ran through all the registration protocols and we arranged the visit." She clicked the mouse once more and said, "Ah. Here it is."

Father Ward moved to her shoulder and read the computer screen. "Maurice Leck. Age fifteen, freshman. Previously home schooled."

Surprisingly, he saw nothing else. "That's it? His father didn't give any reasons for considering All Saints, or for moving his son here?"

"Nope. And this early in the game, with all the privacy policies these days, Father Thomas doesn't let us probe a student's background. If the father calls back after the visit and wants to enroll his son, then we investigate deeper."

She leaned back in her chair and pursed her lips. "How did he strike you? Bit of a cold fish for me. Quiet and distant. Not outright rude, but he sorta acted like . . . " she paused, appearing to search for the correct words, " . . . like he wasn't there."

Father Ward nodded slowly. "Yes. Quietly dismissive. Remote. Like he was going through the motions."

"Yep. As if I was a box on his list to be checked off, nothing more. Could've been talking to a wall, honestly."

"Anyone meet whomever dropped him off this morning?"

Elizabeth frowned. "Now that you mention it . . . I'm not sure. He must've signed in and spoke to someone, because he came to my office wearing a visitor's sticker." She shrugged. "I'll check. Anything comes up, I'll holler."

Father Ward smiled. "Thanks. Now. Any chance you can take my place at the faculty meeting tonight?"

She smirked; suddenly busy shuffling papers on her desk. "You're on your own there, Father. My condolences."

Though he chuckled, a small knot of unease twisted in

his guts. The few answers he'd received only incited new questions. Also, try as he might, Father Ward still couldn't shake the memory of Maurice Leck's cold black eyes.

Thankfully the faculty meeting didn't last long. Father Thomas managed to move things along at a brisk pace. Somehow, they avoided the tedious issue of dress code violations; for once no one complained of untucked shirts, too-short skirts or non-regulation colored socks.

The meeting adjourned at four. Having lasted only forty-five minutes instead of its usual hour and a half, Father Ward had thirty minutes to grade two more essays before heading to Father Thomas's office for his mandatory monthly counseling session.

Father Thomas's office appeared more suited to a college professor than a Headmaster of a Catholic school in the Adirondacks. Everything was polished oak: the desk, bookshelves, and wall-paneling. The two chairs before Father Thomas's desk gleamed of black leather. Books filled the shelves. Having been there many times, Father Ward knew the subjects ranged from Theology, Counseling Practices, Educational Philosophy and World Religions to literary classics. On the wall behind Father Thomas's chair hung the requisite framed degrees and certificates from seminaries and graduate schools, as well as a Certificate of High School Administration.

Despite the decor, the room managed to feel warm and inviting, not stuffy or pretentious. Accompanying the framed degrees were pictures of Father Thomas with former students on graduation night, some of them (judging by hair styles and the gentle progression of Father Thomas's age) going back twenty years. In stark contrast to the weighty literature they housed, knick-knacks lined Father Thomas's two bookshelves from all the institutions he'd attended: Le Moyne, Syracuse, and Binghamton University.

Altogether, Father Thomas's office managed to feel both stately and comfortable, the latter having to do mostly with Father Thomas himself. Standing nearly six foot four with wide shoulders but a trim build, Father Thomas carried himself like an ex-athlete with a quiet grace instead of a fifty-five year old priest. His steel gray hair—thick and wavy—portrayed strength and wisdom, not age. His lined face appeared rugged and weathered, not old.

His eyes glowed an earnest blue. This, more than anything else, gave his office its relaxing warmth. They could, however, cut a person to the quick with one glance. Not coincidentally, All Saints suffered few discipline problems.

Today Father Thomas's eyes were warm and sympathetic, filled with concern as he perched on the edge of his desk, another casual mannerism belying his impressive office. Crossing his arms, Father Thomas regarded him closely and said with no preamble, "So Bill. How's the last month been? Sleeping any better?"

Father Ward shifted, slightly uncomfortable despite the chair's cushion. He opened his mouth, considered lying . . .

But he sighed and admitted, "Not so much. It comes and goes. Some nights, fine. Others—like last night—no."

"Nightmares?"

"Yes."

"Can you describe them?"

Father Ward clenched his hands in his lap, cracking his knuckles. "There's not much to tell. Not any different from the usual. It's always of Afghanistan. I'm part of a detachment providing domestic aide to the locals. There's this sandstone hovel, on the village outskirts. Someone . . . *something* is screaming inside. And, though I *know* I shouldn't go in . . . I do, anyway."

"What happens then?"

He gripped his hands so hard his knuckles ached. "Nothing. Darkness. Then, laughter. Low and cold. The evilest sound I've ever heard. Then, an explosion. And I wake, screaming."

He met Father Thomas's somber gaze, smiling weakly. "Good thing I don't have any roommates. Probably would've scared them all off, by now."

Father Thomas smiled gently in return. "Let's shift our focus. How are things in the classroom? Still running smoothly? I hear nothing but good reports from students and parents."

Father Ward nodded, relaxing. This he could speak genuinely of. "Fine. Great, actually. I've enjoyed working here." He broke into a wry grin. "Teaching high school students has certainly been an eye-opening experience. I'm sure I've learned more from them than they've learned from me. This school year has truly been a blessing. All my students . . . "

He faltered.

Remembering Maurice Leck's cold, dark and empty eyes.

But somehow he pushed on, hardly missing a beat, and if Father Thomas noticed, he didn't show it. " . . . all my students have been a blessing. *Teaching* has been a blessing. I'm thankful to both you and the Diocese for offering me this chance to heal. To rebuild. Especially after what happened."

"You mean your breakdown," Father Thomas said simply and directly, but with compassion. "The nervous breakdown you suffered."

Stated with such simplicity and kindness, Father Ward, perhaps for the first time, felt no shame. "Yes," he breathed. "This year has been restorative, to say the least."

"But not completely."

Father Ward bit his cheek. "No. Still have those dreams, of course. And I'm fine while teaching and hearing confessions at the church. When I'm alone . . . "

"You dwell on it," Father Thomas answered for him. "You wonder if there's anything you could've done differently to save those three soldiers."

Father Ward nodded, swallowing, his throat suddenly tight. "Yes," he rasped. "Also . . . I wonder . . . "

Father Thomas lifted an eyebrow. "What?"

Father Ward looked away. He'd avoided this subject their past several sessions—largely at Father Thomas's insistence, because of how agitated it made him—but he felt compelled to speak of it today, for some reason. "I wonder what I *really* saw in there."

Father Thomas's voice remained level, betraying no recrimination. "How's your . . . obsession been? Been searching the Net for demon lore?"

He shook his head. After Afghanistan, he'd gotten stuck in a rut. Researching demons, their summoning rights, "binding spells" and rites of exorcism. It became an obsession interfering with his duties, ultimately leading to his discharge. "No," he whispered truthfully.

"Sure you want to go into this, then? If you're not ready, it could cause you to regress."

Father Ward looked at Father Thomas, suppressing his fear. "Think so. Yes. The question keeps coming to me, over and over . . . and I think . . . I *know* . . . I have to start dealing with this. If I don't, I'll never put it behind me."

"Indeed." Father Thomas straightened, squaring his shoulders as if readying for an athletic contest. "What do you think you saw in Afghanistan, Father Ward?"

"*EVIL*," he murmured quickly, decisively. "I saw pure, unadulterated, True Evil."

"Of course you did. Insurgents learned of your platoon's movements and were waiting in ambush. They meant to *kill* all of you. And to do so, they'd strapped bombs to a six-year old girl. If that's not evil I don't what is."

Father Ward shook his head, resolution hardening inside. They'd encountered this impasse several times already and each time he'd relented.

Not this time, however.

"There was something else there, Father Thomas. Something *different*. An ephemeral force. A *presence*. Yes, what those men did was evil. Humans are capable of so much evil, born of anger, hatred, jealousy, cruelty, negligence, prejudice, unkindness, pride and greed . . . but what I sensed emanating from her . . . "

He made himself meet Father Thomas's gaze. "It felt bigger. Like a *source*. Also . . . "

Father Thomas shifted his arms, folding his hands at his waist, interested. They'd never gotten this far in their counseling sessions before. "She spoke to you. According to your debriefing this little girl spoke to you. In ways a little girl shouldn't."

where's your faith, priest?

DAMN YOU!

Father Ward barely repressed a shudder. "She was . . . obscene. Profane. Blasphemous. Spoke in a deep, guttural voice. The strange thing was . . . it sounded Arabic, and only knowing basic Arabic, I *shouldn't* have understood it. But I heard the words in English. Well, most of them. Some of it sounded like gibberish. But I still heard it in my head. And the men in the hovel. The insurgents. They may have strapped those bombs to her, may have set things into motion, but they were *not* in control. They were paralyzed with fear, I'm sure of it."

Father Thomas rubbed his chin. "'Set things into motion.' Can you elaborate?"

Father Ward sighed. This was, after all, where his memories grew hazy. "Incense or herbs or something else aromatic was burning in several bowls scattered around the hut. I saw old books. Designs scratched into the floor and on the walls. I couldn't quite tell of what."

"So you believe they . . . "

Father Ward inclined his head. "Invoked a powerful force. Invited something. Offered the little girl to it. I . . . *believe* something was dwelling in her body."

"But consider this, Father Ward: How could such a young, naturally innocent girl deserve *possession*? How could a demon possess an *innocent*?"

Resolve thrummed deep in Father Ward's gut. Setting his jaw, he forced himself to meet Father Thomas's gaze. "You read the report. You know what I said."

"I'd like to hear it from you."

Father Ward exhaled, forcing himself to relax, trying to loosen the tension coiling in his guts. "Dead. She was already dead."

"And you know this . . . how?"

"Her throat had been cut. Blood . . . all over her clothes and the bombs."

"Allowing the demon possession of her body."

Father Ward nodded slowly.

"What do you imagine their plans were?"

He shrugged. "Have the demon march the little girl's

corpse into a crowd? Or right into a group of soldiers. But we happened upon them first, so . . . "

"And after this . . . demon-possessed girl, we'll say . . . shouted obscenities at you, she . . . it . . . "

"Challenged me," Father Ward rasped.

"Excuse me?"

Father Ward swallowed. "It challenged me. Challenged my faith. Challenged the power of God and Christ, the Sovereignty of the Church. It *knew* me. Called me by name. And . . . I failed."

"Failed? You were faced with a little girl strapped with explosives and insurgents bent on your death and the deaths of your escorts. And you believe you failed? The odds, Father Ward. For a moment, consider the odds stacked against you."

He shook his head slowly, understanding how Father Thomas was trying to help . . . but he refused to be swayed. "As I said, the insurgents were no threat. They'd looked paralyzed, weapons pointed at the ground. The only threat lay in what animated the girl's corpse, and when I . . . I tried to banish it . . . I failed. And good men died as a result."

"They'd advanced into the hovel ahead of you. Standard procedure, as I understand. They died protecting you, as was their duty."

Father Thomas folded his arms. "And you were standing nearest the doorway. The explosion threw you ten feet away. You suffered shrapnel lacerations and a grade three concussion. Took you *weeks* to recover. You hardly escaped unscathed."

"But I lived."

Father Thomas grunted. "Survival guilt, nothing more."

Father Ward opened his mouth to protest but stopped at Father Thomas's upraised hand. "I'm not saying you're *consciously* lying. I believe *you* believe what you're saying. But I also believe what's eating away at you most is an age-old question: why *me*? Why did *I* survive?"

The defense he'd been rallying sagged. He closed his eyes and bent his head. Whatever else he believed happened in Afghanistan, Father Thomas was right. It plagued him, hiding in the dark corners of his mind while he conducted his business during the day. Rearing its ugly maw at unexpected times, howling in his nightmares.

Why me?

Why'd I live?

Despite whatever Father Thomas thought, a dread worry nestled in his heart: because It *let* him live.

To *remember*.

And to suffer.

He opened his eyes and stared into his clenching and unclenching hands. "So you think I imagined it? Think it didn't happen the way I remember?"

He looked up and regarded Father Thomas's carefully neutral expression. "You don't believe it was demonic possession, do you?"

Father Thomas paused before answering—perhaps searching for the right words—then said, "I believe you encountered a situation horrible enough to make most grown men fall to their knees. I believe you acted with great courage. I also believe you're suffering under the heavy burden of survivor guilt, which is so common in cases like these. And bearing up under it admirably, all things considered."

"But you don't believe the encounter was demonic in nature."

Father Thomas allowed a small shrug. "I don't believe we can know *anything* for sure, with the scant evidence we

36

have. Also, I don't need to remind you the Catholic Church has developed strict measures in regards to evaluating demonic possession. Not to overstate the obvious, but you aren't trained in those measures. Wartime conditions begat some amount of papal leniency, but in civilian life, your exorcism attempt would've been viewed by the Church as an overstepping of your authority."

He looked out the window. "So you don't believe me."

"*Father Ward.*"

Father Thomas's stern tone brought Father Ward's gaze back, like an adult's reprimand commanding a child's attention. When Father Ward met his gaze, however, all he saw in Father Thomas was compassion and sympathy.

"We'll come back to this, but I think for now we should rest. My advice—and my prayer for you, by the way, over this next month—is you'll focus less on the supposed supernatural elements of your experience and more on immediate issues like your *guilt*. You survived neither by mere chance nor by the whims of some evil entity because it wanted you to suffer. You survived because God willed it and because He has more for you to do in this world."

Father Thomas smiled softly. "And my prayer for you, of course, will be that you'll come to *believe* it over the next few weeks. Even if only a little."

5:00 PM

When Father Ward pushed through the school's front doors he was still thinking about his session with Father Thomas, so he barely noticed the lone school bus exiting the parking lot. He caught its number—253—but dismissed it instantly, his attention drawn somewhere else: Bobby

Mavis standing on the curb, staring into space. Arms hanging at his sides, back-pack slumped on the sidewalk at his feet.

Father Ward approached him. "Bobby. Everything okay?"

Bobby said nothing. Worried but unsure why, Father Ward stepped around him, his alarm growing at Bobby's slack features. "Bobby?"

Bobby shuddered and blinked. "Father Ward? Wow. Sorry." The boy yawned and rubbed an eye with his fist. "Geez. Must be tired. Sorry, Father. Did you want something?"

Father Ward shook his head. "Wondering if you were all right, is all."

Bobby chuckled. "Been up late with a History project the past few days. I'm beat."

Father Ward forced a smile, a chill creeping up the back of his neck, though he didn't know why. "I bet. Hear Mr. Monachino's projects are killer. Hey, don't mean to pry . . . but why are you still here? Doesn't the Boys Home usually come around three-thirty?"

Bobby's smile grew wider. "I advanced to Independent status this year. Means I can do more things on my own if I ask ahead. Like walk home from school or catch the Late Bus."

"Which one did you ask for?"

"Late bus."

"Ah." Father Ward searched the boy's eyes for deception but found none. "So what were you doing here on the curb?"

Bobby's smile slowly dissolved into a slight frown. A shadow passed over his face, his eyes becoming unfocused again. "Uh. I don't . . . huh. I sorta don't remember. I must've fuzzed out. All I remember is standing here with

Moe, shooting the breeze with him while he waited for his ride, but . . . "

Bobby shook his head and offered a weak grin. "I must be *really* bushed."

Father Ward grinned in return, hiding his growing unease. "Aren't we all? Hey. You want to go back inside, give the Home a call? You missed the Late Bus."

Bobby cocked his head, puzzled. "Didn't miss it, Father. Late Bus doesn't leave until five-thirty. It's only five. Late Bus isn't back from its regular route yet."

Father Ward opened his mouth. The image of bus 253 flashed through his mind. He glanced at the parking lot, then back at Bobby. "Didn't the Late Bus . . . didn't it just leave? Bus 253?"

Bobby shook his head. "Didn't see any bus 253, Father."

"Huh." Father Ward glanced at the street, then back to Bobby. "Maybe I need some more sleep, too."

Which made sense. He'd woken early after another nightmare, arrived here early to grade essays, also spent all his free periods grading. All before a faculty meeting and a session with Father Thomas. He didn't exactly feel perky. No wonder his senses were playing tricks on him.

but I saw it

bus 253

I saw it

He shrugged and let it go. "Anyway, have a good night. Glad you didn't miss the Late Bus."

Bobby returned Father Ward's forced smile with a much more genuine one. "Me, too. Have a good night, Father. See you tomorrow."

Father Ward nodded, stepped off the curb and walked across the parking lot to his car. His shoes scuffed against

39

blacktop in the silence. A creeping dread nipped his heels the whole way.

———∿∿———

6:00 PM

Father Ward entered his sparse apartment above Chin's Pizza and Wings on Main Street. Offering only meager furnishings, it appeared more like a modern abbot's cell than a home, but it was more than sufficient for his needs.

There was no one he wished to entertain, anyway. His parents moved to Florida after his father retired as pastor of Clifton Heights First Baptist. His father then passed away. His mother now lived in a Florida nursing home. He was an only child and didn't enjoy close relations with any of his cousins. Most of his childhood friends had moved away. Or, he simply hadn't the nerve to contact them.

He *had* seen one old childhood acquaintance, a man named Nate Slocum. Apart from casual greetings, however, he'd made no attempt to interact with him. Besides a shared affinity for old Universal Monster movies, they hadn't much else in common as kids. Hardly something to resume a friendship on after twenty-some years.

Besides.

Father Ward wasn't sure if he could stomach monsters, anymore. Not after what he'd seen . . .

I DAMN YOU!

Where's your faith, priest?

"I don't know," he whispered. "God help me . . . I don't."

He dropped his satchel next to his old recliner. Gazed into the kitchen, where he knew a bottle of wine waited for him. He licked his lips, a troubling thirst aching in his throat.

one glass
just one glass
Instead, he turned and went to his bedroom to study and pray.

2.

Tuesday, 4:00 AM
April 18th

Father Ward opened his eyes. He gasped and somehow managed not to scream.

It wasn't real.

It *wasn't*. If he waited long enough, breathing slowly, the dream's grip would fade and his heart would relax . . .

Somehow he pushed away the nightmare's lingering dread. He glanced at the digital clock on the nightstand. It read 4:00. Time for his morning studies.

He stood slowly. The nightmare was already fading, but he could still hear those profane screams echoing in his ears.

5:15 AM

When Father Ward again approached the intersection of Hollow and Beartown Road, the same bus idled at the corner, its headlights blazing. Curious in spite of his unease, he slowed and peered out the window. Upon closer inspection, the bus itself looked like a much older model. He couldn't see much more. The glare of its headlights only made its interior darker, but as his headlights panned the bus's grill he briefly saw its number . . .

253.

He drove through the intersection. The number fell back under darkness. As Father Ward returned his gaze to Beartown Road, he thought something *moved* in the bus, behind its steering wheel . . .

A rumble behind him.

A diesel engine revving.

Bright light filled his car, headlights of the bus slowly pulling onto Beartown Road behind him.

It saw me, Father Ward thought. *It saw me. I got too close and it saw me.*

Which made no sense. He'd passed through the intersection as this bus was beginning its route. That's all. In fact, glancing at the clock—which read five-fifteen—he was coming through later than yesterday. Five-fifteen was probably when this bus always began its route. It meant nothing at all.

Still, Father Ward couldn't banish the idea that he'd veered too close, foolishly drawing its attention.

Ridiculous.

Ten minutes later, however, the bus was still following at a distance, driving at a moderate pace. Not threatening in the least.

But still.

Father Ward couldn't shake the sensation of it stalking him. That profane voice from his nightmares echoed in his ears . . .

go fuck yourself, priest!

Where's your faith?

"No," he whispered, gripping the wheel so hard his knuckles ached. "No. It's a bus. A BUS."

However, ten minutes later the bus was still following him. In the slowly graying dawn, Father Ward could see in the rear-view mirror the number under the grill, 253. Another glance in the mirror revealed a shadowed profile sitting behind the bus' steering wheel . . .

"My Jesus . . . "

No. I won't *do this. That's a bus back there. Not evil, not a demon, not . . .*

NO.

His lips moved separate from his mind, however, the litany pouring from him in a frenzied rush. "My Jesus, by the sorrows Thou didst suffer in Thine agony in the Garden," he whispered between his teeth, clenching his hands around the wheel, "in Thy scourging and crowning with thorns on the road to Calvary, in Thy crucifixion and death, have mercy on me, deliver me from this . . . "

No, NOT evil!

a bus

He swallowed. Cracked his neck and forced his gaze ahead. "*From* this evil and protect me with your merciful embrace, Father God in Heaven, cast away this evil thing, Father God . . . "

Don't look. Don't look until . . .

"Amen."

Father Ward slowed to a stop as Beartown Road left the countryside and intersected with Allen Road. He closed his eyes and breathed deeply.

Please, God.

Please.

This is ridiculous. The bus will still be there. It's not evil. It's not. *You can't pray away what's* not *evil.*

He licked his lips. Breathed one last time, opened his eyes and gazed into the rearview mirror.

Nothing.

Nothing but miles of empty road.

He sat still, telling himself nothing had happened. No evil had been warded off. The bus simply turned onto a side road and continued on its route.

But he didn't believe it.

God help him, he didn't believe it.

—⁓—

Father Ward pulled off the road and parked his car. He slumped back and stared blankly for several seconds before glancing at the clock on the car stereo. It read 5:30.

Stupid, absolutely stupid.

There's nothing to be afraid of.

He withdrew his TracPhone from his pants pocket and dialed the number for All Saints' Vice Principal, Anne Wasser. The person to call for arranging substitute teachers, she was always awake by now. It rang only twice before she answered.

"Anne Wasser."

Father Ward coughed—exaggerating a little—feigning a raspy voice. "Mrs. Wasser, this is Father Ward. I'm calling in sick. Got a nasty chest cold. I'm supposed to hear confessions tonight at All Saints Church, but sitting in the confessional is one thing, while being on my feet teaching all day . . . "

Mrs. Wasser clucked her tongue. *"No worries, Father. Stay at home and rest. I'll get someone to cover your classes. You have lesson plans in your substitute folder?"*

"Yes," Father Ward said, feeling ashamed and weak.

Where's your faith?

"Everything's set then. Go home, Father. Don't let it trouble you one bit."

"Thank you, Mrs. Wasser. Tell Father Thomas I'll be in tomorrow, regardless of how I'm feeling."

"Please, Father. Take all the time you need. Father Thomas will understand."

"Right. Anyway, thanks Mrs. Wasser. I'll not abuse the time off, promise."

"Bosh. Get well, Father."

"Thank you."

The line clicked and fell silent. Father Ward turned the Tracphone off and tossed it onto the passenger seat next to him. Feeling cowardly, he put his car into drive, pulled into a K-turn and drove back up Beartown Road.

5:45 AM

Despite his best intentions Father Ward stopped the car at the intersection of Beartown and Hollow. With no traffic behind him, he sat there and stared at the pull-off where he'd seen that bus two days in a row. The bus that pulled onto Beartown Road this morning and stalked him like a predator, until he'd prayed it away . . .

Ridiculous.

Where's your faith?

"Dammit," he muttered, indulging in the rare profanity. He wanted to go home to try and stave off the breakdown looming on the horizon. He didn't want this, didn't want to fool with things best left alone . . .

He slapped the wheel. Put the car into drive, turned off Beartown and parked in the pull-off on Hollow.

He killed the engine. Sat back and folded his arms, debating with himself until he indulged in another curse he hadn't used since college. "Fuck it."

Before he understood what he was doing, Father Ward was exiting the car. He shoved his hands into his jacket pockets and stood there in the cool morning air. He examined the area and saw nothing unusual. Thick stands of tall Adirondack pine. Ditches soon to be filled with Black-eyed Susans and milkweed, come summer. Goldenrod and other weeds . . .

There.

On the opposite side of Hollow Road. An opening in the brush. Beyond, a path wound away into the looming darkness. A trail-head, opening into a trail probably leading to a secluded pond or a lake. There were nearly two thousand lakes in the Adirondacks, literally hiding in the middle of nowhere.

However, Father Ward grew up here. He'd never heard of a pond or lake off Hollow Road. Besides, if it were an official Adirondack Trail, there'd be the ubiquitous wooden sign with gold lettering on a blue background, declaring the trail's name and its destination. Especially if it led to a pond or lake. No such sign stood here.

So where did this lead?

Father Ward squeezed his hands into fists. "Go home," he muttered. "Go home and forget it. Leave this alone."

Where's your faith?

Sighing, giving in, Father Ward crossed the road in brisk strides. He plunged into the trail-head, down the path beyond.

———— ∞∞ ————

A quarter of a mile later, past a metal gate marked 'No Trespassing' and a steep decline, the path descended into a clearing. Father Ward entered it, walked to the middle and stood there for several seconds, not nearly as frightened now, for some reason.

because it's daytime

He turned around, examining the clearing. Nothing

appeared amiss. Someone had cleared and raked the ground, also lined the border with smooth white rocks, the kind outlining flower beds all over the Adirondacks. He stopped looking when his gaze fell on an oddly-shaped fire-pit bordered by those same white rocks. He frowned and approached it . . .

Something cold flipped over in his guts.

He knelt next to the fire pit, which he now saw was shaped like a cross. Black soot filled it, along with powdery splinters of white ash.

Like a cross

white-grayish ash

no

Father Ward lurched back and stood on suddenly rubbery legs, weary of this ridiculous Father Brown Detective Routine. This was wood and paper ash. Nothing more. The shape of the fire-pit was coincidental, too. He should leave before someone showed up and wondered why a priest was trespassing on private land.

But as he stumbled up the path to Hollow Road, he couldn't stop glancing over his shoulder.

Local kids. They sneak here occasionally for some beers and hot-dogs.

That's all.

He almost believed that, except for the strange cross-shaped fire pit and the neat circular clearing lined with decorative white rocks . . .

He pushed those thoughts away as he broke from the tree line and walked to his car. He got in, started it and headed home; never quite shaking the fear of bus #253 lurking around every corner, watching, waiting.

For him.

6:15 AM

Father Ward entered his apartment, flicked on the lights, closed the door and sagged against it. Suddenly his fabricated sick call became a reality. A great weariness settled upon him. His shoulders ached. His thighs quivered. He felt like he could sleep the day away.

Sounds like an excellent idea.

Father Ward dropped his satchel and walked across the den to the kitchenette. Once there, he opened the cabinet next to the refrigerator and withdrew a glass tumbler. From the refrigerator, he withdrew a bottle of dandelion wine. He set them both on the counter and gazed at the bottle. He slipped a finger under his clerical collar and undid it.

He'd never been much of a drinker. In college he'd occasionally enjoyed a few casual beers, but maybe because he'd always known seminary lay ahead he'd never over-indulged. Dandelion wine was the only alcoholic beverage he'd ever consumed regularly. Its light, crisp taste favored his palate and didn't sit heavy on the stomach. *Before* coming home from Afghanistan, he'd only drunk it with certain dinners.

Regarding the bottle and glass sitting on his counter, Father Ward felt some mild alarm. He couldn't recall how many bottles he'd consumed in the last few months.

Pushing those fears aside, he uncapped the wine and poured it gently into the tumbler. Its fizz instantly relaxed him. A bad sign, he thought. Regardless, he filled the glass, recapped the bottle, grasped the tumbler and took a sip, savoring the warmth flowing down his throat.

He grabbed the bottle and glass, returned to the den and sat in an old recliner. He set the bottle on the floor next to his feet. Took another sip and closed his eyes, reclining his head against the chair's lumpy headrest.

Where's your faith?

Father Ward drained his glass in one gulp, coughing slightly as the warmth tickled his throat. He sat forward, glancing at the wall clock as he reached for the wine next to his feet. It was only six-thirty in the morning. He was reaching for his second glass.

But it would be his last. He may have taken the day off from school but he was still hearing confessions at church tonight. His shift didn't begin until five, but the last thing he wanted was to fight his way through a hangover all evening. He'd have one more glass. No more.

He was still making those promises four glasses later.

———————————

7:30 PM

Guilt stung Father Ward in the confessional booth at All Saints Church. Maybe it was his failed promise to only drink two glasses of wine. Maybe it was how drinking too much allowed him his first patch of dreamless sleep in months, which produced in him a conflicted elation. No nightmares! But only because he'd consumed more wine than he'd intended. Regardless, as he'd unlocked All Saints and turned on the lights, he tried clearing his head, but he couldn't stop admonishing himself for his drinking.

Also, his mind kept returning to the student who'd shadowed Bobby Mavis yesterday. Maurice Leck. Try as he might, Father Ward couldn't stop thinking about those eyes and the cold *emptiness* he'd seen in them. And his

49

mind kept flitting around bus 253 and it following him down Beartown Road, pacing him . . .

Stalking him.

The door to the adjoining booth creaked open. Someone rustled inside and sat with a whispery sigh. Father Ward straightened, suddenly alert. He hadn't heard the church's front doors open. Nor had he heard anyone walk down the aisle. But now, through the grate, he could see a shadowed profile bowing its head.

And then he smelled damp earth, moist leaves and fresh Adirondack pine wafting through the grate, spiced with the sharp incense usually burning in All Saints. The outdoor smells weren't unpleasant, but in here, coming from the booth next to him . . .

Who was this, carrying these woodland scents with them?

A voice, barely above a whisper: "*Father.*"

Father Ward swallowed and leaned toward the grate. "Y-yes? Can I help you?"

Silence.

Rustling, a body shifting in the confessional. Then: "*Father. Help us. Please.*"

Father Ward frowned. An icy chill ran down his neck, and he shivered despite his best efforts. The voice sounded vaguely masculine, of a boy not much older than twelve or thirteen. Odd, someone so young seeking confession this late at night, all alone.

"Help who, son? Your family? A friend? Are you here alone? Are you in . . . some sort of trouble?"

Labored breathing.

Sandpaper rasps, as if the boy had just finished running a long distance. A deep, wavering breath, then: "*He . . . He takes us. Takes us away. To the Dark Place. And He won't let us go.*"

The cold unease trickling along Father Ward's spine intensified. With a start, he realized how cold it was in the confessional. "My son . . . are you in danger? Has someone hurt you, in any way? And what do you mean by..?"

"*The ones no one wants. We're the ones no one wants. That's why He takes us. No one will notice . . .*"

A sigh.

" *. . . because we're the ones no one wants.*"

Father Ward opened his mouth, but before he could speak the body in the confessional rose. The door slammed open and steps raced away, in what direction Father Ward couldn't tell.

For a moment, he couldn't move.

He just sat there, trembling, unwilling to stand. After several minutes he breathed deeply, gathered himself and stumbled into the eerie stillness of All Saints.

Alone.

He was alone.

Shaking, he pushed the confessional booth's door open and peered inside. The faint scent of damp earth and wet leaves still lingered. Also, he couldn't tell in the dim light, but it appeared as if the bench *had* been sat on. He saw indentations in the cushions . . .

There.

On the floor.

A rosary, crumpled in the corner. Father Ward scooped it up and stood. He spread it in his palm and examined its medallion.

St. Raphael.

Patron saint of policemen. Something tickled his memory, but for the life of him . . .

Steps running away.

To his left.

A side door—leading outdoors, to the rectory—slammed shut. Father Ward was already in motion before he knew what he was doing, walking briskly toward the door, clutching the rosary of St. Raphael tightly. And it was odd; he realized calmly, how unafraid he felt.

He closed the distance in several strides. Grabbed the handle—wincing at how *cold* the brass felt—and jerked the door open. He slipped outside into the cool spring night.

Silence covered everything like a velvet shroud. Before him stood the rectory, where Father Thomas lived. Porch lights burned above the front door but the windows were dark, which was no surprise. Father Thomas was speaking tonight at St. Mary's over in Indian Lake, nearly two hours away. He wouldn't return until after ten.

Father Ward listened to the dark night, trying to discern the rustle of cloth or the scrape of shoes on sidewalk. There was nowhere to hide in the decorative garden between the church and the rectory. However, Father Ward supposed the mystery visitor could've ducked around the back corner and into the woods, or turned left toward Henry Street.

In fact, Father Ward was ready to admit defeat when he caught the smell of something sour, coppery. Something slightly spoiled, floating on the night breeze.

He faced the garden, to the left of the rectory's front walk. The smell came from there. Father Ward clutched the rosary of St. Raphael as he approached the smell. Halfway to the rectory, the stench intensified . . .

At the statue of the Virgin Mary, in her nave.

Small ground-lights cast her face into a haunting, beatific glow. They also highlighted the reddish-brown streaks on her cheeks, illuminating what lay at her bloodied porcelain feet.

A cat.

Or what remained of one. Gutted, its entrails piled at Mary's feet and, he saw, looped around her neck like a profane rosary. Purplish flesh glistened in the groundlights. With an obscene touch, someone had painted Mary's beseeching hands with the cat's blood and viscera.

As Father Ward fought the gorge rising in his throat, Mary's hands dripped, as if fresh from a kill.

8:30 PM

At the entrance of All Saints Church, Father Ward recounted the evening's events to Sheriff Beckmore. He'd known Beckmore since the man served as deputy, when Father Ward was young. Beckmore was ponderous and slow-moving back then. Nothing had changed, past a thicker body, rounder face and a sheriff's star.

"Father, I don't mean any disrespect," Beckmore rumbled, "but let's go over this once more. You were sitting in the confessional when you heard sounds coming from outside, in the direction of the rectory?"

Father Ward nodded, pressing his lips together. He hated withholding information . . . but what was he withholding, exactly? He *might* have heard a boy creep into the confessional next to him? He *thought* he'd heard someone whisper strange things? He'd no proof of anyone actually being there. The rosary he'd found could've easily been dropped any time in the past few days.

He clenched the string of beads in his pocket, felt the rosary's tiny cross and the medallion of St. Raphael, wondering again why it seemed so familiar.

"Yes. I was praying when I heard noises in the garden."

"What time was this, Father?"

"Can't say, for sure. Didn't have a watch, and there aren't any clocks in the sanctuary. I called you . . . "

Beckmore flipped back a few pages in a yellow notepad. "Received your call around 8:00."

"Then it must've happened around 7:45, best I can figure."

Beckmore nodded slowly, licked a thick fingertip and flipped a page. "Outside, you heard footsteps running away, too. But you couldn't tell which direction. Didn't see anyone, either."

Father Ward shrugged. "It's dark out. And I was a bit scatter-brained, a little frightened. I didn't see anyone, and you're right. Couldn't exactly tell which direction I heard them running."

Beckmore huffed a little at 'frightened' but Father Ward ignored him, well aware of what the sheriff must be thinking. He'd gotten used to it. He wondered if everyone in town thought the same: poor jumpy Father Ward, who'd gone to war and was now scared of his own shadow . . .

Of course, no one ever said as much. But he saw it in their eyes, all the same.

Always in the eyes.

"So you found the dead cat after coming out here."

"Yes."

Sheriff Beckmore flipped his notebook shut. Which, more than anything else, spoke volumes. "Well, can't say for sure, but I don't think this is anything too serious."

It was Father Ward's turn to snort. "Other than knowing some kid is running around mutilating animals." *A kid*, he added mentally, *also visiting confessionals and whispering nonsense about Dark Places and someone taking someone away.*

54

Which didn't sound right, at all. Those two things didn't sync, and he couldn't exactly put his finger on *why*.

"Father Ward, I know you're a man of the cloth and all. Supposed to believe the best in everyone. But most kids're bent these days. It's all those damn video games like Grand Theft Auto and the Internet, where they can watch any sick video they want. Stuff messes with their heads."

"I suppose, but . . . "

"Course, kids've *always* been bent," Sheriff Beckmore offered almost gleefully as he stuffed his notepad into his breast pocket. "I remember when I was a deputy, when you were a kid, in '92 or so, someone finding six dead dogs skinned and laid in a row by the railroad tracks on Bassler Road. Same summer, staties got called to Tahawus, back before it was abandoned? Some kids found a bunch of skinned *cats* next to their railroad tracks. Kids get into weird shit, Father. Happens all the time."

Father Ward nodded mutely. Something still didn't make sense.

"Course, we'll investigate. Have one of my deputies drive by next few nights. I'll leave Shackleford here to touch base with Father Thomas when he gets in, and I'll call in the morning. You say he's speaking somewhere?"

"St. Mary's. Indian Lake. Won't be home for another hour or so."

Beckmore nodded, meaty hands on his hips. "Like I said, I'll leave Shackleford here to touch base. I'm sure Father Thomas'll be upset it's happened again, but like I told him first time, hard to keep up with kids 'n their shit these days. Especially in *this* town."

Father Ward said nothing immediately, because it took a moment for the *happened again* to register. When it did, he frowned. "Wait. Are you saying this has happened before?"

Beckmore shrugged and crossed his thick arms over his barrel chest. "Yep. Happened about six years ago. Sort of different, then. A dead rat, hanging around Mary's neck by a string."

"I see. No suspects then, either?"

"Naw. Probably a bunch of kids. We don't have any gang-bangers here or any major junkies or pushers, but our kids wreck their share of mischief. Hell, this week alone, someone found big piles of—uh, *dog* leavings—dumped on the front lawn of First Methodist. Week before, someone wrote gibberish and drew circles with squiggly lines in them all over First Presbyterian's Welcome Sign with red paint."

Father Ward raised his eyebrows. "Sounds like an epidemic."

Sheriff Beckmore shrugged his shoulders. "Whaddya gonna do, right? We can patrol all we want, but I haven't got the manpower or funds to post guards all over town or enforce a curfew. Doubt if I could get the Town Board to approve one. Besides," he waved dismissively, "folks wanna wreck things bad enough, they'll find ways to do it, guards or not. Some people like to destroy shit, for no other reason than they *can*."

Father Ward thought of a sandstone hovel in Afghanistan, shivered and whispered, "Yes. I suppose so."

Fifteen minutes later, Father Ward drove numbly home. He forced himself not to think of the gutted cat and its entrails sprawled at Mary's feet and looped around her neck. He just drove.

When at his apartment, limbs still trembling with fatigue and leftover adrenaline, he undressed in a fog and slipped into bed, falling into an uneasy sleep. And, as he had so often for the past few weeks . . .

He dreamed.

3.

He stands before the looming dark of the sandstone hovel's door. Profanities and gibberish pour forth from the darkness . . .

fuck me priest, fuck me fuck me I know you wanna
motherfucking ph'nglui mglw'nafh wgah'nagl hastur!

. . . but he's here to do Good Works. How can he face himself tomorrow if he can't face *this*, standing firm in his faith?

So he steps into the darkness as always, but instead of being swallowed by the screams he finds himself in his classroom at All Saints. He looks around, gaze sliding over the neatly ordered desks.

This isn't how the dream goes.

Something else is supposed to happen. Something . . .

"He takes us."

He sees a slightly built and gangly boy staring out the window. The boy rasps, "The Faceless Man takes us. The ones no one wants. The Faceless Man drives the black bus and sends His shadows to bring us to Him, and He takes us away. To His court by Lake Hyades, in Carcosa, under black stars."

He steps toward the boy, but he can't say anything. He doesn't have the words.

The boy faces him.

Revealing a thin and pale face with dark, sunken eyes. A face Father Ward *knows* from somewhere.

"He takes us. He's always hungry and is never satisfied and He always comes back. Always."

The boy steps closer, his dark eyes swirling with a dizzying intensity. "He saw you. He saw you, and knows you *know*. He knows you know. He knows you . . ."

———∿∿∿———

Father Ward opened his eyes.

It wasn't real.

His bed. His bedroom. *Those* were real. The dream wasn't. As always, if he waited long enough, the dream's grip would fade . . .

But this was different. That boy, and what he said . . .
the Faceless Man, the dark bus, His shadows
His court near Lake Hyades
in Carcosa, under black stars

Slowly he pushed away the nightmare's lingering dread and glanced at the digital clock on the nightstand.

4:00.

He eased out of bed. The nightmare was already beginning to fade, but the boy he'd seen there still whispered in his ear.

———∿∿∿———

Father Ward sat at his small dining room table, staring with heavy eyes at a page open in Microsoft Word on his iBook. His morning devotions faltered so he'd opened his laptop and tried to write something, *anything*, even if only through stream-of-consciousness thinking. He'd generated random paragraphs of nothing, and then deleted them. Every ten minutes he stood, paced, sat and repeated the cycle. Try as he might, he couldn't shake his dream. Scattered refrains from it echoed in his head over and over . . .

the Faceless Man
motherfucking ph'nglui mglw'nafh wgah'nagl hastur!
His shadows take us to him
to His court near Lake Hyades
under black stars
shadows
His shadows

Something bothered him about those thoughts, but he didn't know what.

He sighed, leaned forward and typed "a Faceless Man took us." He paused, fingertips hovering over the keys. Then he typed, "the Faceless Man takes the ones no one wants."

He sat back and stared at those words, shock running through him: *takes the ones no one wants.*

Last night's mysterious visitor in the confessional.

He takes us
because we're the ones no one wants

"God in Heaven," Father Ward breathed, "what *is* this?"

On a hunch, he minimized Word, opened Google Chrome and typed "missing children," which produced results ranging from stories of kidnappings to runaways. Most of them were national cases, except . . .

A result at the bottom read: "NO NEW LEADS IN ADIRONDACK PARK CASE." Father Ward clicked on it and found himself at the Utica Herald's website, reading an older article detailing the disappearance of Martin Spencer, a freshman from All Saints. He'd apparently gone missing six years ago.

Father Ward stopped reading for a few minutes, his

mind refusing to process the rest. *Martin Spencer. I know that name. How? Something to do with St. Raphael . . .*

He sighed and continued reading. As he did so, a chill crept over his shoulders. Martin Spencer went missing six years ago on the night he'd walked home from All Saints to the *Boys of Faith Residence Home.* He'd recently been granted Independent status . . .

like Bobby Mavis

. . . and requested permission to walk home after school.

like Bobby Mavis, who'd wanted to take the Late Bus
the bus
sitting on the corner of Beartown and Hollow Road

Martin Spencer never made it to Boys of Faith, and was never seen again. According to the article, authorities concluded—as unlikely as it seemed, given his excellent reputation—Spencer ran away.

Father Ward snorted and shook his head. No doubt other authorities joined the search, but he wondered how strongly Sheriff Beckmore pushed the runaway theory. It reeked of his laissez-faire passivity.

Troubled, Father Ward clicked on Martin Spencer's school photo embedded in the article, feeling little surprise when he recognized the boy in his dream as Martin Spencer.

Impossible.

Coincidence.

Father Ward minimized the photo and continued to read the article, which became more surreal with each line. All the academic and social awards Martin won, all the clubs and causes Martin belonged to . . .

like Bobby Mavis

. . . didn't indicate a boy intent on running away. Which,

of course, according to the article, compounded the "tragedy." Father Ward continued to read, not surprised to see Martin was vice-president of the freshman class, on the Honor Roll, member of a group called Letters to Soldiers . . .

Father Ward straightened, his mind screeching to a halt.

Letters to Soldiers.

no, couldn't be

Father Ward pushed away from the kitchen table, stood and walked down the hall toward his small bedroom. There, from under his bed he withdrew a small metal lock-box. Fingers trembling so badly he could hardly hold it, he returned to the kitchen table and sat, gently placing the box next to his laptop as if it were an explosive device. For several seconds he stared at it, once again filled with the urge to forget all this, to leave it alone.

But he couldn't.

Taking a deep breath, he pushed the 'release' button on the box. The lid clicked open, uncomfortably resembling a slit mouth waiting to sever unsuspecting fingers. Pushing his dread fancy aside, Father Ward lifted the lid and opened the box. He stared at its contents for several seconds before rifling through them.

Letters. Postcards. His dog-tags. Notes from casual childhood friends and loved ones, sent to him while he'd served in the military. And, somewhere in here, letters from . . .

His hand shaking, Father Ward pulled out several envelopes held together with a rubber band. He gazed at the address: Father William Ward, Fort Benning. Above his address, LETTERS TO SOLDIERS was carefully written in adolescent block letters. In the upper left corner, the return address.

Martin Spencer.

At the Boys of Faith Residence Home.

The details felt so abruptly clear Father Ward couldn't believe he'd ever forgotten Martin Spencer—then in 8th grade—who'd written him as part of All Saints' "Letters to Soldiers" campaign. He didn't remember every word, but he clearly remembered Martin's desire to become a police officer, to help those in need, to help kids with lives like his.

"Because we're the ones no one wants," Father Ward rasped, holding the packet of letters in trembling hands. He didn't have to read through them, he *knew*. Martin Spencer wrote those words several times, words spoken to *him* in the confessional last night, and in his dreams afterward.

The voice in the confessional *hadn't* been responsible for the desecration last night. An air of quiet, sad desperation had accompanied that voice, clashing with the creeping malice he'd felt in the rectory's garden. The voice in the confessional hadn't been *responsible* for the desecration . . .

It led Father Ward to it.

As a warning?

And there was the rosary with the medal of St. Raphael, the patron saint of policemen, purchased for a few bucks at The Catholic Shop near Fort Benning. A standard rosary, one of thousands like it, most likely mass-produced . . .

And yet he knew, without a shadow of a doubt, the rosary he'd found in the confessional last night was the same one he'd sent to Martin Spencer, the 8th grade boy who'd wanted to be a cop someday, to help kids like him.

Father Ward swallowed. He placed the packet of letters back inside the box. Closed it and sat there, feeling numb.

Too much.

Too much to process, to make sense of. Too much to *believe*.

Where's your faith?

Father Ward took a deep breath and released it, slowly. He closed his laptop, stood on weak legs and headed to shower and change. His mind buzzed with dark thoughts he didn't want to examine right now. He needed to get on the road while it was still early, take the back way to school again and see if bus 253 was waiting on the corner of Beartown and Hollow Road.

No bus. As his headlights splashed over the dark intersection, Father Ward saw nothing except a dark stretch of road winding off into the countryside . . .

that strange clearing shaped like a cross

. . . but he didn't feel any better, because it only made him wonder if the bus had already taken its next passenger.

Bobby Mavis

And when Beartown Road wound toward Allen Road, Father Ward saw what appeared to be a school bus turning the corner. He nudged the gas but by the time he reached the intersection, Allen Road was empty of all vehicles save his.

Shamefully, he felt relieved.

Father Ward tried to spend the hour before school grading more essays but fragments of his nightmares interrupted his thoughts. His mind wandered down dark alleys populated by shifting shadows . . .

His shadows take us to Him

motherfucking ph'nglui mglw'nafh hastur!

This continued for an hour. Reading and re-reading the same essays. Making lame notes in the margins. His attention drifting off and snapping back.

The wall-intercom crackled. Father Thomas said in a scratchy voice, *"Father Ward? Could I see you for a moment?"*

Father Ward glanced at the clock. Fifteen minutes remained before homeroom. "Certainly."

The intercom crackled again. *"Excellent. See you shortly."*

Father Ward glanced down and saw he'd only graded two essays the whole hour.

"Father Ward. Thanks for coming. Glad to see you're feeling better. Won't take too much of your time. Know you've got homeroom in ten minutes."

Father Ward nodded and stepped into Father Thomas's office. Father Thomas sat behind his oak desk, completing paperwork. He smiled at Father Ward, blue eyes warm and kind, as always.

For some reason, Father Ward felt anxious under Father Thomas's gaze. He'd no reason to. Obviously Father Thomas only wanted to know what had happened last night. Still, he felt nervous all the same. He couldn't quite put his finger on *why*, which only made him more nervous.

"So I heard some interesting visitors stopped by the church last night. Deputy Shackleford was strutting around like he was guarding a homicide scene when I returned home from St. Mary's." Father Thomas shook his head, chuckling. "Heaven help us if Shackleford ever succeeds Beckmore as sheriff."

64

Father Ward opened his mouth but forced himself not to spew forth a rush of apologies. "I swear I didn't hear anything, Father Thomas, except a little noise, right before I found . . . it. I . . . "

The lie caught in his throat. He swallowed it, for some reason feeling it would be a mistake to tell Father Thomas of the voice in the confessional and the rosary . . .

he'd sent to Martin Spencer seven years ago

. . . he'd found there.

Father Thomas smiled and waved away his worried apology. "No worries, Father Ward. Clifton Heights certainly suffers its share of young ne'er-do-wells. Nothing you could've done to prevent it, for sure."

Father Ward relaxed slightly. Still, something inside stayed wary. "Sheriff Beckmore said there's been vandalism all over town this last month. Especially at the local churches. They sound like . . . desecrations."

Soon as the word slipped, Father Ward knew he'd committed a crucial mistake.

Father Thomas's smile faded, eyes growing somber. "Desecrations. A necessary rite in summoning a demon. Supposedly."

A rush of instinctual guilt tightened his chest. Father Ward rubbed his temples. "Father Thomas. I'm *not* falling back on old habits. I swear. And I know we've talked of this. The other day, in fact. But . . . isn't this disturbing? All the religious institutions in town vandalized at once?"

Father Thomas sat back in his chair, expression grave. "Disturbing, absolutely. A sign of our youth's general disdain for the sacred. Unusual, given the general decline of our youth? I'm afraid not so much."

Father Ward nodded, letting it go, ashamed he'd felt the need to prove he wasn't again sinking into the obsessions which ended his Army career. But something *was* going on. The dreams. The strange bus. The voice in the confessional last night, the rosary, his unexpected and eerie connection to the long-missing Martin Spencer . . .

All things he couldn't bring himself to share, for fear of finding himself the subject of an unwanted Diocesan review.

Or maybe.

Maybe he didn't want to tell Father Thomas these things for *other* reasons.

"Anything else unusual happen last night? No odd visitors at the church?"

Father Ward smiled broadly, forcing himself to meet Father Thomas's bright blue eyes, which, for the first time, weren't as comforting as usual.

"No," he said, "no one at all."

Bobby Mavis wasn't in Catechism class that afternoon. Worried, Father Ward's attention drifted the rest of the day. Fortunately, however, ninth period was free. Soon as his eighth period class ended he went to the office and confirmed Bobby's absence. He then called Boys of Faith and spoke with the resident manager, a man by the name of Harold Connelly. The news of Bobby's absence came as an unwelcome surprise because Bobby had left for school—walking—at 7:30 AM sharp.

Barely listening to Connelly's reaction, Father Ward thought of the bus he'd seen turning onto Allen Road, which wasn't so far from Clarke Street and Boys of Faith. A ball of icy dread formed in his stomach. He left the main office for the guidance-counseling wing.

Elizabeth Hull glanced up at his knock and smiled. "Afternoon, Father. Feeling better? Heard you were absent yesterday."

Father Ward offered a fake grin. "Better, thanks. Listen, I've got a question. Might sound odd."

Elizabeth pushed back from her desk and spread her hands. "Shoot. I'm a high school guidance counselor at a Catholic School. Odd questions are what I do."

"Do you keep records of visiting shadow students?"

Elizabeth nodded. "Sure do. For recruitment purposes. With the parents' permission we keep their email addresses on file so we can send them our seasonal newsletters and other school updates. For example, say a family initially decides against All Saints. We'll send them our newsletter at the end of the year and over the summer, keeping a point of contact. Maybe they'll change their minds; maybe they won't. But it doesn't cost us a thing to email our newsletters."

Father Ward nodded, wheels turning in his head. "Okay. Here's another. Do you remember a student named Martin Spencer? From six years ago."

Elizabeth frowned, brow wrinkling. "Kristen and I have only worked here five years, but that name . . . I was working at Inlet High six years ago. Didn't he go missing, or something? I remember my sister-in-law freaking about her kids staying out late because of it."

Father Ward pursed his lips, searching carefully for the right words. "Official story is he ran away, but they never solved the case. Here's the weird question. Can you check through our records; see if a prospective student shadowed Martin Spencer . . . "

His shadows take us to Him

" . . . before he went missing?"

Elizabeth shrugged, scooted toward her desk and began typing. "Sure. Six years ago? Information should still be on file. Let me check . . . "

Several seconds filled with clacking keys, and then, "Ah. Here we go. Six years and two days ago, a Hammon Bale shadowed Martin, and . . . "

She frowned and peered closer. "Weird."

Father Ward straightened. "What?"

"Says here Hammon Bale lived with his father downstate, was being home schooled, and he was staying with an aunt in . . . "

"Inlet?"

"Yes," Elizabeth said, "an aunt who was frequently unavailable to answer calls. Also, the reason given for considering All Saints . . . "

"Let me guess. He needed more 'structure' in his education?"

Elizabeth frowned. "Bingo. And I don't have an email address here. Father, what the hell is this?" Her eyes widened at her slip. "Oops. Sorry."

Despite the circumstances, Father Ward chuckled. "Don't worry. It's a perfectly appropriate sentiment." He nodded at the computer screen. "What date did Hammon Bale shadow Martin Spencer?"

Elizabeth checked her laptop. "April 17th."

A cold weight settled onto Father Ward's shoulders. "So this Hammon Bale shadowed Martin Spencer two days before he ran away. And another prospective student—Maurice Leck—with disturbingly similar background information shadowed Bobby Mavis two days ago . . ."

"Oh, God. On the 17th. Is Bobby absent today? You don't think . . . but I mean, how could..?"

Elizabeth met his gaze. "Father. What the *hell* is this?"

Father Ward couldn't say. Half-formed ideas and fears too fantastic to believe swirled in his head until he didn't know anymore what was down and what was up. But he refused to speculate in front of Elizabeth.

"Father," Elizabeth whispered, "should we call the Sheriff?"

Father Ward shook his head. "No. I've got nothing concrete to say."

"Right," Elizabeth breathed, "because maybe it's nothing. I mean, doesn't Boys of Faith have a history of run-aways? No offense, Father, but it *is* a half-way house, so . . ."

Father Ward offered Elizabeth what he hoped was a convincing smile. "Perhaps. Either way, I don't want to raise a big fuss over nothing. Best I think on this, then speak with Father Thomas before calling the Sheriff."

He nodded. "See you tomorrow."

"Sure thing, Father."

He left her office, stomach churning.

Father Ward knocked softly on Father Thomas's open door. Father Thomas paused in typing on his laptop and smiled. "Father Ward. Good afternoon. Wasn't expecting to see you again so soon. Everything all right?"

Father Ward entered the office, warring with himself. What could he possibly say to Father Thomas? How could he ask questions without appearing as if he was fully in the grip of the paranoia which drove him from the military last year? Worse yet . . . could he *trust* Father Thomas?

maybe you can't
because maybe you are *crazy*
again

Father Ward smiled weakly. "Doing fine. I wanted to mention. Bobby Mavis missed school today. He acted preoccupied the last time I spoke to him. I was worried, so I called Boys of Faith. According to them, Bobby left at 7:30 sharp this morning, packed and ready for school. But he never showed."

Father Thomas sagged back into his chair and sighed, his expression grave. "Lord have mercy."

"The man from Boys of Faith," Father Ward barely avoided a cringe at yet another lie, "mentioned another runaway. A Martin Spencer?"

Father Thomas frowned slightly. "Yes. From before your time. Unfortunately, residents run away from Boys of Faith quite often. Given their clientele, it's the nature of the beast. Runaways like Bobby Mavis and Martin Spencer, however, are more dismaying. Boys who've made such great progress, have attained such growth . . . and then, for whatever reason, they regress. Fall off the wagon, so to speak."

Father Ward frowned. "Bobby Mavis was a model student. Never a behavior problem, from what I understand."

Father Thomas steepled his fingers. "No *discipline* problems. Unfortunately in his early years Bobby tried to run away from the Home often. He was classified a 'flight risk' until around the fifth grade. I was so proud when he'd attained Independent Status recently. A sadly premature promotion, apparently."

Father Ward opened his mouth to speak but stopped.

He hated holding things back, feeling as if it was another form of lying. Worse, he hated his sudden wariness of Father Thomas, but the last thing he wanted right now was to be reported back to the Diocese as unfit.

But was that *it*? The only reason for his distrust?

Or was there something . . . more?

"Something else, Father Ward?"

Father Ward swallowed and said, "It's a shame. I held high hopes for Bobby."

Father Thomas nodded, smiling sadly. "As did I. Boys of Faith does tremendous work. I know, personally. My mother left my father when I was seven, for good reason. He wasn't of sound mind. He never recovered from his time in Vietnam, I'm afraid. Which I'm sure you can appreciate."

Father Ward nodded stiffly, somehow keeping his expression neutral. *Wait. What the hell does he mean? Was that a . . . a threat..?*

Unperturbed, Father Thomas continued. "Eventually, circumstances required my removal from his care. For all intents and purposes, I grew up at Boys of Faith. They *saved* me, literally, as they've saved hundreds of boys over the decades. Which is why I eventually petitioned for a seat on their Board of Directors, then became Chairman of the Board. So I have a vested interest, you see. Every boy they lose . . . *I* lose. Suffer the little children to come unto me, as Jesus said. Yes?"

Still reeling from Father Thomas's comment . . .

was that a threat?

. . . Father Ward could only nod.

"Did you know we nearly lost Boys of Faith? Nearly twenty-four years ago this month, right before I joined the Board. So many budget cuts, a lower than usual popularity

71

of the Church at the time, parish giving at an all-time low . . . but I joined the Board and, thanks to a miracle, I helped save that which saved me. A wonderful turnabout, if I do say so."

Father Ward nodded, oddly desperate to be away from Father Thomas and what felt like an uncharacteristic posturing.

"Anyway. I apologize. Gathering wool there, wasn't I? *Was* there anything else? Boys of Faith will deal with Sheriff Beckmore regarding Bobby Mavis. He'll want to question us, of course, and perhaps a few students, but I didn't notice anything amiss with Bobby. Did you?"

There.

Something lurking in Father Thomas's quietly inquisitive gaze. A question. Curiosity. And, also . . . a curious sort of . . .

Hunger.

Father Ward swallowed, and for the second time in fifteen minutes and the third time in one day, lied.

"No. Not at all."

Half an hour later, after a numb and mindless drive home, Father Ward sat at his kitchen table, staring at the open Google Chrome browser on his laptop. An insistent, traitorous thought kept banging against his brain: Father Thomas was *hiding* something.

Ludicrous.

Impossible.

A man who'd played such a crucial role in giving him peace of mind. A man universally respected in the community could be party to . . . what? Kidnapping? Murder. Or . . .

the fire pit
No.
Father Ward refused to speculate on what Father Thomas did or didn't know. He instead turned his focus on the two names of those shadow students, which he suspected were fakes. Something in them rang familiar. If only he could place from where . . .

His hands hovered over the keypad as he realized what he was doing: searching on the 'Net. His paranoia, his obsession, coming back?

No.

This is different. Something is happening. I know it. Besides, I'm only searching some names. Nothing more.

He sighed, typed into Google Chrome's search field "Maurice Leck" and hit ENTER.

The results offered nothing of importance at first glance. Facebook, Twitter and Instagram profiles, all for Maurice Leck, Maurice D. Leck, and several other derivatives. Two or three address-finder services offered to find Maurice Leck for "reasonable" fees. The search results also offered several hits on a Maurice G. Leek, an MD at Georgetown University Hospital.

He stared at the results, thinking. Then it came to him . . .

his name's Maurice, Father Ward

Moe for short

He typed "Moe Leck" and hit ENTER. Google Chrome received several more hits on various social media profiles. Even an old Myspace account for a punk rock band MOLOKSTAR. He was ready to quit when he saw Google's suggestion at the page's head: DID YOU MEAN MOLECH?

"I know that name," Father Ward whispered. He clicked the link. The page refreshed, offering new hits . . .

There it was. The first result. MOLOCH/MOLECH, at

JewishEncyclopedia.com. Father Ward clicked the link and scanned through the first several paragraphs. He read of King Solomon's last days, his reign over Jerusalem and how he created a 'high place for Molech.' Also noted where Molech's 'Ammonite origins' . . . .

The words leaped from the text, stabbing cold little daggers into his guts: Passage through fire. Right of initiation. Appeasement.

And child sacrifice.

He takes us
the Faceless Man takes us
the ones no one wants

The cross-shaped fire pit.

His heart thumping, Father Ward clicked IMAGES along the page's header. Immediately, several different pictures appeared. Paintings and drawings of a great bull-headed figure looming over congregations of supplicants, gigantic hands outstretched, accepting infants from the hands of robed acolytes. Several other pictures depicted stone statues of the same figure cradling small children.

Father Ward swallowed.

Closed his eyes.

And wished desperately he could stop. Wished he could continue as if nothing ever happened, as if he'd never seen that strange dark bus. He wished he'd never met Moe Leck, or heard a voice whispering in the confessional, or found that dead cat . . .

But he couldn't.

The memories of a gaping black doorway to a sandstone hovel in Afghanistan wouldn't let him. So he returned to Google, typed in "Hammon Bale" and clicked SEARCH.

His first results produced nothing but websites for law

firms and LinkedIn business references. He stared at the name, wondering why it bothered him so much, thinking of the transformation of Moe Leck to Molech . . .

He cleared the field and typed 'Hammon Baal.'

The first hit read: "Baal-hammon." Here, his seminary studies proved more useful. He of course recalled the Old Testament contest between God's prophets and Baal's worshipers. Baal was unable to light its sacrifice, while God was able to light a sacrifice drenched in water. He clicked the link, which this time took him to a Wikipedia page.

Scanning the text, Father Ward found a more detailed description of Baal-hammon: a fertility god of sky, harvest and prosperity. Also, similar to Molech, many of Baal-hammon's followers sacrificed their children as burnt offerings.

the cross-shaped fire pit

A fragment from his nightmare came to him, of a little girl screaming obscenities and things in a strange, inhuman tongue . . .

fuck me priest!

go ahead and fuck me!

motherfucking ph'nglui mglw'nafh hastur!

hastur

Father Ward's trembling fingers typed 'hastur.' This produced several images of a spectral figure cloaked in yellow, one of which reclined on a throne made of skulls, and another Wikipedia link. The entry proved vaguer than the others, but no less disturbing.

"Hastur," he whispered. "The Unspeakable One. He Who Shall Not Be Named. Also known as Assautuu, Yastur, H'aztre, or Kazum. Mythical deity said to reside in far off Carcosa, along Lake Hyades. Often associated with gods of pagan and child sacrifice."

takes us to his court
near Lake Hyades, in far off Carcosa
under black stars
Carcosa

Father Ward typed 'Carcosa.' Again, the first link went to a Wikipedia page. He scanned the first few paragraphs, which detailed Carcosa as a fictional lost city written by several 18th century speculative writers. He was skimming the page, ready to dismiss the entry as irrelevant until his eyes snagged on a bit of verse: *The shadows lengthen/In Carcosa.* He stopped scrolling and read the full poem, his skin growing cold with gooseflesh as he did so.

Along the shore the cloud waves break,
The twin suns sink behind the lake,
The shadows lengthen
In Carcosa.
Strange is the night where black stars rise,
And strange moons circle through the skies,
But stranger still is
Lost Carcosa.
Songs that the Hyades shall sing,
Where flap the tatters of the King,
Must die unheard in
Dim Carcosa.
Song of my soul, my voice is dead,
Die thou, unsung, as tears unshed
Shall dry and die in
Lost Carcosa.

The poem, credited to a play he'd never heard of entitled 'The King in Yellow,' made him feel weary and afraid, though he didn't know why. Something about the desolation in its lines, about the emptiness of a lost city in which everything—including soul songs and tears—was dead. And of course, there was his dream, in which Martin Spencer claimed the 'Faceless Man' had taken the 'ones no one wants' to Carcosa.

Father Ward exited Google Chrome and sat at his desk. He stared at nothing, reluctantly fitting pieces together to form an insane puzzle.

Two days ago on his way to school he saw a strange-looking school bus idling on the corner of Beartown and Hollow Road. A bus dark inside.

the Faceless Man drives the black bus

That day a prospective student shadowed Bobby Mavis . . .

sends His shadows to bring us to the bus

. . . a boy named Moe Leck, which was a derivative of an ancient god named Molech or Moloch, which demanded child sacrifice. The next day the bus followed *him* down Beartown Road . . .

stalked

. . . and afterward he'd found a clearing in the woods near the intersection, with its strangely-shaped fire pit. At night he'd dreamed of Martin Spencer . . .

he takes us

the ones no one wants

to His court . . . near Lake Hyades . . . in far off Carcosa

. . . a former resident of the Boys Home who "ran away" six years ago after being shadowed by Hammon Bale, which also was a derivative of the child-consuming god Baal-Hammon. Martin Spencer, who'd written *him* several letters seven years ago as part of a school-sponsored Letters to Soldiers campaign. Martin Spencer, who'd expressed dreams of becoming a policeman someday, to whom Father

Ward sent a rosary with a medal of St. Raphael, patron saint of policemen, a rosary Father found in the confessional the night a voice (his imagination? his paranoia?) whispered to him: *He takes us*. A voice which lead him to the desecration at the foot of Mary in the rectory's garden.

And then today, after everything, Bobby Mavis "ran away." After being shadowed by Moe Leck (Moloch?). Also, on the morning Moe first appeared in class, Father Ward swore he'd heard a bus leaving the empty parking lot. Thought he'd seen a shadow dart around the front of the school. He remembered later that day coming upon Bobby Mavis standing on the school's front sidewalk, dazed and confused, as a bus—number 253—pulled away. A bus Bobby didn't remember seeing. He thought again of bus 253 following him yesterday morning . . .

stalking

he sees you

. . . thought of it turning the corner onto Allen Road this morning . . .

Clarke Street, near where it cuts across Allen Road

And now Bobby Mavis had 'run away.'

253.

Bus number 253. On a whim, Father Ward re-opened Google Chrome and typed in '253.' All he got were various telephone numbers and area codes. He typed in #253 and got the same thing.

Next, he typed 'number 253,' which produced an interesting result third on the list: Numbers 25:3 at biblepedia.com. He clicked the link, which led to a Bible verse from Numbers—chapter twenty-five, verse 3. He cleared his throat and in a thin voice he whispered . . .

"So Israel yoked themselves to Baal of Peor. And the Lord's anger burned against them."

Baal.

Hammon Bale.

Baal Hammon.

He tried one last entry into Google search, "bus number 253" and the first hit referenced a site titled "Adirondack Park Journalism Archives." He clicked on it and found himself staring at a scanned image of a yellowed newspaper article dating back to 1959, about the solving of a child homicide case. A little boy walking home from Clifton Heights Junior High had vanished without a trace. No leads ever surfaced. The case remained unsolved until a fifty-five year old school bus driver, Eli Thomas, swallowed the muzzle of his own shotgun, leaving behind a hastily scrawled note confessing to the rape and murder of the little boy, whose body was never found.

And then Father Ward stopped and stared at the next sentence . . .

. . . *on April 25, 1959, after finishing his route, Eli Thomas killed himself in his school bus—bus number 253—while it sat idling on the corner of Beartown and Hollow Road.*

Numb with disbelief, Father Ward sat back in his chair and closed his eyes.

Impossible.

Outlandish. Fantastic. *Insane.* A child-devouring demon was lurking around Clifton Heights? And somehow it had harnessed the bus in which a pedophile and murderer killed himself over forty years ago?

Ridiculous. He should have his head examined for thinking of it. This was *obviously* the result of his paranoia rearing its ugly head.

But still, that strange bus he'd been seeing looked like a much older model. And Father Ward wondered fearfully what answers he might get if he researched *how* many residents had 'run away' from the Boys Home over the years.

the ones no one wants

Eyes still closed, Father Ward leaned forward and put his face into his hands. He rubbed his forehead with his fingertips. For the sake of speculation, say someone *had* raised a demon demanding child sacrifice in exchange for bounty and good fortune.

Who?

Who would do such a thing? Who possessed the knowledge, and *why?*

A thought clicked in his head, one he didn't want to face, but couldn't avoid.

Father Thomas was hiding something

The bus driver's name was Eli Thomas.

my mother left my father

he wasn't healthy

circumstances . . . required my removal from his care

Eli Thomas.

Father Ward opened his eyes and finished the article. The old cliché of 'blood running cold' didn't feel so old, at all.

The article closed with:

"A single parent, Eli Thomas is survived by a six year old son, Archie Thomas. The son has been remanded by social workers to the Boys of Faith Home in Clifton Heights."

Father Ward exited Google Chrome and closed his laptop gently, fingers trembling.

Archie Thomas.

Father Archibald Thomas, Headmaster at All Saints High, priest at All Saints Church and Chairman of the Board for Boys of Faith Residence Home.

Son of a child molester and murderer.

"And the sins of the father shall be visited upon the sons," he rasped in the silence.

Of course, he didn't believe that completely. Father Thomas was *not* a puppet. No human being was. Despite his own sagging faith, Father Ward still believed in free will. There existed *choice*. There *always* existed choice. If the truth was as insane as it sounded—Father Thomas was dabbling in the occult—it wouldn't be because 'Daddy' had been evil. There must be a reason, a cause . . .

Why?

Why did people pay homage to these . . . beings? Usually for bountiful harvests, for prosperity and gain, short-lived as they may be. The scripture passage he'd found in Numbers chastised God's people for turning to Baal, desperate for immediate deliverance instead of trusting upon the Lord . . .

Father Ward sat straighter in his chair.

we nearly lost Boys of Faith
I joined the Board
I helped save that which saved me

The horrifying question was: How did Father Thomas save Boys of Faith?

Father Ward's mind raced. He possessed no hard or even circumstantial evidence. But in his heart, he knew.

He *knew*.

And he felt betrayed on the deepest of levels. Father Thomas—son of a confessed child murderer and rapist—had made an unholy deal to save Boys of Faith twenty-four years ago, and Bobby Mavis was the next payment.

But one last thing. He needed something more to make this real.

Father Ward sat forward, typed in St. Mary's in Indian

Lake's website, found their phone number. He grabbed his TracPhone from next to the laptop, took a breath and dialed.

A few rings, a click, and then: *"St. Mary's of Indian Lake."*

With false cheer—his insides twisting at yet *more* lies—Father Ward said, "Good evening. This is Father Bennington, from St. John the Evangelist in Binghamton. A relative of one of my parishioners attends your church and heard Father Thomas of All Saints speak there last night. We've been searching for special guests for an upcoming series, and we were wondering what you thought of him?"

A pause, and then the secretary's polite voice. *"I'm sorry . . . but I'm looking at our schedule, and there must be some mistake. There was no special speaker here last night, no Father Thomas."*

"Are you sure? Because your parishioner's cousin was raving . . . "

The secretary's tone sounded firm. *"I'm quite sure. Perhaps you're thinking of St. Mary's in Blue Mountain?"*

Father Ward offered a fake chuckle. "Now, that would be like Dorothea, wouldn't it? Wonderful woman, but easily excited and confused. Thanks for your time, anyway."

"No problem. God bless."

"You, too."

The secretary hung up.

Nauseated to the point of dizziness, Father Ward dropped his TracPhone to the table, put his head into his hands and whispered, "Dear God. Father Thomas. What the *hell* have you done?"

4.

Father Ward spent his childhood and teen years rambling through the Adirondack forests. During his military service, his active upbringing served him well. He'd never considered himself 'combat ready' by any means, but he'd held his own in PT. As a result, he now moved through the night woods with adequate ease.

Along his thigh he held a semi-automatic Springfield .45. He'd quietly and legally purchased it not long after coming home. He'd been practicing regularly since, visiting a firing range in Utica, dressed as a civilian. While he wasn't an expert marksman, he could mostly hit what he aimed at. Also, shooting wasn't exactly foreign to him. He'd grown up in the Adirondacks, after all.

And as he slid past trees and eased over uneven ground, he flexed his grip on the .45, trigger finger lying alongside the barrel. After his call to St. Mary's, he'd gotten the Springfield from its locked box under his bed and loaded it. He'd collected his Tracphone and the rosary he'd found in the confessional, traded his black dress shoes for hiking boots, but left his clerical clothes and collar on. Maybe it was vain—especially considering his recent struggles—but he believed the clothes and the collar stood for something bigger, something more powerful than what he was heading to face. Even if he was weak, what they represented was *not*.

Or so he'd dearly hoped and prayed.

He'd then driven past Beartown's intersection with Hollow and parked at the old abandoned Disbro Farm three miles past it, pulling his car behind the dilapidated barn. Then, with a small flashlight, he'd slowly picked his way through the woods in the general direction of Hollow Road.

He was nearly there.

Light flickered through branches and brush. What would he find over the rise? He still didn't know or understand what he'd uncovered. Father Thomas, a demon-worshiping killer who'd been kidnapping children from the Boys Home, children no one would notice?

the ones no one wants
runaways from Boys of Faith occur quite often
nature of the beast

And he'd been . . . sacrificing them? Or was someone *else* to blame? What of the ghostly bus, stalking him? Same number as the bus Eli Thomas—Father Thomas's *father*—killed himself in, after admitting in a letter to the rape and murder of a child?

suffer the children
come unto me

And here he was, digging into something he didn't understand, investigating something he'd no proof of, without contacting proper authorities.

Father Ward shifted the .45 to his side, muzzle pointed down. He ascended the gradual rise, eventually pausing at the edge of the clearing he'd found yesterday. He raised the Springfield and peered through the trees. Scattered points of light—torches?—flickered in the dark.

Who *could* he contact? Who would believe? Sheriff Beckmore contented himself with wrangling town drunks, investigating vandalism and petty larceny, and handling the occasional domestic abuse. Should he approach Sheriff Beckmore with his fears, he'd be gently humored and told the matter would be investigated. By then, it would be too late for Bobby Mavis.

84

And Father Thomas?

What if Father Thomas wasn't involved with this at all, despite the lie he'd uncovered? He was the diocesan-appointed Headmaster at All Saints High, the priest-superior at All Saints Church. He held considerable influence at the Utica Diocese. Quite simply, Father Thomas could do much more than ignore him. He could remand Father Ward back to the Diocese for review. In short, Father Thomas could set into motion the stripping of his ordination. If, of course, he wasn't involved in this.

Or worse . . . *especially* if he was involved.

To keep Father Ward quiet.

Father Ward braced his shoulder against a tree as he examined the clearing. The torches secured to trees around the clearing bathed the scene with a hazy, surreal glow. Past the torches, he saw nothing but an inky blackness. Despite his best intentions, he couldn't keep from wondering what spirits swirled in the depthless dark.

Why was he doing this? Why take the risk? Why drag his limping faith into something so uncertain, so dangerous . . . and possibly *evil?*

He could tell himself it was because no one would believe him, because he was the only one who cared enough to investigate. He could tell himself that, but he'd be lying, because it was really about what had happened in an Afghani hovel a year ago, when three soldiers died because he'd been afraid. If he let himself believe this *was* happening and it wasn't a manifestation of his guilt, then there was no choice but to face a horrible truth. As a demon profaned a dead little girl a year ago, *here* in his hometown a demon was going to consume another child.

And though his faith was cracked and torn, Father Ward would be *damned* if he'd let it happen again without a fight.

He closed his eyes and pressed his forehead against the tree's rough bark. "Merciful Lord," he breathed, "come alongside me now. I don't deserve You or deserve to serve Your Holy Church. But Bobby Mavis doesn't deserve to die, either."

A deep sigh.

He tightened his grip on the .45. "*Please*. Amen."

He pushed off the tree, opened his eyes, raised the .45, flicked off the safety and stepped through the brush and into the clearing beyond.

"Dear *God*," Father Ward breathed as he moved into the clearing, gripping the .45 so tight his knuckles hurt. His arms and legs trembled at the sight before him. "Holy Mary, pray for us. Dear God in Heaven, shield Your unworthy servant in this hour, pray for us . . ."

He tried to continue, but fear snatched the words away. He swallowed, his heart pounding, lungs thundering. New to the clearing was a statue made of thick tree branches, a stick-figure extending pine-branch arms, like the images of Moloch and Baal he'd seen on the Internet. And lying before the cobbled-together abomination, naked and spread-eagled in the cross-shaped fire pit, lashed to stakes driven into the ground . . . a boy.

Bobby Mavis.

Father Ward tore his gaze away, further examining the scene. Small flickering torches lined the path leading away to Hollow Road. The night lay deathly still. No owls or night birds calling, no wolves howling. No sounds at all save the sighing of the wind and the fluttering whisper of the torches against the night. From what he could tell, they were alone. Which, of course begged the question: Who lit the torches? And how soon before they returned?

For a moment, the silence and the profane tableau overwhelmed Father Ward. His legs quivered. The .45 dropped to his side as his arm went limp. He swayed on his feet. It was Afghanistan all over again. Someone was going to die because of his weak faith . . .

"No," he rasped. "Not again. *Not. Again.*"

Father Ward switched off his flashlight, stuck it into his jacket pocket and withdrew the rosary of St. Raphael. He looped it over his wrist, clutching the medallion in one hand, gripping the .45 in his other, comforted by its cool steel against his skin. Holding it pointed to the side, he approached Bobby Mavis, gaze darting back and forth between him and the torch lit path leading to Hollow Road.

Though it felt like forever, he eventually reached Bobby's side. He knelt, pointing the .45 at the path. With his other hand he clumsily felt the boy's neck, without letting go of the rosary of St. Raphael.

Two fingers found the boy's pulse. Weak, but there. He risked looking down. In the flickering light, Bobby was deathly pale. Slight tremors shook the boy.

He was *alive.* Weakened and sick, but alive. And for him to remain so, Father Ward needed to move him somewhere safe and warm, immediately. He laid a hand on Bobby's forehead, then cupped his face. The boy's eyelids twitched, but he remained unconscious. Too weak? On the verge of a coma? Drugged, perhaps?

Awkwardly, the rosary's medal still dangling from his wrist, he dug into his jacket pocket and withdrew his Tracphone. His heart twisted, however, when he saw that—not surprisingly—this deep in the forest, he got no service.

He was on his own.

Didn't matter. He must get Bobby away from here, now.

Father Ward put his Tracphone away and from the same pocket retrieved a pocketknife. He flicked the blade free, bent over the boy and gently sawed at the bonds holding Bobby's wrists to the stakes pounded into the ground.

After several seconds of awkward cutting, trying not to slash the boy's wrists, the ties fell away. When he shifted near Bobby's head to work on the other wrist, Father Ward couldn't help but stop and stare at what had been slashed into Bobby's chest.

Bile rose at the sight. The cuts were shallow and would eventually heal, but Father Ward knew Bobby would carry around internal scars for much longer. Perhaps the rest of his life.

It was a circle. Inside the circle, three hooks spiraling from the center.

And as he sawed the ties on Bobby's left wrist, glancing between the path and the design, he knew he'd seen it somewhere, though he couldn't remember where. One thing he did think, however . . . it was a seal or a brand.

The kind denoting *ownership*.

Father Ward pushed the chilling thought from his mind. He'd worry about it later. If he didn't get Bobby away from this unholy place soon, whomever . . . *whatever* cut the sign into his chest would return to claim its prize.

A few more draws of the knife. The lashing fell free. Father Ward slid near Bobby's feet. Maybe because he'd gotten into a rhythm, or maybe because of the situation's urgency, he made short work of the lashings on Bobby's ankles.

He closed his knife and stashed it, bent over and placed his hand against Bobby's burning forehead. "Father God . . . give me the strength to endure, make my path through this trial clear . . . "

Bobby Mavis groaned and arched his back. He thrashed and kicked, hands and feet drumming against the ground. Father Ward tried to secure Bobby so he wouldn't hurt himself, but a deep cold spread through him . . .

The sigil on Bobby's chest.

It was blazing yellow.

"Bobby! It's Father Ward!" He desperately fought the boy, trying to grab his arms and legs. "Please! You're going to—"

From the path, he heard it: the throaty rumble of a diesel engine.

Father Ward stood, one hand gripping the rosary and its medallion, the other tightening around the .45's grip, finger against the trigger. As he turned and faced the path, he wondered what good such an earthly weapon could possibly do.

Yellow light spilled down the path leading in from Hollow Road. As Father Ward stared in horrified fascination, a figure approached, its features cast into darkness . . .

the Faceless Man

. . . as it approached him in measured steps. Father Ward raised the .45, finger tensing on the trigger. "Dear

God in Heaven, protect us, now." As he said the words, however, an empty wave of cold despair washed over him.

Because he wondered if God was listening, anymore.

The figure drew near, the dark shadows falling away. Father Archibald Thomas stood before him. Face wooden, eyes wide and black. Though he wore his vestments, around his neck hung a strange, glowing medallion. Father Ward knew with a curdling stomach: It had burned the mark into Bobby's flesh.

And on the heels of his dread realization came another: The medallion's symbol was the same as the etchings he'd seen on the floors and walls of the little sandstone hovel in Afghanistan.

The *same* demon.

Father Thomas stepped closer.

Father Ward raised the .45, his finger pressing against the trigger. "Father Thomas," he whispered. "What . . . What in God's name . . . "

He trailed off.

No recognition sparked in Father Thomas's fathomless black eyes. He wore no expression, only a blank, pitiless stare.

A machine.

A force of unholy nature. Whatever Father Thomas was during the daylight hours, whatever he'd been when Father Ward met with him earlier today, he was no longer. What stood before him was an automaton, possessing no conscience or soul.

And it wanted to feed.

Father Thomas leaped. Father Ward shouted and squeezed the .45's trigger one-two-three times, hitting

Father Thomas center mass, jerking him with each shot. Father Thomas stumbled and fell to one knee. He caught himself before collapsing. Father Ward stepped forward and pressed the .45's muzzle flush against Father Thomas's forehead. "I'm sorry, GOD I'm so sorry . . . "

His finger tensed against the trigger.

But Father Thomas surged upward, swiping the .45 from Father Ward's hand, clamping onto his neck with an icy, iron grip. Father Ward kicked, hands clawing weakly at Father Thomas's clenching fingers.

His eyes a cold swirling black, chest oozing from several gunshot wounds, Father Thomas hurled Father Ward away. He landed onto his back, head cracking against the stones around the clearing. Pressure filled his head, vertigo rising and swelling, threatening to sweep everything away.

He'd failed.

Again.

no

He'd survived his failure in Afghanistan by filling every waking moment with service and volunteering, doing what little the Church allowed him to. He'd found a true measure of enjoyment, a semblance of peace. But he couldn't fail again.

He'd rather die.

"No!"

Forcing his dizziness aside, ignoring the throbbing in his temples, Father Ward scrambled to his feet, slipping on damp leaves. He lurched forward and leaped at Father Thomas, who was bending over poor Bobby, something sharp and gleaming in his hand . . .

God, please!

me for him!

. . . which he slammed into Father Ward's belly.

Father Ward's momentum carried him into Father

91

Thomas, impaling him on the dagger. Father Thomas staggered back but didn't fall. Father Ward clutched onto Father Thomas's arms, his gut somehow on fire *and* freezing where the knife dug into him.

Waves of pain radiated from the knife in his belly, washing over his abdomen. Father Ward coughed, gagging on a small flush of blood against the back of his throat.

But *power* surged through him.

It didn't wash away the pain, but it gave him the strength to grab Father Thomas by the throat as an all-consuming conviction blossomed inside. Driven by an instinct Father Ward didn't understand, he pressed his other hand and the medal of St. Raphael *against* his wound, and the blood.

"You cannot have this child," he rasped, managing to speak despite the roaring pain. "By the power . . . and blood. *My* blood. Which belongs to HIM, I deny YOU."

He slapped his bloody hand and the medal of St. Raphael against Father Thomas's face. Father Thomas gaped in a wordless shriek. Smoke rose from sizzling, popping flesh.

"In . . . in the name of . . . "

A coughing fit bent him over, raking his tortured muscles against the blade, but he grit his teeth, spat and straightened, staring into Father Thomas's black eyes. "In the name of Christ: *Leave!*"

Father Thomas shuddered, opened his mouth impossibly wide and screamed.

Marshaling what little strength remained, Father Ward placed both hands flat onto Father Thomas's chest and *pushed*. Father Thomas, still screaming an inhuman wail, staggered back, his hands slipping off the knife's hilt. The knife's edge twisted against Father Ward's belly, sending icy shocks of pain across his abdomen. He clapped his hands to the knife embedded in his stomach, but lacked the strength—or courage?—to yank it out.

He collapsed sideways.

The world spun.

Father Ward felt cold, especially in his extremities. Darkness seeped into his vision. The world was spinning and tilting and falling.

Father Thomas—or whatever it was, now—staggered back, still screaming, face smoking where Father Ward had pressed his blood-smeared hand and the medal of St. Raphael, patron saint of the police, and Martin Spencer. Under his feet, soil began to shift and *move*. As if something was tunneling from the ground below.

And *they* burst forth.

Dirt, pine needles and leaves flying as dozens of hands exploded from the ground, reaching for Father Thomas.

As the darkness closed in, Father Ward saw them . . . *perhaps*. Like the hands reaching up from the ground, maybe a hallucination, a figment of a dying mind. But he *saw* them. Standing behind a screaming Father Thomas as those hands pulled him into the earth.

Children.

Rows of children. Standing still, watching. Before them, Father Ward thought he recognized two children. One, a little Afghani girl. The other, standing next to her . . .

Martin Spencer.

And they were smiling, and it was horrible to see.

Father Ward gasped and shuddered.

Then darkness came.

———∿∿———

KEVIN LUCIA

Utica General Hospital
Two Days Later
April 21st

"One last time, Father Ward. You were heading home from working late at school," Sheriff Beckmore droned. "You were driving Beartown Road because of construction on Main Street, and you saw . . . "

He heard Beckmore flipping pages in his small notepad. "Here it is. You saw lights at the intersection of Beartown and Hollow Road. A school bus? An older one. From the fifties, you say."

Father Ward nodded, shifting slightly in his hospital bed. He was rewarded with a dull stab of pain from the stitches in his abdomen. "Yes."

"Okay. You doubled back, parked your car at the old Disbro Farm and made your way through the woods from the opposite side. And you had a *gun*. Which you've kept around for protection ever since you came home from Afghanistan."

Sheriff Beckmore paused here. "Weird. A priest packing heat. But you were in the Army, so I guess it makes sense. Anyway, your piece checked out nice and legal. Of course . . . strange how you happened to have it on you, in the car, on your way home from work."

Father Ward shrugged, wincing again as the motion tugged on his stitches. "Intuition. God was whispering in my ear, that day . . . "

"Yeah. Good thing you're a priest. Anyone else, that'd be reason enough for the psych ward. Anyway," Beckmore consulted his notes. "When you found the clearing, you saw Bobby Mavis—who the Boys Home reported as a runaway—tied on the ground, naked. And with a damn

94

brand on his chest, poor kid. You also saw someone dressed in black, wearing a mask . . . "

Yes.

A mask. He was wearing a *mask.*

One looking like Father Thomas's face. But whatever it was . . . it hadn't been Father Thomas, anymore.

" . . . getting ready to perform some sorta satanic ritual on the boy. You charged in there John Wayne style, fought with him . . . the clearing showed signs of struggle . . . and knocked him out cold. While he was dazed you cut Bobby free but this guy came to and attacked you again. You plugged him three times in the chest, but he *somehow* closed the distance and stuck *you* in the gut. And that's how we found you. Knife in your gut, unconscious, nearly bled out and damn near to the pearly gates."

He gestured at Father Ward's bandaged abdomen. "According to the doctor you're awfully fortunate. That knife cut you a little deeper at a different angle, sliced your intestines, we might not be talking right now."

Father Ward nodded, a memory flickering of him lying on the forest floor, bleeding into the dirt, and a little Afghani girl pressing her small hand into his wound, waves of soothing warmth flowing from her into him . . .

He cleared his throat.

The vision faded. He coughed, winced at the throb in his stitches and said, "Yes. Lucky. Or blessed. Depends on your perspective, I suppose."

Beckmore grunted. "This guy musta been jazzed on his Satanist kick to shake off getting clocked in the head, and for him to get away after being shot three times. Maybe he was high. Probably will never know, unless we find his body, or him. Got men searching the area . . . "

Images flashed again.

Of hands dragging Father Thomas screaming into the ground.

" . . . but between you 'n me, I'm not so hopeful. Deep wilderness out there. Either he's somehow escaped, or he stumbled into some ravine and no one's gonna find him until they happen on his bones."

"I suppose so," Father Ward said, forcing himself to meet Sheriff Beckmore's gaze with a blank expression. He hated lying. After everything he'd endured, it was such a small thing, indeed . . .

But he still hated it.

Beckmore closed his notepad, becoming uncharacteristically somber. "Considering the set-up there in the woods, we've been excavating that clearing. I bet you can figure what we've found."

Father Ward swallowed, remembering again those grasping hands pulling Father Thomas into the earth, but also strangely sure, wherever Father Thomas was *now* . . . it wasn't under a clearing off Hollow Road. "Yes."

"Most of em are burnt to hell, nearly impossible to identify. I figure . . . you don't wanna know how many."

runaways are a fact of life at Boys of Faith
nature of the beast
the beast

"No. I'd rather not."

"Bobby Mavis'll be okay. Thanks to you. Was a bit dehydrated and he's fighting a cold, and he'll need some more skin-work to cover that damn thing burned into his chest . . . but I suspect he'll make it okay. Physically, of course. In his head? Probably another story."

Despite the circumstances of his survival and Bobby's rescue, a wave of grief rose in Father Ward's heart. "What does he remember?"

Sheriff Beckmore pushed his hat higher on his forehead with a thick, sausage-like finger. "Not much, thank God. Remembers walking to school, hearing something big—like a school bus—behind him, and then . . . BOOM. Nothing until he woke here. Luckily, they'd already finished the first set of skin grafts on his chest by then."

Beckmore shook his massive head. "Who knows what kinda shit's gonna be in his dreams, though."

Father Ward said nothing to this. But he knew of dreams, indeed.

Sheriff Beckmore turned to go, but stopped. "Y'know, some strange things I can't quite figure. First of all, this business with the bus. An old bus, from the fifties, like the bus you saw, and the bus Bobby Mavis says he heard pull behind him before he blacked out. No schools in the area run buses that old anymore, and no one's running a bus 253. Also, we didn't find any bus tracks."

Father Ward didn't say anything to this either, simply because he hadn't expected them to find traces of the bus at all.

"Another thing is this 'Moe Leck' and 'Hammon Bale' stuff the guidance counselor at All Saints said you two talked of. Far as we can tell, though you and Mrs. Hull and Bobby himself swear they met him, no Maurice Leck exists. Further back, we couldn't find any records of a Hammon Bale, either. They don't exist, and I can't for the life of me figure what they have to do with all this." He paused. "And honestly? Don't think I want to know."

his shadows
his shadows take us to him

"I do have one last question. Something no one knows what to make of." Sheriff Beckmore eyed him closely again, his stolid expression blank, unreadable. "You've got no next of kin to call. Dad passed on, Mom in a Florida nursing home, so we tried Father Thomas. No dice. We visited the rectory, but no one was home. Car's gone, place looks empty. Two days later, he's still gone. Doesn't show at the church or school. Family relations and superiors at the Diocese have no idea where he is, or why he left so suddenly without telling anyone where he was going."

Sheriff Beckmore bent over slightly, his gaze bright and penetrating. "Father Ward . . . you haven't any idea where Father Thomas might be . . . do you?"

Father Ward forced a blank, confused expression, shook his head slightly and rasped, "I have no idea."

And that, more or less, was the truth.

Sheriff Beckmore stared at him for a heartbeat longer. Then he sighed, his face relaxing, as if resigning himself—gratefully—to no answers.

"Besides that, most everything else has been settled. Got some loose ends can't be explained, course. Like how Bobby Mavis managed to call 911 from your Tracphone despite the spotty service out there, then pass out again, all without remembering him doing it. Of course, 911 never got a *name*, did they? Only identified the caller as 'young teen boy.' So that's sorta hanging, with a few other things. But that's life here in Clifton Heights, son. Probably didn't notice much growing up, but now you're an adult? Well, suppose this might be your first lesson there. One you're gonna need, with what's coming for you next."

"Next? What do you mean?"

"Well, unless Father Thomas shows up with an air-tight explanation as to where he's been and why he left, All Saints Church and Academy are in need of a priest and Headmaster. And right now, you're the hero of the hour, saving Bobby Mavis and all. Don't know how the Diocese works, not being Catholic and all, but seems to me their choice for a successor would be clear."

Sheriff Beckmore touched the brim of his hat. "Get some rest, Father. You're gonna need it."

Sheriff Beckmore turned and left.

Father Ward lay back in his bed. He stared at the shadows shifting on the walls until fatigue claimed him, pulling him under the warm, dark covers of sleep.

Where he didn't dream.

YELLOW CAB

MOST KIDS GROW up being afraid of the dark, or of spiders and snakes or of the monster hiding under their bed. When they get a little older they're afraid of not fitting in, or zits, or they have nightmares of standing naked in front of gym class because they forgot to get dressed before leaving the locker-room.

Me?

Far back as I can remember the only thing I ever feared was letting my parents down. Failing. Not being able to handle things like they'd trained me to. Disappointing them by being a nobody.

Well.

If they could only see me now.

I drive a taxi, which I guess probably doesn't meet their original expectations. But I'm somebody. I get things done. There's that, at least. I like to tell myself they'd be a *little* proud. After all the time and effort they invested in me, I'm the type of person who *handles* things.

And on some nights? It helps me sleep.

Some nights.

I don't think anyone counts hitting bottom as one of their future goals. Driving a taxi in a small Adirondack town while living in a shoe box apartment over a pizza place? Sure wasn't on my future agenda. In high school I bought the same guidance counselor bullshit everyone else did. Get good grades, join a club or two, play a sport, run for class office or Student Council, be active in the community. Anything to make my transcripts appear "well rounded."

Take my SATs and ACTs multiple times to achieve the best possible scores. Shoulder a heavy course-load of advanced classes so I could graduate college early.

I swallowed it like everyone else. The old cliché, right? Hook, line and sinker. But in college I realized an awful truth: None of it meant a damn because there was something *wrong* with me. Something was missing, inside.

And I discovered exactly what my sophomore year.

The rainy Sunday night I pulled up to The Relief Pitcher around eleven PM—*that's* the night things started getting weird. My fares emerged from the bar: three guys around my age. They ran to my cab, shoulders hunched under the rain. The back door opened and they clambered in, swearing and jeering at each other. The last one—a guy with broad shoulders and a crew-cut—slammed the door, leaned forward and rasped, "Dude, crank the heat? My shit's *cold* back here. Fuckin' rain."

I raised the heat a notch. "Sure. Where to?"

The lanky kid on the far right shook his mop-top in disgust. "Guys, let's bail. I'm tired as shit and outta cash."

Crew Cut waved away the complaint. "Fuck that noise. Got plenty of cash. I'll stand you."

"What the hell else is there to *do* around here?" This came from the one in the middle. A round-cheeked guy you'd call *stout*, which is code for *kinda fat*. "We've already hit the only three bars in town. They were beat."

I cleared my throat, glancing over my shoulder. "You guys from Webb Community College?" They nodded. "Well, if you're looking for something a little more exciting, I know this place . . . "

"Damn straight," Crew Cut muttered.

"The Golden Kitty. On Route 28 toward Whitelake. Fully nude and the dancers are pretty wild. Word is, anyway."

They grinned and Crew Cut nodded. "Hell yeah. Drive on, Jeeves."

Jeeves.

Like I hadn't heard *that* before.

I nodded without saying anything, however, grabbing the mic off the dash and calling Dispatch. When you're lost at sea you don't complain about the thing keeping you afloat. You swallow your pride and keep paddling as best you can, in hopes of one day making it to shore.

But pulling away from The Relief Pitcher, I thought the same thing as always. Getting to shore wasn't happening anytime soon. Treading water and keeping my head above the waves was probably the best I could manage for the foreseeable future.

Maybe forever.

The worst part?

I'd done everything my guidance counselor and parents told me to. All the things they'd promised would pave the road to success. I didn't make top of the class, but I graduated fifth. I received an academic scholarship to Binghamton University for their Secondary Education Program. I was going to be a high school English teacher. Not because I wanted to, or even liked the idea of teaching, but I'd always read a lot, and I'd grown up the son of a retired principal. Since age thirteen my parents fed me plans of teaching, tenure, future administration and early retirement. Becoming a teacher appeared inevitable, regardless of *my* feelings. At the very least, I wasn't averse to the idea of having summers, holidays and snow days off.

Also, at the time I'd no ideas of my own about the future. Someone else's seemed as good, because I figured I was like every other high school student who didn't know what to do with their life. That's all. There's wasn't anything wrong with me. I just didn't know what I wanted to do when I grew up.

Two years after graduation I learned how mistaken I was.

So there I was after dropping those guys off, sitting in The Golden Kitty's nearly empty parking lot and smoking a Marlboro Menthol, when the rear door of my cab opened.

My car sagged a little on its shocks.

The door slammed shut.

I dragged on my Menthol, tapped ash out the window and without turning around muttered, "Where you wanna go?"

Silence.

A body shifted on the cheap vinyl seats. A slight cough, and then in a smooth voice, "Well. I believe a better question is: Where do *you* want to go?"

I snorted, took another drag and exhaled. I glanced into the rear-view mirror and saw nothing but a shadowed profile. "Where would *I* like to go? Home, man."

A chuckle. "Don't we all."

"Which I can do soon as you tell me where *you* want to go. You're probably my last fare tonight, so soon as I get you where you need to be . . . "

"Pardon my presumptuousness, but I believe a much more apt question is where do *you* need to be? Why are you *here*, in this car, this late at night? Why not some place better, doing something more *important*?"

I rubbed my temples with my fingertips. It never ended.

I was *forever* getting fares who thought it was their duty to give me uplifting life-advice. You know, the old 'what's a young, bright fella like you doing in a dead end job like this?' speech.

"Listen. Thanks for the Pysch 101 self-esteem pep talk, but right now? Where I need to be is in bed, so if you could hurry up and tell me where you want to go, I can make that happen."

"It must be frustrating. Not being able to go where you most need to be. Frustrating. Maddening, even."

"You know what's maddening? A fare who won't tell me where he wants to *go*."

"So sad, a life of unfulfilled dreams. A life left alongside the road like a discarded candy wrapper or a blown tire."

Why didn't I flick the dome light on and see who was yanking my chain? In all honesty, I can't say. I remember *reaching* for the dome light. I remember my hand hovering over the switch. I also remember thinking maybe I didn't want to see this guy's face, though I didn't know why.

Anyway, I drew another stinging menthol breath, held it for a second, then thought—*what the hell, it's my cab*—and exhaled without bothering to shunt it out the window. "Listen. Give me a destination or scram. Make up your mind, or I'm gonna dump you right here."

"Indeed," the fellow said. "But before I tell you where I need to go, may I ask one more thing?"

"Pal, if it'll get you to your destination and me home to bed any quicker, you can ask me anything you want."

"Don't you want something more from life? Something more worthwhile? With *purpose*?"

I'd heard the same speech from half a dozen people over the years, but from this guy it sounded . . . *different.* I couldn't have told you how at the time. He placed more emphasis on certain words, and it sounded more than the rhetorical "improve your life" spiel I usually got.

Of course, I understand *now* why it sounded different. Invitation.

It was an invitation. A what-do-you-call-it, an invocation. But back then it flew over my head as I snapped, "Sure, pal. I want something better. Who doesn't? But there's not much I can do about it right now. Not that it's any of your business. Now, you gonna tell me where you want to go, or am I dumping your ass here?"

Though I couldn't see his face in the shadows filling the back seat, I could *hear* his smile as he told me his destination.

Exasperated, I shook my head, put the cab in gear, flicked the meter on and left The Golden Kitty's parking lot, happy to be on the road and one step closer to being home in bed.

If I'd only thought a little harder about the destination he'd given me, however, I probably wouldn't have felt so relieved.

<hr />

Here's the thing which should've got me thinking right from the start. That night I dreamed of driving along an endless country road surrounded on both sides by strange black trees stretching to a strange black sky. Ahead of me—though I couldn't get any closer, no matter how fast I drove—was a lake stretching across the horizon, like the road itself descended into its waters.

It was a strange lake. From far away, the water appeared silver and turbulent, as if in the midst of a windstorm, though I heard no wind. And I caught the barest glimpses of . . . something . . . thrashing around in the water. Something yellow, scaly, and huge.

THROUGH A MIRROR, DARKLY

I didn't wake from that dream. It faded into another (one I was more familiar with) like changing channels on television. One minute, I was driving along a strange road cutting through weird black trees toward a bizarre lake with things thrashing in it, the next I was in my dorm room back in college, getting the phone call which changed my life forever.

And honestly?

I would've rather have stayed in the first dream, instead of going back to the night Andie McGovern called me for the last time.

So how'd I end up driving cab in the little nowhere town of Clifton Heights? I'll give you the short version. The long version involves all the drama you'd expect when the son of a career-obsessed family drops out of college for no reason.

To the quick?

When living at home under the suffocating intensity of parental condemnation became too hard, I moved to my current residence over Chin's Pizza in Clifton Heights. I took the first job I found: driving taxi.

That's how things were before Mystery Philosophical Guy boarded my ride. Dad told me I wasn't welcome back until I'd "gotten my shit together." That suited me fine. I'd no plans of going home any time soon.

See, I know "they don't understand" is usually hysterical teenage bullshit. An over-emotional cop-out. But they *didn't* understand. They couldn't. First of all, they hadn't known about Andie McGovern. They'd never met her, hadn't known she existed, much less known what happened when she called my dorm room sophomore year.

Second?

Neither Mom nor Dad have much in the way of empathy. Dad has always been "all business." Spent all his time at school before he retired, and after retirement, traveling and giving seminars. He always made sure my summers were busy, full of athletic and academic camps, day programs, chores and the books he wanted me to read. We never played catch, went fishing, or flew any kites.

Don't get me wrong. He was never cruel or abusive. He just acted distant. Detached. He never yelled at me, never cursed or derided me. He always listened, tried to be fair in his judgments, and often compromised. But he wasn't *Dad*. He was more like an efficient administrator who desired a healthy working relationship with one of his teachers.

And Mom?

Well, best you can say of Mom is her "evolved sense of civic responsibility," which she spent a lot of time trying to instill in me. When Dad didn't have me hopping she was volunteering me at church functions, cleaning the community center or mowing its lawn, visiting the Webb County Assisted Living Home, and anything else you could imagine. She wanted to make sure I "gave back to the community."

Even church was largely important only to "instill values." Honestly, the concept of a God or Higher Power was often incidental to my parents, sometimes nonexistent, but they insisted I be involved in every church function there was.

So they kept me busy. Way too busy for me to get into trouble, way too busy for me to ever figure out what *I* wanted to do with my life. Which, in retrospect, is probably why Mystery Philosophical Guy's questions bothered me so much. In a way he was asking me what I'd never been allowed to ask myself: Where do *I* want to go? What do *I* want to do?

I suppose because Andie's death still haunts me, I have a little more soul than my parents. But to me, that's like running a car on fumes instead of running it on empty, which isn't enough of a difference to make much of a difference, if you get what I mean.

———∕∕∕———

When my alarm rang at 9:00 AM Monday morning after Mysterious Philosophical Guy first hopped into my cab, I lay there in bed, arm thrown over my eyes to shield me from the sunlight leaking through the blinds. One of the few upsides to driving taxi the evening shift: I can sleep in to nine or ten in the morning.

Which is fine, because it's not like I did much socially. Occasional drinks at The Stumble Inn with a few bar hounds I'd gotten to know, the occasional NBA game on the big screen at The Sports Bar on State Street. I'd gone on a few dates; if by dates you mean a quick bite at The Skylark or Henry's Drive-In, then either a movie or a pub walk ending in some bounce 'n tickle at either her place or mine. Both parties always went their separate ways after. Most the girls I met at bars, although a few I met driving cab, though none of them ever offered sex in place of payment, like they do on Real Confessions of a Cab Driver, or in porn.

The morning after meeting Mystery Philosophical Guy, however, I had no such obligations. So I lay there awhile, trying to pull together my thoughts to face the day. A vague unease lingered in my brain. For some reason I was having a hard time shrugging off sleep. As my mind cycled through all the reasons why, however, the day's date clicked in my head.

October 14th.

The night everything changed three years ago when Andie McGovern called my dorm.

I grunted, lurched upright and headed to my apartment's small bathroom for a handful of Advil and a glass of water. Then, I stripped for a shower, ignoring a dull emptiness inside, which has gotten easy to do these days. I'm good at it, because after all . . .

I've had lots of practice.

<hr />

Ever read Flannery O'Connor's short story "Good Country People?" I've read it half a dozen times over the years. It's the one in which Hulga—a sophisticated, college-educated nihilist—takes a naive, innocent Bible salesman named Manley Pointer (really?) into the loft of this barn, hoping to seduce the poor guy because, you know, he's a Bible salesman and she's a college-educated nihilist who believes in nothing.

Thing is, our Bible salesman Manley Pointer (REALLY?) isn't nearly as innocent as he appears. Apparently he wants to play some hanky panky. Some *weird* hanky panky. He wants to touch Hulga's wooden leg (can't remember why she had one).

So he manages to con Hulga into letting him remove her wooden leg (by unscrewing it, or something), pretending he gets a big sexual charge from it. Because it's intimate or taboo or something. Soon as she removes her leg—all the while "humoring" this poor, innocent Bible salesman—he takes off laughing with it, leaving her stranded in the hay loft with only one leg. See, while she's been *playing* with the idea of nihilism and believing in nothing, good old Manley Pointer really *does* believe in nothing.

What's the point?

Well, I'm a lot like Hulga, I guess. I cruised through high school and into college thinking I was superior to everyone else because I believed in nothing. But Andie McGovern snatched away my wooden leg with one phone call, and I've been stranded in a hay loft ever since.

———∿∿———

I remember clearly when I first thought maybe something vital inside me was missing. I can't remember the exact circumstances (I was at the bathroom sink, shaving for school or church or something), which is exactly what makes the memory so disconcerting. No traumatic catalyst preceded this revelation. It wasn't a precursor to some life-changing milestone. It came in the most mundane of ways, on what was another day in the life of me. Finished shaving, I dribbled some aftershave on both hands, glanced into the mirror as I rubbed it onto my slightly reddened cheeks . . .

And didn't recognize the face staring back at me.

As if on cue, a voice whispered in my head: Who the *hell* are you?

A host of answers leaped to mind: Mitch Reynolds. Senior at Inlet High. Son of James and Harriet Reynolds. A+ student. Regents Scholar. Captain of the lacrosse team. Member of Mock Trial and Student Council. Future teacher/principal/superintendent who will be efficient, punctual, timely, and retire early like Dad. All of those things were labels I'd become accustomed to. They fit. They applied to me. They'd been accepted as valid definitions of *me*.

But a gnawing emptiness mixed acid in my stomach as I stared into the glass. Those things meant nothing. They were labels. Names. Roles. Different masks I showed to different people as circumstances demanded. They weren't, however, *me*.

I felt a numb sort of panic. My legs actually trembled, thighs quivering as a wave of nausea rippled through me. I grabbed both sides of the cool porcelain sink as the voice continued.

Who *are* you?

I don't know.

Who are you? *What* are you?

I don't know.

What's stopping you from going to the kitchen, grabbing a knife and gutting Mom right now? Or punching the first person you see at school? Or standing up in the middle of church and screaming at the top of your lungs: "Pastor Babbet likes to diddle little boys and girls!"?

What's stopping you?

Again, a litany of stock answers sprung up: I'd go to jail. Ruin my future. Get fined. Destroy my reputation. Get detention and ruin my perfect academic and disciplinary record or worse, get expelled. Exiled from church. Disowned by my family. Punished by my father, lose money for college.

Not once did it ever occur to me I shouldn't do those things because they were *wrong*.

The awful truth lay before me, naked and cold. But I did what I've done so often since: I shied away, lest I disturb a slumbering beast. Numbly, I wiped my hands, dried my face, walked away and thought doggedly to myself . . .

I'm *me*.

And I buried that truth beneath those labels, roles and

masks. I did a good job, too, because it lay hidden there until my sophomore year when one phone call stripped those masks away, laying bare the Truth so I could see myself for what I was.

As maybe you can imagine I avoid mirrors as much as possible. Can't be managed all the time, obviously. I do have to shave, comb my hair and brush my teeth occasionally. There's also the rear-view mirror in my cab, too. That's somehow the worst. It focuses on my eyes. Everyone's heard it by now. It's used in countless stories, poems and movies when someone wants to sound insightful. Eyes are the windows to the soul.

Cliché, but remarkably apt. I *hate* looking into my eyes. They're dead and flat, which spooks me. I usually angle my rear-view mirror so when I absolutely *have* to use it, I see mostly the road behind or whoever is riding in back.

The morning after I took those college boys to The Golden Kitty, I spent as little time as possible before the bathroom mirror, as always. Wasn't sporting much scruff so I skipped shaving, opting to swig some mouthwash instead of brushing my teeth (lazy, I know). I ran my fingers through my hair, brushing a few locks into place. Still, I caught my reflection's flat gaze and couldn't stop the voices whispering in my head . . .

who are you?

As always I ignored the question. Snatched my coat off the back of a chair at the dining room table, grabbed a few bills and headed to the post office. I'd walk there, then head over to Yellow Cab.

Business as usual.

For some reason, I couldn't shake a nagging little voice

in my head. I muted it, to be sure, pushed it away from my conscious mind. As I hit the sidewalk, however, that question—*who are you?*—kept nagging at me, a lingering splinter in my thoughts.

------ ✦ ------

After I'd slipped my bills into the post office's mail slot, my TracPhone started ringing in my pocket. I dug it out and answered. "Yeah?"

"What the hell kinda gag you pulling, Mitch? Think yer some kinda goddamn comedian?"

It was Buster Malfi. The short, squat, hot-tempered Italian who owned Yellow Cab. He sounded pissed. "Buster, I've got *no* idea what you're talking about."

"I finished counting last night's take from your route. What the hell you think we're running here, some kinda charity? Think we're back inna medeeval times, so we can barter 'n shit? What, maybe today you'll take a sack a potatoes or a few chickens?"

Getting a little pissed myself and not wanting my voice to carry, I headed toward the post office's exit. "Buster, you're not making any sense."

Buster fairly growled on the other end. *"Just get your ass here and explain yourself if you still wanna work here, kid."*

"All right, relax. I'll be there in a minute or so. Don't know why you're so upset. If I was short last night for some reason, I'm good for it."

A grunt. *"You better be."*

He abruptly hung up, which in itself wasn't so odd. Buster didn't have much in the way of etiquette. But I'd caught something else in his voice, some slight inflection I couldn't quite place at first because it wasn't something I'd ever heard from him before . . .

Unease.

Maybe fear.

Sure, Buster sounded pissed. But he also sounded spooked, which spooked *me*. If I knew anyone who didn't rattle easy it was Buster Malfi. If he was as unsettled as he'd sounded over the phone . . .

I exited the post office and headed toward Yellow Cab, my pace quickening.

"So," Malfi said as I walked into his office in the rear of Yellow Cab's garage, "what the hell is *this*, anyway?"

Buster flipped a coin at me. I caught it neatly in my palm. "Looks like a silver dollar."

Buster scowled and pointed at me. "Take a closer look, smart ass. Sure as hell ain't no silver dollar."

I opened my palm and examined the coin lying there. It was certainly the same circumference of a silver dollar, but sure enough, it wasn't one. First of all, it was thicker and heavier. Also, not silver at all, but a tarnished bronze, a dull yellow. And it appeared old. Like a collectible or an antique you'd find at Handy's Pawn and Thrift.

A design was etched on both sides. I rubbed my thumb over it, peering closer. A small circle, with what appeared to be three crooked question marks spiraling around the circle.

"Huh. This isn't a silver dollar."

"Amazing. It's like there's an echo in here or something. What I wanna know is, whaddya think yer doing turning it in with your take? And where the hell you get it, anyway? Not that I care, past the money you owe me."

I didn't look at Buster, all too familiar with his pinched, red, pissed-off face. I stared instead at the coin, lying flat in my palm. "You said I was short in my count for last night."

"According to last night's logs, yeah." Papers rustled. I glanced up to see Buster flipping through the Dispatch log. "After dropping your fare off at The Golden Kitty, you took a fare to Shelby Road. Shoulda been 5.50, which you're short by."

Shelby Road.

I'd taken Mystery Philosophical Guy there.

Hadn't I?

"Shelby Road," I said slowly. "Past Samara Hill, isn't it? Past Raedeker Park?"

"Yeah. Where the hell you take your fare? Ain't nothing there except the old Shelby Road Cemetery, far as I know."

I raised my head, suddenly gripping the coin with the strange design on it. "Does the log say?"

Buster scowled at the Dispatch log. "Shit. It don't. Maybe the system was screwy last night. Or maybe *Jimmy* was screwy and didn't enter it."

Buster peered at me and frowned. "You saying you don't remember?"

I closed my hand over the strange coin, avoiding Buster's piercing gaze, staring at my clenched fist. "It was late. I . . . "

"Hey." Buster's voice lost some of its edge, a note of concern creeping into his rasping grumble. "You okay, kid?"

I coughed and waved him off. "I'm fine. No problem."

"You ain't been sneaking the wacky tabaccy on those late runs, have ya? I ain't the feds or no holy roller; don't care what ya do in your off time but I gotta business to run and if you're getting high while driving one of my cabs . . . "

"No. No way. I was tired. Careless, and this guy pulled a fast one. Take it from my pay. He tries to get a ride again, I'll ditch him."

A grunt. "What'd he look like? Case this guy tries to pull it on one of my other cars."

I rubbed the back of my neck with my free hand, still staring at the clenched fist holding the strange coin with its odd design. "Uh. It was dark. Can't remember. He was tallish. I think."

I salvaged the courage to meet Buster's gaze, offering him a weak smile. "Take it from my pay. Okay?"

Buster stared at me for several seconds, face blank, likely weighing some vague concern for my personal welfare against his desire not to get involved. After several seconds, he grunted. "I'll cover the difference with petty cash this time. Next time, it'll be double outta your pay. Got it?"

I nodded eagerly, strangely desperate to get away. "Got it."

Then he was all business again, dismissal clear in his voice as he turned back to the old PC on his desk. "You're on the road in an hour."

I said nothing and beat a hasty retreat, a corner of my mind wondering. Buster hadn't asked for the weird coin back. Weirder, if he did, I wouldn't have given it to him.

I sat in my cab as it idled in the parking lot, staring at nothing, trying to piece together what happened the night before. Mystery Philosophical Guy got in after I'd dropped the college boys off at The Golden Kitty. He'd spouted some shit about where I wanted to go, where I *really* wanted to go, some crap about me choosing my destiny or life or whatever, I couldn't remember. He told me his destination, except I couldn't quite . . .

Shelby Road.

Buster said I'd called into Dispatch a fare going to Shelby Road, which is past Samara Hill and Raedeker Park Zoo, in the middle of nowhere. He'd offered the lame excuse of Jimmy Radici—who'd been working Dispatch last night—entering the wrong destination, which certainly held precedent. Everyone sort of knew (Buster too, I think) Jimmy kept a little tin flask hidden in the bottom drawer of his desk, which he sipped from when he worked Night Dispatch. Wasn't inconceivable Jimmy entered the wrong destination last night after hitting his flask. He'd certainly done it before.

I rubbed my temples with my fingertips, squeezing that coin with its weird symbol. Somehow, I knew this hadn't been another Jimmy-I've-Been-Nipping-the-Firewater-Again screw-up. Somehow, I knew I'd taken Mystery Philosophical Guy to Shelby Road . . .

But why couldn't I remember?

Believe it or not this sort of thing happens more often than I'd like to admit. The end of a long night shift gets fuzzy. Don't know what driving a cab in Utica or Syracuse is like, with the rush of traffic and the constant business and all, but here it sometimes feels like I'm floating aimlessly along a winding backwoods stream with no clear destination in sight.

I mean, for a small town I got more calls than you might think, but they were usually spread out over a shift.

Memorizing all the streets and dead ends wasn't hard, so often I drifted semi-consciously from one pickup to the next. Dispatch hissed and squawked in the background, I answered and confirmed fares unconsciously because it was more like muscle memory than anything else. Believe it or not, I'd come off shifts with a blank memory before. If it weren't for the call log and my earnings, some nights I'd have sworn were completely uneventful.

But though I'd suffered a little "missing time" occasionally, I'd never experienced shortfall in my earnings. I'm conscious enough to make sure I get paid. So what the hell happened? How could I *not* remember where I'd taken Mystery Philosophical Guy, and how did he pass off that weird coin to me?

Cold unease rippled down the back of my neck.

I put my cab into gear, left the parking lot and turned onto Alice Street, heading toward Samara Hill and Shelby Road. I drove with one hand, gripping the weird coin so hard its blunt edges pressed painfully into my palm.

Twenty minutes later, five miles from town on a narrow asphalt road, I parked and stared at the remains of Shelby Road Cemetery. An access road cut down its middle from Shelby Road, curving into the forest's darkness at the tree line. Off to one side leaned a gray weather-beaten shack. Presumably the caretakers' tool shed, from the days when Shelby Road Cemetery was still in use. The door was closed. From the car, I saw nothing but darkness through its small, dirt-grimed windows.

The cemetery had fallen on hard times. The plots appeared as if they hadn't been maintained in years. Most of the headstones barely peeked above the weeds. Some of them tilted sideways, others broken off at the base and lying face-down, barely visible through the stands of goldenrod and brush.

There was no reason to bring anyone here.

Yet in the pit of my stomach, I felt sure the Dispatch log was correct. I came here last night and dropped off Mystery Philosophical Guy. He'd given me some weird-ass coin as payment, and I'd somehow forgotten the whole thing, except . . .

I couldn't quite remember *where* the guy asked me to take him. It was on the tip of my brain and wouldn't quite come, but I somehow *knew* he hadn't *said* Shelby Road. I called Shelby Road in, of course. Vaguely remembered saying . . .

oh, that's on Shelby Road

. . . but I knew, somehow, he'd used a different name, not Shelby Road . . .

Carcosa.

That was it.

Carcosa.

But what the hell did *that* mean? Wasn't any place in Clifton Heights or Webb County named Carcosa *I* knew of.

I peered closer at the road. Though years of driving had worn the ground bare in twin earthen stripes, grass grew high in the middle. From my vantage point, it didn't appear as if anyone had driven to the woods in a long while, except . . .

There.

It had rained the night before. Craning my neck, I could see a strip of damp earth in one of the access roads' tracks. Hardly aware of my own actions, I opened the door, stepped from my cab, crossed the road and found myself examining it.

Tire tracks.

Fresh. Made within a day.

I'm not one of these CSI guys you see on television; I didn't know what kind of vehicle made those tracks. They looked too big for a dirt bike but not big enough for a truck. A three or four wheeler would've left tracks with more studded treads. These looked regular and smooth, like a car would make.

Still.

Didn't necessarily mean anything, right? Could've been a bunch of college kids like the ones I'd picked up last night, or high school kids partying. It didn't necessarily mean anything.

Still, I straightened and began following the access road back toward the tree line. The damp strip ran for several feet, disappeared into dryer ground, then reappeared, then disappeared in alternating strips. In each I saw the same tire marks. They led to the caretaker's leaning shack and abruptly stopped at its front door.

I stood and stared for several seconds at the shack. At first glance it appeared to be nothing more than an old tool shed barely still standing. Leaning to one side, its roof sagging in the middle. Probably where the former caretaker stored picks, shovels, weed-whackers, rakes, even a push mower. Maybe a cot and a small heater for overnight stays, like Whitey Smith occasionally enjoys at Hillside Cemetery when he's gotten too drunk to face the wrath of Mrs. Smith. I knew this because I'd taken Whitey to his much nicer shack at Hillside Cemetery many times.

This, of course, appeared far worse for wear than Whitey's humble home away from home. Gray-mottled, the wood looked damp and spongy. If I opened the door too hard, it'd fall off its hinges. And yet there it still stood, apparently intact, nothing amiss past its worn, rotten appearance, its sideways lean and sagging roof . . .

As I peered closer, the shack's doorknob glimmered. It looked shiny and polished, as if someone had installed it yesterday, gleaming a golden-yellow under the clear, October morning sun. And it looked like . . .

I stepped closer.

Bent over.

And saw, engraved on the doorknob, the same design as on the weird coin Mystery Philosophical Guy gave me. The weird coin I was holding in my other hand, which was *vibrating*.

A chill rippled through me as I raised the hand holding the coin. I hadn't meant to bring it with me. Thought I'd left it on the passenger seat. But there it was, lying in my open palm. I couldn't *see* it vibrating, but I felt it, all the same. Like a low grade electrical current pulsing from the coin into my hand.

I glanced from the coin back to the strangely new and shiny doorknob on the old shack. They indeed both shared the same strange design. And for a moment—a second—a mini-film ran through my head of me stepping forward, grasping the shiny new doorknob (which would feel cool against my skin, and would be humming, too, like the coin), turning it and opening the door and seeing nothing but a deep blackness lit by black stars and a black moon . . .

I chucked the coin with its weird-ass symbol past the shed and into the forest. I didn't bother tracking its arc, just jerked around and walked stiffly to my cab. I shut down my brain and didn't think about anything, just like I'd done the night Andie McGovern called me in my dorm to tell me she'd slit her wrists in the tub and how it didn't hurt that bad and how dreamy she felt, like she was getting high for one last time . . .

I pushed all thoughts away. Got into my cab, put it in gear, executed a clumsy K-turn and drove back into town. Mercifully, on the way, the CB squawked with my first fare of the day. I slowly lost myself in the usual routine. Everything went numb and quiet in my head, until the end of my shift, when I picked up Everett Boyers outside Paddy's Place.

———————

You might be wondering how I could brush off such crazy stuff, right? Yeah. Fucking weird, I'll admit. But see, here's the thing: Like I said, my parents raised me to be "efficient." "Productive." Feeding the poor and "doing unto others as they have done unto you" wasn't what my parents preached, it was *crisis management*. How will you handle yourself in a "situation?" How can you achieve the most optimum results from unfavorable circumstances?

You compartmentalize. Cordon things off. Focus on the goal you most want to achieve and drop everything else to the wayside in your exclusive pursuit of said goal. Whatever gets in the way of that pursuit must be eliminated mercilessly, as well as emotionlessly. In other words, no fuss, no muss. Easy-cheezy, Wheezy.

So that's what I did.

I couldn't explain the coin. Couldn't explain the guy whose face I didn't want to see. Couldn't explain how I could forget where I'd taken him. Couldn't explain what the hell Carcosa was. Couldn't explain any of it, so I *didn't*. Buster needed to get repaid; he could take it from my paycheck. No fuss, no muss.

Easy Cheezy, Wheezy.

I walled it off. Drove away from Shelby Road Cemetery and went to work. I stopped for supper at The Skylark

Diner, enjoyed a passable conversation with Sheriff Baker and one of the town's holy rollers, Father Ward, from All Saints Church. Then I got back on the road. Picked up fares. Called in destinations. Received new fares from Dispatch. The usual. Over and Out, Come Back, ETA ASAP and all that happy horseshit.

I took care of business, as I'd been raised to. Like I took care of business when Andie McGovern slashed her wrist open in a warm bath. I took care of it, like my parents taught me to.

Sort of wish they knew about Andie, sometimes. If they could've overlooked certain details, I think they might've been proud. I sure handled my shit that night, like I handled my shit after Mystery Philosophical Guy boarded my ride.

Until the morning after I picked up Everett Boyers.

<center>~~~</center>

I was sitting at the curb in front of Paddy's Place, a little pub over on the East Side, not far from the lumber mill. Smoking another Marlboro Menthol, which, despite Buster's insinuation about "wacky tabaccy" is the only poison I inhale. Anyway, my mind buzzing pleasantly on nicotine, a solid evening of work screening off the weirdness of the morning, I felt okay. I didn't think anything of it when the door opened; someone clambered in and shut the door behind them.

No.

Not exactly true.

For a minute—hell, maybe only a second—my mind blurted: *It's him shit it's him again I don't wanna see his face* but quickly, coldly, efficiently I squared myself away and muttered around my cigarette, "Where to, pal?"

126

Like the other night, however . . . silence. Then a slight cough, and in a whispery rasp, "I . . . I need to go home."

I snorted, took a drag of my cigarette, then exhaled out the crack of my window. "Don't we all?"

A thought snagged in my head.

Why did that sound so familiar?

I quickly brushed the question away, saying, "I'll need more specific directions, chief."

I glanced in the rear-view mirror. This close to Paddy's, weak green light washed into the back seat, illuminating a kid who didn't appear much older than nineteen. He wasn't really dressed for the weather, wearing a thin denim jacket over a white T-shirt. From what I could see, the kid's face was thin, emaciated, damn near cadaverous. My first thought was he looked sick. Exhausted, too.

My second thought? A junkie near his last hit. Though the Adirondacks doesn't have dealers peddling crack on every street corner, we do have our fair share of drugs floating around here.

I sucked in some more menthol smoke. Exhaled and said, "C'mon, kid. Ain't got all night."

The kid's deep-set eyes focused a little. He licked his lips and with a tremendous effort repeated, "Just . . . home. Please. I can tell you The Way."

It was how he said it that stands out to me, now.

The Way.

As if both words should be capitalized. A proper noun. Like it was a calling. A way of life. A pilgrimage, or something.

At the time, however, I closed my eyes, rubbed my forehead and thought: *Just what I need. An underage kid who probably snuck into Paddy's with a fake ID, got*

*himself smashed and is now trying to get home without
getting busted by either the cops or his folks.*

I sighed.

What the hell, right?

I could start driving, and if the kid couldn't get his shit
together, I'd drop him off somewhere and hope he could
pay me *something* (Buster could be forgiving in his own
hard-ass way, but he had his limits). At the least, the kid
was trying to be responsible (despite him probably illegally
drinking) taking a cab home instead of trying to drive.

The kid leaned forward, looking confused and maybe a
little scared . . .

*like you were when Andie called
but you handled your shit
like Mom and Dad taught you*

. . . and he whispered, "Please. I need to go home."

I shook my head, put the cab into gear, flicked the
meter on and pulled away from Paddy's Place. "Sure, kid,"
I muttered around my cigarette, "like I said. Don't we all?
But one last time: Where's home?"

Quietly, he told me.

And I drove him there.

God help me, I did.

I had another strange dream, later. It started with me
driving down the access road leading to the old caretaker's
shack at Shelby Cemetery. The night was deathly quiet. Not
a sound, no animals, birds . . . anything. I left my cab and
approached the shack, weird coin buzzing in my hand.
When I grasped the shack's shiny, strangely new doorknob,
something *pulsed* from it, up my arm. I pushed the door
open and ice cold wind howled from the darkness . . .

128

Then I was driving along an endless dark country road in my cab. But not alone. The back seat was packed with . . . ten? Twelve? Twenty people? I couldn't see their eyes or their faces in the shadows. They sat silently, expectant and patient . . . for the moment. Deep inside I somehow knew if I didn't take them where they *needed* to go, they'd become a lot less patient. Sitting next to me was Mystery Philosophical Guy. I still couldn't see his face, subconsciously grateful for the way he hid in the shadows, or the way the shadows rode along with him, whichever it was.

I was driving with only one hand, because he was holding my other one, clasping to it something round and metallic, something which burned like acid against my palm.

The coin.

He was branding me with it, sure as a farmer brands a cow. Though its cold burning scorched my skin I said nothing, driving along that endless country road, while he mumbled words which flowed from his lips with an odd, foreign lilt sounding intimate and familiar, strange and alien all at once.

And the night sky.

It burned with black stars. I know this probably doesn't make sense. How can you see black stars against the blackness of night? Of course, a night sky is never *completely* black. It's a dimness lit by faint, ambient light. Against this burned great stars of *utter* blackness. Gazing at them made my blood freeze.

The road ended abruptly at a wide lake. Its glass surface shimmered under the black moonlight as yellow, misshapen things frothed in its waves, lurching from the waters and onto the shore . . .

I sat up with a gasp, clamping both my hands to my mouth, muffling a shriek. My heart pounded, my breath roared in my ears, and my shirt and boxers stuck to cold, sweat-slicked skin.

What the hell.

What. The. Hell?

I kicked my covers off, swung my feet to the floor, bent over and put my face into my hands. I swallowed deeply, forcing myself to calm down. After a few minutes numbness stole over me. The nightmare's grip faded, its intensity leaching from my system. Slowly, fearfully, I flattened my right hand, spread my fingers and gazed at my palm.

Nothing but smooth, unblemished skin.

"Jeez," I muttered, my guts quivering. "What the hell were you expecting to find?"

that sign

three pronged hooks or question marks swirling around the center

HIS sign

I sat, squeezed my right hand into a fist, running my other through damp hair. "A dream," I muttered. "Just a stupid dream."

Yeah, I know.

How could I possibly have sold myself such a bullshit line?

just a stupid dream

I'm gonna be honest here.

I haven't a clue. Maybe it's human nature. Scary stories and movies have turned it into a clichéd vehicle: "The lame denial of something weird and unsettling happening to us" or the "It's only a dream" defense.

Thing is, I think—hell, I *know*—it *is* a defense. So many strange things happen on a daily basis. We live in a massively fucked-up world. These fucked-up things are shoved down our throat daily. We're force-fed them through television, radio, movies, the newspaper, YouTube and Facebook and Twitter and Vine and hell knows what else. The only way our brain can cope with all this strange shit, I think, is to codify it in dreams. And when strange shit actually happens *to* us . . .

like Andie McGovern calling
saying she's slit open her wrists
has bled but she can't die
why won't she die

. . . the "It was just a dream" defense becomes a necessary coping mechanism. It helped me survive trekking across Binghamton University's campus to Andie's dorm on a cold December night to hold her under the water until she died (which took way longer than it should've). It helped me survive seeing her later in my shower, in the rain, in lakes and streams and standing next to my bed, dripping water and blood.

"It's only a dream" helped me survive all those things because, as my efficient, practical and logical parents pounded into me since infancy: dreams, fears and nightmares were childish and impractical. They served no purpose but to distract, and were best dismissed and disposed of.

So for several months after Andie slashed her wrists I told myself "It Was Only A Dream." I told myself the same thing after my nightmare of driving under that black sky. Sitting on the edge of my bed, rocking back and forth with my face in my hands, I told myself *it was just a dream*.

And I gotta tell you, it worked like a charm.
For a day.

———— ∽∽ ————

A few hours later I was again leaving the post office (I don't
get anything but bills but for some reason I check my box
every day) when I stopped dead before the bulletin board.
There, from a "Missing" poster stared the kid I'd picked up
outside Paddy's Place. The confused kid who'd wanted to
"go home." His picture offered me a dead, flat stare.

After the initial shock passed, I sighed, figuring I'd been
right about the kid, sort of. He'd acted scared and lost not
necessarily because he'd been drinking illegally, but
because he was on the run. He'd been on his last legs when
he stumbled into my cab. This, of course, raised an
important question, one which oddly enough I hadn't
thought of until seeing this poster.

Where did I take him?

I couldn't remember.

Like I couldn't remember where I'd taken Mystery
Philosophical Guy.

I frowned and peered closer at the Missing poster, my
mind skittering around the question for a moment, looking
for this guy's name—Everett Boyers—and his address,
figuring it to be local. Maybe it would jog my memory.

why couldn't I remember?

Something unpleasant stirred in my belly. First: Everett
Boyers was from Dewitt, Syracuse. So whatever he'd meant
by "go home" he hadn't meant his real home, only the place
he was currently crashing. I sure as hell hadn't driven him
to Dewitt and back. Would've been a four hour round trip.

But, try as I might . . . I couldn't remember where I'd
taken the kid.

Another disturbing thing?

The date he'd gone missing.

According to the poster, he'd gone missing six years ago. *Six years.* Maybe the kid looked young for his age. How much did a person age in six years anyway? But far as I could remember (because I *did* remember Everett Boyers's flat eyes) he looked last night exactly the same as he did in his missing poster.

Exactly.

My mind was on the verge of throwing some serious sparks when my TracPhone rang. Icy dread curdled in my stomach.

I knew who it was.

"Yeah?"

"Get yer ass over here. Right now. You want to keep yer job? My office, ten minutes."

Buster, of course.

He hung up. Slammed the phone, sounded more like.

Feeling as if I'd been thrust into the middle of a hallucinatory fever dream . . .

it's only a dream, only a dream

. . . I stuffed my TracPhone into my pocket, exited the post office and shambled my way to Yellow Cab, knowing already what I was going to find there, knowing, but still telling myself the whole time . . .

it's only a dream

"You were short last night *again.* $6.50 this time. Thought I told you no more of this shit?"

I stood at Buster's desk, hands in my pockets, staring numbly at him. Memories from my dream the night before . . .

so many faces I can't see

Mystery Philosophical Guy, holding my hand
the coin
the coin
. . . flickered in my head. I licked dry, chapped lips and stammered, "Uh. I don't know how . . . I mean, I got some kid at Paddy's Place . . . "
who went missing six years ago
from Dewitt
how the hell is he way out here?
where did I take him?
"Yeah, yeah." Buster consulted his ancient PC's food-splattered screen, "And it says here you took him to Bassler Road. But *where* on Bassler Road? The Commons Trailer Park? Only place you could've taken him, unless some of the jocks were partying at Old Bassler House last night. But they only do that over the summer, so . . . "

I could only run a trembling hand through my hair and stare, because, of course . . . I couldn't remember.

Buster turned a piercing yet weirdly compassionate gaze onto me. "What gives? You need some time off? You got personal problems? I'm asking this once, you understand. I'm running a business. Not a charity."

Personal problems?

Like lingering guilt I couldn't compartmentalize, despite all my parents had taught me? Guilt from helping someone commit a suicide?

"Yeah," I began slowly, choosing my words carefully, my tongue feeling heavy. "Something . . . personal. Haven't been sleeping well. I . . . I don't know what to do, honestly."

At least the last part was right.

Buster leaned back, laced his beefy fingers over his belly and sighed, appearing strangely more paternal than my father ever had. "Kid, you're the youngest driver I got. And smarter than most. Way you carry yourself screams 'college' but you're here, driving cab. Kids your age with your brains don't drive cab in a nowhere town like this because they *want* to. Three years I ain't said nothing cause I figured it weren't none of my business, and you've been one of my most reliable drivers. That's the only thing standing in the way of you getting fired, so's you know."

I swallowed, clasping the back of my neck which felt cold and clammy. My head spun, my stomach clenched and I felt like I was standing right on the edge of passing out, so I nodded gently.

Buster clicked his dingy PC's equally dingy mouse. "All the time you've worked here, you ain't never taken time off. Pascucci is coming back from his vacay today. Run your route tonight, and then you're on *paid* leave for a week."

He stopped clicking and glanced up, face still a mixture of sympathy and admonition. "Get your shit together, come back next week. I'm taking this short-fall from your paycheck. Next time it happens you're done. First time was your verbal warning. When you get in from your shift tonight, there'll be a written warning waiting for you. Sign it, leave it on my desk and get outta here for a week. Go relax, drink some booze, get laid, whatever. Come back next week with your head screwed on straight. Got it?"

I nodded. "Thanks, Mr. Malfi. I'll sort it all out, I promise."

Malfi grunted, fixing me with an introspective gaze. "Whatever. You know . . . at the end of the week, you decide to blow this one-horse town and go back to wherever it is you're running away from, I won't be heartbroken. Can always find another schmuck to take your place."

He dismissed me with a wave, turning back to his old PC. "Get the hell on the road."

I left his office quickly, wishing he hadn't added the "going back" part, because when you help your secret lover commit suicide over the guilt from the horrible thing you'd both done, there wasn't any going back. There was only going forward, no matter how aimless the path, in a vain effort to put as many miles between you and the thing that exposed the lessons your parents taught you for a lie.

Like the day before, I sat in my cab for a few minutes as it idled. Staring. Thinking. Filling my head with white noise, desperately trying to drown the clamoring voices in my head, trying my best to deny and compartmentalize.

where do you really want to go?

But it wasn't working.

where do you want to be?

Despite my best efforts, I couldn't quite push aside the weirdness of the past few days . . .

the anniversary of helping Andie die

after what you both did

. . . forgetting where I'd taken not one but *two* passengers, coming short on the till, the nightmare . . .

missing six years ago

from Dewitt, how'd he get here?

. . . and that damned coin . . .

My focus snapped back into place. The weird coin I'd thrown into the woods behind Shelby Road Cemetery yesterday. I'd forgotten *where* I'd taken Everett Boyers . . .

somewhere on Bassler Road

. . . and came short on the till again, but apparently this time there wasn't a weird coin . . .

Or, at the least, I hadn't turned it in.

I glanced at the glove compartment.

Stared at it for several seconds before reaching toward it. But as my fingertips grazed the latch, I clenched my hand into a fist, pulled it back, put my car in gear and pulled away.

I wasn't planning to go there. Not consciously, for sure. But twenty minutes later I found myself parked on Bassler Road, idling before old Bassler House itself. And you know the funny thing? I wasn't surprised. Not in the least.

I left my cab slowly, feeling distant, as if someone else was working the strings and moving me along like a puppet. I staggered across Bassler Road, through the brush clogging the ditch, and then stumbled to a halt in the middle of the old drive leading to Bassler House.

I gazed upon its ruins.

Honestly?

I didn't understand at first why folks whispered about the old place so much. Far as I could tell, standing in front of Bassler House on a slightly chilly but sunny October morning, it was a broken-down Victorian farmhouse in the middle of an old cornfield left fallow for years. Sure, it exuded a creepy *Children of the Corn, Chainsaw Massacre* vibe, but it was only an old house, right?

I told myself so, anyway, as I continued up the drive. Slowly, I felt better and more in control, no longer so detached. And I felt a bit silly, to be honest. So I'd probably taken Everett Boyers here last night. So what? If he'd run away . . .

six years ago?

. . . he was probably squatting here. Since he wasn't from around here . . .

all the way from Dewitt

. . . the rumors about this old place probably didn't bother him much, either.

Of course, the minute I climbed those rickety steps onto the old front porch, I was thinking twice about dismissing those rumors. It wasn't how the empty windows leered darkness like eye-sockets in a skull. Or how the old house kind of loomed over me while I stood on the porch. There was something in the air. A sense of lingering dread. A foulness I could taste, a taint or malignancy pressing in on me the longer I stood on the porch.

Despite all this, however, I found myself reaching for the front door . . . but I stopped when I saw two things. One: a shiny new doorknob exactly like the one on the old shack at Shelby Road Cemetery, with the same weird design. Two: something yellow spray-painted on the front door. I hadn't looked at it ascending the front steps, dismissing it as nothing but graffiti.

Looking closer, I saw it was the same design as on the coin and those shiny new doorknobs. It was shaky, as if sprayed by the hand of a child, but still. The spiraling question mark design was unmistakable.

A coincidence.

It only looked like the design on the coin because some crazy part of my brain wanted it to. The brain's weird that way. It was graffiti. It didn't mean anything. In a burst of reckless bravado (desperate to prove it to myself), I grabbed the door knob and yanked the old door open.

Light and riddled with damp-rot, it slammed open on its hinges. A wonder it didn't come off. A satisfied, smug corner of my mind noted I'd felt nothing when I grabbed the door knob . . .

nothing pulsing from it into my hand up my arm like in my dream

I looked into the foyer. Past a few damp leaves and twigs, it was empty. Just the foyer to an old house, and that's all.

No howling blackness. No ebony skies hung with black stars. No strange road surrounded by strange black trees reaching for the sky. Nothing but a dusty, littered foyer, beyond which was a second door leading into the house proper.

Nothing.

Just like I'd thought.

Except.

Except, whispered a sly little voice, sounding a lot like Mystery Philosophical Guy, *you don't have a coin. What if you were holding a coin when you opened the door? Maybe you should check in your glove compartment, get the coin you* know *is there and try this door again, see where it takes you . . .*

I spun sharply on one heel.

Bounded down the stairs, amazingly not tripping and breaking my neck. I'd be lying if I said I didn't run all the way back to my car.

The mind is a strange, sometimes wonderful (and horrible) thing. Given the right circumstances, it can become extremely flexible and absorb a lot more weirdness than we give it credit for. All it takes is the right combination of desperation and the dogged determination of someone frightened to death (in a suppressed sort of way) of losing his grip on a rigidly constructed, routine-oriented world.

Mystery Philosophical Guy was an asshole who'd messed with me two nights before. He'd passed off a bum coin on me, probably something from an old novelty store.

And it was old, which was probably why its design was similar to the one on the doorknobs of the caretaker's shack at Shelby Cemetery and Bassler House's front door (though both doorknobs were shiny, polished and new) because it was probably a common decorative design used on lots of things at some point . . .

and there wasn't *another coin in the glove compartment*

The yellow design spray-painted on Bassler House's front door was graffiti. My mind made it look like the design on the coin and the doorknobs because minds do weird shit sometimes. Besides, when I opened Bassler House's front door nothing happened, right?

because you didn't have a coin

Everything was all right.

Everything was *fine.*

But though my morning proved uneventful—I took a few fares to ordinary destinations, and nothing strange happened at all—that afternoon the dyke I'd built in my head sprung another leak, and I officially ran out of fingers.

Around two o'clock I parked before Clifton Heights First Methodist. One of my regulars, Bobby Watson, was standing on the curb, bags of food pantry goods huddled at his feet. Standing six foot four, weighing enough to make my cab sag on its shocks, Bobby must've been quite the physical specimen once. Though his pendulous gut hung over his belt, his chest sagged and his face was puffy and soft, his arms and legs were the size of tree-trunks, and his hands looked like they could pop my head like an overripe grape. He'd told me many times in a dreamy voice of his days playing middle linebacker for Clifton Heights High, of being All County, leading the Conference two years in a row in both tackles and sacks.

Apparently he'd been offered several scholarships to play college football, but according to my fellow drivers, he enlisted soon as he graduated back in 1991. Not too long after came the war. Operation Desert Shield in Kuwait. In one of the initial skirmishes, shrapnel blew apart his right knee. It was repaired (after a fashion), but ever since he'd worn a metal-hinged leather knee brace.

Apparently he'd found work at the lumber mill for a while, but as the years passed and his knee deteriorated, so did he. He hit the bottle more and more and also, dogged by bad luck, took several falls at work. Wasn't long until he was staying at home, declaring disability and drinking full time. This was his station in life by the time I started picking him up every Tuesday outside the Methodist Church after its weekly food pantry.

He wasn't a bad guy. I felt sorry for him. He was always friendly and upbeat in a dreamy way. He talked of his football days without bragging. He also talked about how much he missed the military, because in the military he was always doing *something*, following a routine he could count on every single day. The only thing he could count on these days was waking to pain every morning, drinking until it went away, the food bank once a week, and me taking him home afterward. Somehow, he managed to talk of all these things without crying. He sat there and chatted with me, eyes seeing something far away, smiling his distracted smile.

The day Buster Malfi gave me his last pep talk, Bobby appeared happier than usual. More alert, aware . . . hell, excited. He got into the cab and I pulled away without asking for his destination, noting his big smile and bright eyes in the rear-view mirror. "Bobby. What's up? Hell, you look like you won the lottery, pal."

Bobby smiled wider, showing yellow-stained teeth. He shuffled his food-pantry bags aside and actually clamped my shoulder in an excited squeeze. "It's the most awesome thing. It's amazing. I'm so excited, I'm afraid I'll burst."

I raised an eyebrow. "Yeah? What's to tell, Bobby? You meet someone in there? Got a hot date tonight?"

Bobby shook his massive head. "Nope. Way better. I'm being *reactivated*. They want me *back*."

Somehow I managed a poker face. So Bobby had gone around the bend. Lost it. Slipped into Never-Never Land. Sad, but I supposed it was inevitable. Forty-something with no job or purpose, a busted knee that hurt all the time, dropping full-on into a fantasy world to cope with it all? Who could blame him?

I offered him a smile in the rear-view mirror, wondering if there was someone I should call, or if it was any of my business. I didn't want Bobby to hurt himself, but the last thing I wanted was to be responsible for the guys in white coats hauling him away.

"Great, Bobby. Awesome. When did you hear? And do you know what you're gonna be doing? I mean . . . well, no offense . . . but I don't think you'll be doing a lot of marching or walking or anything. Not with your knee and all."

Bobby grinned wider. My heart sank a little, seeing his wet lips glistening with drool. "No marching. I mean, they'll get my ass whipped into shape, definitely. Get me back on only three meals a day, no booze, and some PT . . . but my knee's busted for good, sure enough. No, they want me for a special division. Recruiter called me this morning, offering to reactivate me. Told me I'd been chosen. For training at Camp Hyades. Isn't that fucking great?"

I nodded slowly. A sick feeling crawled around in my gut. How awful for Bobby. He'd lost a football career because he'd wanted to serve his country and got his knee wrecked and his future along with it. Now, he was losing it. Imagining recruiters calling his house, enlisting him in fantasy special divisions.

"Did you get the guy's name?" I asked gently. I didn't know what I was doing, but as happy as Bobby was acting, I couldn't bear to see him like this, so lost in his delusion. "Not saying I don't believe you. Just want to make sure everything's legit. Don't want you to get hurt."

Bobby's grin looked so painful, my own cheeks hurt in sympathy. "Yep. Lt. Hastoor. And don't worry about a thing. It's all legit. I can tell. I know about these things, see."

He paused for a moment, glancing out the window. "Hey. Where we going?"

I shrugged and said, eyes straight forward, "Back to your place. Right?"

"No, no," he gushed, "I need to meet Lt. Hastoor so he can brief me on what I'll be doing in the special division at Camp Hyades."

Realizing I needed to talk to *someone* about Bobby's obvious break with reality, I said casually, "Sure thing, Bobby. Where do you need to go?"

He told me.

And I took him there.

I decided to eat dinner at Henry's Drive In after dropping Bobby Watson off, mostly because my route took me past there and I was too hungry to drive across town to The Skylark, where I normally ate dinner. I usually didn't like eating at Henry's because a bunch of other drivers—on duty and off—ate there. They always wanted to get together and gab over their dinners, and I mostly liked to eat alone.

And of course with all the strange things going on, I was in less of a mood than usual to talk to my coworkers. But my stomach won and soon enough I found myself seated in a booth near the back of Henry's, enjoying an open-faced hot-turkey sandwich. Some of the other guys were there, but they'd settled a few booths away. They showed no inclination of joining me, so at first it appeared I could dine in peace.

Unfortunately, my solitude didn't last long. I'd gotten halfway through my meal when Ike McPeak stood from a booth where he'd also been sitting alone and wandered over to me.

Ike is an odd duck. The kind found in any small town, I suppose. He lives alone in a neatly-kept trailer in The Commons. His is a genuinely sad story. He'd fought in Vietnam and saw some bad action. Story goes he survived by playing 'dead' under the corpses of his platoon while Charlie moved through the rubble of their position. If you believe the stories, he'd hidden under the mangled body of his best buddy while a Cong slipped a watch off his wrist.

In some ways, the rest sounds like a story arc from a TV show. Ike survived his close encounter with the Cong and finished his tour without a hitch, but he arrived home to Syracuse Hancock International Airport to the news of his wife and only child, a little girl, getting killed by a drunk driver on the way to meet him.

The stories vary afterward. One: He tried to settle into a career teaching Math at Clifton Heights High, only to get fired and nearly arrested when he throttled a student in a drunken rage because the kid forgot his protractor. Or, he'd been fired from the lumber mill after his teaching career ended, for reporting to work drunk too many times.

The 'best' story is when he was pumping gas at the Quickmart on Haverton Road and slashed the tires of a leftover hippie's YUGO. Apparently, the hippie (wearing old Army fatigues peppered with Grateful Dead patches) gave Ike attitude for not cleaning his windows. Ike didn't say a word, just drew a box-cutter from his pocket and proceeded to slash the hippy's tires. Don't know if it's a true story, but it's certainly the most entertaining one. I don't really like leftover hippies myself.

The common denominator in all these stories, of course, was Ike's drinking. Ike spent the first fifteen years after returning from Vietnam blind drunk. Considering his experience I don't blame him. From what I've gathered, no one else did, either.

Thing was, Ike's drunk wasn't the kind you could easily dismiss with a sad smile, like Cletus Smith, a nightly regular at The Stumble Inn. Cletus is an amiable, friendly, sad-sack "tear in ma beer I wish I could make somethin of maself but it's too late" kind of drunk. No one paid Clete any mind, nor took him seriously after he'd downed a few.

Ike on the other hand was mean and a little crazy. From what I understand, not even Deputy Shackleford (biggest guy on the force) liked tangling with Ike when the old boy was deep in his drink. I've heard it mentioned several times that Sheriff Baker's biggest relief was Ike McPeak sobering up long before he was hired.

And he'd gone sober *hardcore*, or at least the stories told. Back in the nineties, when he'd first started driving for Yellow Cab. He'd been sober ever since.

Ike stopped at my booth and stood there. Hands in his

pockets, staring at me with sharp green eyes which didn't look as if they'd ever seen a drop of alcohol. If I hadn't heard the stories, I'd never have suspected, because his eyes could peel layers of skin off you, cutting to the quick. They weren't the eyes of a sad-sack drunk like Clete, or the eyes of a man who'd lost his wife and kid to a drunk driver. Those eyes belonged to stone-cold-death striding through the misty Cambodian jungle, M-16 ready to speak hot lead in an instant.

"Uh. Hey, Ike," I managed, feeling ridiculous with a forkful of turkey and gravy-sopped bread frozen halfway to my mouth. "What's up?"

Ike kept staring at me, his green eyes blazing. Age lined his face with deep cracks, but he didn't look like an old man or somebody's grandfather. He looked savage and primal, weathered by the harshest elements imaginable. His square jaw formidable, his receding hairline squared-away in a bristling white crew-cut. He wasn't tall and wasn't 'big' by anyone's standards, but he carried himself with a whip-cord erectness *I* wouldn't put my twenty-two year old self against.

And, damn. The way Ike looked at me.

Sober, sure.

But still mean and crazy.

Behind the wheel, however, Ike McPeak was all business. He was the most meticulous driver at Yellow Cab. He logged more time on the road in one week than I want to think about. I have no idea what laws govern how many hours a week a guy can work, but they didn't apply to Ike McPeak. Word was he'd driven every single road, street, avenue, cul de sac, dead end, traffic circle and intersection in town. He'd mapped the 'Heights and driven as far as you possibly can in Webb County while staying within Yellow

Cab's jurisdiction. He was Buster's most experienced driver, his go-to guy.

But he was still mean and crazy, no doubt.

Without speaking, Ike slid smoothly into the booth across from me, pulling his hands from his pockets and folding them on the table.

I glanced at them. His hands and fingers were strong and lean. No arthritis knotting those joints. I realized Ike could crush my fingers in a handshake. Those hands around my throat would probably be the last thing I'd ever feel.

I opened my mouth to say something else—what, I have no idea,—when he rasped in a sandpaper voice, "You've seen them. Haven't you?"

Cold unease trickled down the back of my neck. "Seen . . . who?"

Ike peered closer at me, narrowing his eyes, as if judging me. Like I'd never spoken, he continued. "Yep. Can see it in your eyes. Like I saw it in boys' eyes back in 'Nam."

As if a switch flipped in his head, Ike sat back smoothly and said in a far less confrontational voice, "One thing no one understands about 'Nam. Damn jungles were haunted. Every goddamn thing in there was haunted, and those Cong didn't just *believe* it. They *lived* it. They lived *with* it. Goddamn ghosts every goddamn day every goddamn-where. Vietnam was *lousy* with ghosts. Boys in brass and folks at home didn't understand. Charlie couldn't just move *like* a ghost, dammit. Half the time, Charlie *was* a ghost. For real and for certain."

His switch flipped again. He leaned forward, eyes blazing, hands clasped before him on the booth's table. "And it wasn't only the Cong who were haunted. *We* were haunted. By gooks we'd killed. By our pals. Guys we'd tried to save but couldn't. Worse, guys we'd been too pissed-pants scared to save. But they weren't the worst. *Linh hon da mat.* They were the worst, by far."

I swallowed and managed a weak, "What were they?"

Ike rambled on. "*Linh hon da mat.* Lost souls. Gooks believed when a body lost its way, it wandered off this plane of existence in search of a new one. Maybe when the body got so it didn't know what it wanted anymore or where it was going. Or maybe somehow it knew its time was up, so it got to wandering. Problem was, once it started, it hardly ever found where it was going.

"It's the *land* over there. The jungle. The ground we walked on. It was cursed or haunted or more . . . aware. It *knew* you. Wasn't in country too long before I started hearing about the *linh hon da mat.* Stories of ghost soldiers joining platoons on marches. Not ghosts of gooks we'd killed or guys we could've saved, though we all saw plenty of those, too. I'm talking strange soldiers nobody recognized. They came from nowhere and joined the ranks, moving through the jungle like they were one of us. Like they belonged, except deep inside you knew they *didn't.* At *all.* Lt's would tell stories of swearing an extra man was with their platoon, but when they reached their LZ or took a break, they sounded off to the usual number. But soon as they got back to humping it, they swore they had one or two more men then they should. Boys in brass waved it off as jungle fatigue, but I knew better. We all did. Those extra soldiers were *linh hon.* Soldiers who'd lost their way. Their spirits had gone wandering, and they never made it back."

He paused, peering at me. "I saw it in their eyes. Men who'd seen the *linh hon.* Same exact look *you* got in your eyes. Like you're drifting, too. Lost. Like it won't be long before *you* start wandering yourself. Because you seen *him,* too, haven't you?"

I sat back in my booth, stomach churning, feeling slightly feverish and nauseated. "Him? Him *who*?"

"*Vua linh hon.* King of lost souls. Only ever heard talk of him in 'Nam. He's some chief spirit, the one who entices folks to start wandering in the first place. But I saw him *here,* boy. Twenty-five years ago. Why I dried out so fast. I was driving on Bassler Road after a bender, cruised right on past the trailer park and didn't notice until I was way past Bassler House. I turned myself around, got headed back the right way and saw someone hitching for a ride. Must've been stone-cold drunk, because I stopped to give him a lift, and everyone around here knows you never give *anyone* a lift on Bassler Road. Never. Place is lousy with *linh hon.*"

I shivered a little at this.

dropped off somewhere on Bassler Road

"Anyway, I picked this fella up. Can't remember how long he rode with me, and for the life of me I can't remember where I dropped him off. And I don't recall what-all we talked of, except . . . "

Ike paused again.

Leaned back and stared away, at some unfixed point across Henry's Drive In. I followed his gaze but saw nothing except hungry patrons paying us no attention.

"What? Except what?"

"An invitation," Ike whispered, continuing to stare at nothing. "I think . . . I think it was an invitation. To . . . follow him? Work for him. Or something. I can't remember."

Ike visibly shook himself and looked back at me. "Somehow, drunk as I was, I didn't accept anything. I don't remember if I dropped this fella off, or if he sorta . . . left. All I know is, next morning I dumped all the booze down the drain and got dry. Went through hell doing it, went through awful shakes and bad dreams in which this fella came to me every night, offering me the same thing . . . "

My nightmare flashed in my head.

Of me riding with Mystery Philosophical Guy in the front seat of my cab, pressing a weird coin into my hand.

" . . . but somehow I made it through, got clean, and I haven't swallowed a drop of booze since. Somehow, I know if I fall off the wagon he's gonna come looking for me and if he finds me, start right in on me all over again. I still see him, now and then. Standing on the side of the road, thumbing for a ride. But I always pretend I don't see him and drive by."

He gave me a pointed look. "And you've seen him. Seen the *Vua linh hon* and his ghosts. I can see it in your eyes. You're set to go wandering, sure enough, to become one of his, or some other damn thing. You best be careful, son. Or one of these days you're gonna go driving and never come back."

Done, Ike clapped his hands onto the booth's table, stood and headed toward to door.

All appetite completely gone, I stared at Ike's receding back. "What the *hell*?"

But deep in my heart some part of me knew. A subconscious adding machine was tallying the score: Mystery Philosophy Guy; Everett Boyers who wanted to "go home" (somewhere on Bassler Road), who'd also been missing for six years; Bobby Watson and his delusional ramblings about getting "chosen" for some special division . . .

The strange coin.

Like fare for passage.

It occurred to me. Like the other two, I couldn't remember where or when I'd dropped off Bobby Watson before coming to Henry's for dinner.

My stomach flipped over. I pushed aside my unfinished turkey sandwich (now a pile of cold, sodden bread and meat in congealing gravy), stood and headed to the front counter to pay.

I was in line at the front counter, waiting to pay when Derek Brown sidled next to me. He nudged my shoulder with his, nodding toward the door through which Ike had exited only moments before. "He give you the whole 'wandering spirit-king' shit?"

Something in Derek's gap-toothed, stained-yellow grin always made me uneasy. Ike may be the stereotypical intense and slightly-unhinged town Vietnam vet, but Derek is, unfortunately, how most people think of small town taxi drivers. Skinny, with greasy hair slinking to his shoulders around a narrow face pock-marked with old acne scars, Derek always smelled of smoke, tobacco juice and something peppermint, like cheap schnapps. Derek Brown was high on the list of people I'd rather avoid.

His question, however, took me aback. "Wait. What? He's told you, too?"

Derek snorted, shaking his head like I was a moron, which made me want to bury my fist between his eyes. "Hell, he's told *everyone* that story. Bout some Thing wanderin the roads, lookin for someone to bring 'im all the lost souls in the world. So he can eat them or some such? Shit, some folks he's told it to two or three times. Myself, think I've heard it four."

Derek winked, leering, as if letting me in on the secret

holes he'd drilled in the wall of the girls' locker room at school. "Don' pay old Ike no mind. He's one of Buster's best drivers, but he's crazy an full of shit. Crazier 'n a shithouse *rat* full of shit. Ain't no spirit king wanderin the roads, lookin for someone to bring 'im all the spirits to gobble. Only thing wanderin is Old Man Sykes lookin for little boys' peckers to gobble, you dig?"

Derek leered wider, nudging me again with his shoulder for good measure. He broke into a rasping cough, thin shoulders shaking, as if he were about to hack up some vital organ.

I managed a weak grin. "Sure. I dig."

Derek, still shaking with hawking laughter, slapped my shoulders like we'd been buddies since the day he'd drilled those holes in the girls' locker room wall. "Have a good run tonight. Don't pick up no oogie boogies!"

He raised his hands and clenched his fingers into claws, snarling, then exploded into more coughing laughter as he turned and left. Not surprisingly, Derek's reassurances didn't overly inspire much confidence.

I sat in my cab for several minutes at the curb outside Henry's, unpleasant thoughts mixing in my head. I was trying my hardest to do as Mom and Dad taught me: rationalize and compartmentalize. Fears, nightmares, feelings, emotions in general were all distractions weakening efficiency and performance. Nothing was mysterious. Everything was explainable. Mysteries and the unexplained were distractions, and therefore unproductive.

But these things happening to me . . . I couldn't explain them. Starting with Mystery Philosophical guy, who'd gotten into my cab two nights ago in The Golden Kitty's parking lot rambling on about "Where I really wanted to go and do . . . "

he looks for ones to bring souls to him

Everything tracked back to him. Whoever he was, all the weird shit started after Mystery Philosophical guy got into my cab.

he recruits

those to bring lost souls to him

I looked at the glove compartment again for several minutes. Then—my hand remarkably steady—I flicked it open, spreading my palm wide . . .

And into it rolled those damn coins. One for Everett Boyers, and one for Bobby Watson.

I raised my hand, gazing at their strange designs, thinking about a mysterious person who'd acted overly interested in my future, about fares I couldn't remember taking anywhere, about Ike McPeak's crazy Vietnam stories, and of how he'd picked up a Mysterious Philosophical Guy of his own.

You've seen them, haven't you?

I can see it in your eyes.

I closed my hand around the coins but this time didn't throw them away. Instead, with them still clutched against my palm . . .

and they burned slightly, they burned

. . . I turned the ignition, starting my Caprice. I pulled away from the curb, heading somewhere I knew I shouldn't, doing the worst thing possible, the only "sin" my parents could've ever conceived: I was going to get some answers (of whatever kind) and blow my compartmentalization wide open, destroying my rationalizations once and for all.

153

I sat in my idling cab in front of Bobby Watson's trailer in The Commons Trailer Park, warring with myself. I was ready to break every bit of compartmentalizing I'd done my entire life. Standing before a door that, once I opened, I sensed I'd never be able to close.

But I needed to know.

Because I should've taken Bobby *here* after the food pantry. I'd been doing so once a week for the past three years. Parking outside Clifton Heights First Methodist around noon and taking Bobby Watson from the food pantry to his home here in The Commons. Which I should've done, except . . .

I couldn't remember.

The door to Bobby's trailer was cracked open, showing only darkness beyond, a darkness filling the trailer's windows with thick, oily blackness.

I shut my cab off. Got out and on numb legs, stumbled toward Bobby's trailer and its cracked-open door. I pushed it open. Felt against the wall, found the switch and flipped on the lights. A sickly yellow—the kind you associate with sickness and decay—bathed the living room, throwing into stark relief the words and symbols scrawled on the walls in what looked like black sharpie or magic marker.

The same design as on those coins.

Scribbled all over the cheap paneled walls, along with words which sounded hauntingly familiar but strange at the same time: Lake Hyades . . .

a lake in which hideous, rubbery yellow things thrashed

. . . Crawling Chaos, Nyarlathotep, Hali. Words I

recognized dimly from history lessons: Crotoan, Roanoke. Written there several times was the name of that *place* I supposedly took Mystery Philosophical guy, Carcosa. Also, Assatur, Xastur, H'aaztre, Hastur . . .

Lt. Hastoor

. . . and He Who Shall Not Be Named. He'd hastily written phrases, as well. Things like "I'm going home to Carcosca," "Yog-soth is the Key and Gate," and "I'm for the Undiscovered Country," which is a campy installment in the *Star Trek* movies but also a snippet from Shakespeare. The most disturbing of them all, for some reason, was, "He waits in Lake Hyades to bring me home."

Crazy.

Bug-shit crazy, like I'd figured when he'd been rambling in my cab about getting a call "choosing" him for a special division. He'd absolutely lost it, broken free from reality, except . . .

Where the hell did I take him, if not home, like always?

Carcosa

Lake Hyades

They paid me with those coins, a dim corner of my mind muttered. *Paid me for passage and I took them . . . I took them . . .*

Away.

Where?

To *him*.

A freezing numbness filled me. I spun and without thinking twice, without bothering to switch off the light, stumbled from Bobby Watson's trailer and to my cab.

———✷———

I don't know how long I sat there. I may have fallen asleep or passed into some sort of fugue, I don't know. All I know is, one moment I was drifting in a hazy place, the next jerking awake at the tell-tale *thump* of my back door closing.

Another fare.

I glanced into the rear-view mirror, not batting an eye when I saw who sat back there. I felt no fear, no remorse, no pity or anger or anything. In fact, more than anything, I felt relieved, because I think (subconsciously)I'd been waiting for this fare ever since Mystery Philosophical Guy boarded my cab.

In the back sat Andie McGovern, her face looking much different from the rounded, soft pretty-little-girl I remembered from college, her features sharpened, thin and angular, drawn with fatigue. Her eyes, focused on the bundle swaddled in her arms, glittered blackly, stone-cold and distant.

In her arms?

Our baby, of course.

The one she'd given birth to at 3 AM in the deserted parking lot behind the Utica Walmart. Initially Andie wanted the baby. To spite her parents maybe, or to fill the same hole inside her as I'd discovered inside me. But at the last minute, Andie changed her mind. In labor, on the way to Utica General, she demanded I get off the highway and park behind a dumpster behind Walmart. She couldn't have this baby. Couldn't care for it, didn't want it, didn't want the life we'd dreamed and talked of and (of course) hidden from our career-oriented parents. As Fate or Blind Dumb Luck would have it, no cop cars or security cars swung by. Andie survived labor with no complications. She gave birth to a healthy, average sized baby boy.

She made me smother it.

Ditch it in the dumpster.

Because she hadn't wanted to bond with it. She'd

wanted to make a clean break. She figured because I'd never wanted the baby in the first place . . .

at least that's what she'd thought

. . . I wouldn't mind. She figured I could handle it, like I'd always handled things.

And of course I did.

Because my parents raised me to handle things. And I'd thought Andie had been handling things, too, until she was dead by her own hand . . .

and mine, always helpful always handling things, as usual

. . . five months later.

Thankfully, whatever Andie was cradling in the back seat had most of its face covered. As she made all the senseless, cooing noises new mothers make, it gurgled wetly, and didn't sound remotely human. What little skin I could see was gray.

I looked forward, and in the flattest voice I could manage, "Where to?"

Her voice rasped, like dry leaves scratching across autumn pavement. "Home. I need to go . . . home."

I nodded and put the cab into gear. Home, yes. But not home in Florida. The place Andie McGovern and our dead baby wanted to go was somewhere much farther away, and without question, I drove her there.

They say your career picks you, not the other way around. I never used to believe that. Of course my logical, rational, efficient and motivated parents would've completely disagreed also. To them, it was opposite. You trained yourself for the career *you* wanted, taking control of your destiny with your own two hands.

Who knows?

Maybe both ideas are sort of right. Because I never *intended* on this life. But I certainly claimed my career when I sent my first passenger (Dylan, we were going to name him) to his faraway home with my own two hands. Whether I knew it or not, I chose my career right then and there.

I don't work for Buster these days, though I'm still getting lots of fares. But I never took my cab back to him, or officially quit. Funny how neither Sheriff Baker nor any of his deputies have ever come searching for me, seeing as how I basically stole a cab and still live in the same apartment and all. Of course, with all this new traveling I've been doing to Old Shelby Road Cemetery, the abandoned church on Sanctuary Street, Bassler House, the abandoned La Pierre place by the tracks, I'm not exactly on the map anymore.

And I don't know what the hell I'm going to do with all these weird coins. It's not like I can spend them anywhere. But I suppose I'll figure something out. I'll handle it. That's why I'm so perfect for this job, I suppose.

Handling things is what I do.

ADMIT ONE

BOBBY MASKEL'S SOCKET wrench slipped off the bolt he'd been trying to loosen for the past twenty minutes. His knuckles slammed against metal. Pain flashed across his hand. He cursed, barely stopping himself from tossing the wrench against the wall, remembering at the last second Mr. Greene's lectures about "respecting the workplace and the tools with which we make our living."

"Living my ass," Bobby mumbled as he clenched his hand into a fist, examining the damage. "Only one making a living off this shit is Greene and his dumb-ass son."

After a brief inspection, it was clear he'd done nothing worse than scrape his knuckles. It stung all the same. Still pissed but calmer, Bobby regarded the dismembered snowblower on the work bench, glaring as if he could lay the blame for his life's misfortunes on its engine block and chassis.

He was working 'The Pit' this month. He *hated* working The Pit. Greene's Metal Salvage accepted all kinds of scrap metal and paid competitive rates. If scrapping pure aluminum, brass, copper, copper wire, or returning cans and bottles for deposit, you visited the main warehouse. Associates there weighed your metals and counted your cans and bottles. Everything else went into The Pit.

The Pit was aptly named. Upon entering Greene Salvage, if hauling a load of "scrap" metal (tin, iron, steel, cast iron) you drove your truck or minivan onto a giant set of scales. After getting weighed, you pulled off the scales, took a right and backed down an incline into a recessed, fan-shaped area. The Pit. You chucked your metal, returned to the scales, got re-weighed, then reported to the main office and cashed out.

At the end of The Pit was the compactor. Throughout the day, whenever The Pit filled up, someone in the mini-dozer pushed scrap back into the channel leading to the compactor. Old rolling chairs, tool chests, tricycles, odds and ends, toaster ovens, scrapped sheet metal, old ventilation ducts and more were then compacted into rectangular metal cubes. These were then conveyed by a belt to the loading area. A crane loaded them onto a flatbed, destined either for storage or raw metal processing plants.

But not everything thrown into The Pit was "junk metal." Lots of times whole pieces of equipment—like the snow-blower he'd labored over for the past hour—were tossed in simply because their former owners hadn't the patience, the know-how or the tools to strip off the precious metals.

Case in point: most snow-blowers, lawnmowers, and weed eaters had aluminum engine blocks. Market value for aluminum was currently 90 cents a pound. Copper was 3.23 a pound. Any aluminum or copper gleaned from The Pit was a bonus for Greene's because they'd only paid baseline tin rates for it. Collect enough precious metals from The Pit in a month, you saved Greene's some cash.

When he was working The Pit, once an hour Bobby drove in the company four-wheeler and its trailer. Between customers, he searched through piles of twisted, rusted, and bent metal for any aluminum or copper pieces worth stripping.

Like this Briggs and Stratton snow-blower engine, circa 1975. The engine block was aluminum, but probably its former owner simply hadn't known how or hadn't cared enough to strip the block. So he'd pulled it from The Pit and lugged it into four wheeler's wagon (along with several tires on aluminum rims and a transmission for an old pick-up truck) and brought it back to his station to strip.

It was proving to be a pain in the ass. He'd needed to pull apart five other things to reach the engine block's mounts. After wrestling with five of the six bolts mounting the engine block to the chassis, the sixth was frozen, rusted to hell. All told, he'd blown an hour on the snow-blower already.

Luckily the aluminum rims would be an easy job. Greene's owned an automated dismounter which popped the sealant holding the tire to the rim, dismounting it in seconds. The transmission, however, looked like a son of a bitch. Was going to take forever. If he didn't make any headway with this snow-blower, he'd have to put it aside and search through The Pit again to keep on schedule. The place was hopping today. This would put him behind. If he didn't clear his station by 4:00, no way old man Greene was going to let him out early like he'd wanted. That, in his humble opinion, would be the fucking icing on a suck-ass cake.

Because Mr. Jingo's was in town. An annual fair which always visited Clifton Heights every August for a week, and it opened *today*. Free admission until 6 PM. If he didn't get his work done early, he'd have to work until closing (six-thirty) and then waste money he couldn't afford on admission.

And there, Bobby Lee thought as he grabbed a can of WD-40, is a shitty statement about *my* life. I'm so goddamn poor, paying admission to the county fair cripples my funds.

He triggered the WD-40 and soaked the rusted bolt with a hissing stream of rust-solvent. Life hadn't been *all* bad since graduating high school four years ago, but it hadn't been a party, either. He'd tried attending Webb Community College like everyone else (they took anyone, after all), majoring in Arc Welding and Mechanics, but though he'd found those classes interesting, he'd still been required to take other prerequisites like English, Math, and Life Sciences. After skipping most of those classes he flunked out after only one semester.

He spent the next year bouncing around different jobs. First came The Can Man, a bottle and can recycling center out on Route 434. He'd thought it'd be a cinch. He loved beer and pop and knew all the brands. How hard could it be?

But after a week of standing on a cement floor for six hours in the sweltering warehouse twisting at the waist all day and sorting piles of wet and slimy cans into different bins sorted by their distributors, his feet aching and his lower back throbbing, he simply stopped going. Next, he worked as a cashier at The Great American Grocery. That hadn't been so bad. Air conditioned, and business never moved too fast or too slow. Problem was, he kept seeing people he *knew*. Old classmates. Old teachers. Ms. Whipple from church. Friends of his mother. They always acted polite and didn't *seem* to pity him, but he quit there after only a week.

Then came a week at the lumber mill. Too much heavy lifting, and working the line with those huge saws scared the shit out of him. Then the rock quarry for a week or so, but once again, all the lifting killed his back. There was the Mobilmart out on Haverton Avenue, but he got stuck on the overnight shift and was fired for falling sleep behind the counter his second week there.

Through it all, he managed to earn enough cash for rent

on his little rat-box apartment over Chin's Pizza and to keep cheap frozen dinners and discount beer in the fridge. Things started looking financially desperate, however, after quitting as a stock boy at Handy's Pawn and Thrift because . . . well, because that place gave him bad vibes, period.

Afterward he couldn't find another job. With rent and utilities due, he'd gotten desperate. Inspiration struck one day when he saw an old '93 Dodge Caravan creeping around town on garbage day, stopping at curbs, the driver getting out and sifting through the junk left for trash pickup. He'd been looking for anything metal. Scrap metal to turn into Greene's. Bobby thought maybe *he* could score some scrap metal and turn it in, somehow collect enough cash to help him squeak through the month.

So the following Wednesday night he got into his beat-up Isuzu pickup and prowled the streets of Clifton Heights, looking for scrap metal. He passed that Dodge Caravan several times. It felt weird (like they were competing) though the driver of the Caravan never appeared to notice him.

He'd done okay. Collected several aluminum lawn chairs, a filing cabinet and some old aluminum molding. The next day he took it all into Greene's and actually came away with forty bucks. On the way out he noticed the Help Wanted sign. He turned around, got an application from the secretary, filled it out and turned it in. A week later he was gainfully employed at Greene's Salvage.

For the most part, his experience at Greene's evened out, which he supposed was probably the best anyone could hope for in a job. Some days the work was easy, especially when it was his turn to weigh out the precious metals or to count bottles and cans (unlike The Can Man, Greene's used an automated bottle and can sorting machine). Other days, the work was interesting. Especially when he rode around in a Greene's salvage truck to clean out closing businesses, old barns, or to dismember cars abandoned in the woods decades ago.

Of course, there were days he didn't enjoy so much. Day like these, working The Pit and wrestling with rusted pieces of trash, trying to salvage whatever little aluminum or copper he could. At least he hadn't found any insulated copper wire today. The chemical bath used to melt the insulation off the copper gave him headaches. He'd take wrestling with a frozen bolt over smelling *that* shit any day.

Bobby applied the socket wrench again and tried to turn it. This time it rotated at least forty-five degrees before it seized again. He gritted his teeth, clenching his hands around the socket wrench's grip and applied more pressure. He was rewarded with a screech as the bolt jerked a whole 15 degrees before getting stuck.

He released the socket wrench—still locked onto the bolt—took his battered Yankees cap off and ran a hand through matted, damp hair, regarding the bolt sullenly. Maybe if he kept wrenching it, *maybe* he could eventually get it off and get this thing torn apart. Maybe he'd be able to hit the fair while it was still free admission. In all honesty, if he worked to six-thirty he'd probably *still* hit the fair, but if he could get free admission, that would leave more cash for food, sideshows and the beer tent. As luck would have it, the fair had arrived near the end of the month (bills were due) and he was running on fumes.

But he pushed those thoughts away and applied himself to the reluctant bolt once more. He'd bust his ass and finish as much as he could. Maybe Old Man Greene would show mercy and let him out early. If so, he'd have enough cash for the beer tent, which would let him forget for a while how lame life was. Hell, maybe he'd get drunk enough to beer-goggle his way to a little female company for the night, too. The fair brought out all kinds. Especially bar whores tired of dark, dingy, stale pubs.

Bobby pressed his hat back onto his head and was about to renew his attack on the engine block's rusty bolt when a meaty hand clapped him on the shoulder. A deep voice rumbled, "Damn, Bobby. How long you been busting your ass on this?"

Bobby snorted and shook his head. Tommy Grummel was the biggest, hardest, toughest guy he knew . . . with a heart like a melted marshmallow. At 6'4 and 230 pounds he didn't seem to realize he could crush anyone he wanted. Instead, he befriended everyone, especially all the other square pegs . . .

losers

. . . like Bobby who didn't fit the world's holes. Bobby didn't think he could call anyone his best friend, but if push came to shove, he'd name Tommy.

"Yeah. Thing is rusted and stripped. I wanna say 'fuck it' but the engine block's aluminum. Greene would blow a gasket if he saw it tossed back into The Pit."

"Wanna hand?"

Bobby thought for a moment, then shrugged, handing the socket wrench to Tommy. "Sure, Tom-Tom. Knock yourself out."

Tommy accepted the socket wrench with a grin. Unlike everyone else at Greene's, he *liked* working The Pit. He loved wrestling apart scrapped appliances, lawn mowers, bikes and motorcycles. Of course, if Bobby's biceps were like Tommy's, he'd probably enjoy prying apart junk, too.

Instead of applying the socket wrench right away, Tommy grabbed a small hand sledge from the workbench. He tapped the bolt three times. Then, he set the sledge down, applied the socket wrench, and with one hand, turned.

At first, the bolt wouldn't move at all. Though he didn't want to see Tommy fail, Bobby felt a small thrill of perverse vindication. Wasn't just him and his weakling arms. Damn bolt was rusted fast.

But Tommy narrowed his eyes and turned the socket wrench harder. Muscles in his corded forearms twitched and jumped. The dragon tattoos there pulsed and breathed as Tommy strained . . .

With a screech, the socket wrench turned all the way around, the bolt coming loose.

Bobby clapped Tommy's bulging shoulder. "Yes! Dude, you're a lifesaver. This is gonna save me some minutes, big time."

Tommy—looking embarrassed as he always did under the focus of someone's praise—stepped back, wiping his hands on his shirt. "Whatever. You probably loosened it for me."

Bobby snorted. "Yeah, the ole 'you just loosened it for me' line. Right. Anyway, I owe you a beer tonight at the fair. You going?"

Tommy nodded, smiling. "Yeah, Sandy and me will be there. She loves the fair." He nodded toward the front. "Gotta get back to the aluminum and copper scales. See you later?"

Bobby attacked the snow-blower with renewed enthusiasm, nodding. "Yeah. Thanks again, man. Saved me some serious grunting on this piece of shit."

Tommy waved again, still looking embarrassed. "Nothing to it. Glad to help. See you."

He turned and walked away. Bobby's smile faded as he returned his attentions to dismantling the snow-blower, doing his best to focus on his gratitude and the possibility of getting to the fair free tonight, trying hard to ignore the bitter spark of jealousy flickering inside (especially at the mention of Sandy's name) and failing miserably.

———— ∼∼∼ ————

At the All Saints Junior High dance of 2009, Sandy Clem actually danced with Bobby for several songs before ditching him. Whether she'd felt bad or had been a little drunk or high (Bobby always assumed the latter), he never knew. But when a shy thirteen-year-old Bobby had asked her to dance, she'd yelped "Sure!" and grabbed his hand, dragging him directly into the gym's jostling center, away from the inattentive eyes of bored teachers serving out their required chaperone duty. She'd woven her way through sweaty adolescent bodies, pulling him along. When they reached the center of the gym—where there was hardly room enough to dance, let alone shuffle side to side—Sandy spun, faced him with a wide smile, clasped her young and lithe body against his and proceeded to grind him with a passionless sort of abandon.

For Bobby the experience was anything but passionless. Full of a mind-scrambling pleasure burning every vein, Bobby stumbled numbly along. A great breathtaking *SOMETHING* rose inside, and at the end of the third song he shuddered and clutched Sandy tight as a fountain of emotion and a bright silvery *RELEASE* exploded within. To his dismay, he discovered later in the boy's bathroom something else had exploded, in a much more physical fashion.

Whether or not Sandy sensed this and ditched him out of disgust or amusement or simply decided to move on to something better, he'd never known. At the end of the third song she'd pecked him on the cheek, grimaced regretfully, pulled him close and yelled into his ear over the pounding bass, "Gotta piss! Be right back, kay?"

He'd nodded wordlessly, gaping like an idiot. She gave him a smile he still remembered as being affectionate, placed a soft hand on his cheek (which felt like the finest silk), turned away and melted into the crowd of dancing and jumping adolescents in the general direction of the bathrooms.

Of course, she never came back.

On Monday (after he'd spent the weekend agonizing over a letter expressing his true feelings for her; a letter he never finished), she walked by him in the hall on the way to homeroom, never once glancing his way, clinging like second skin to the muscled arm of some upperclassman who played football, basketball, lacrosse or something else Bobby could never play himself. And, of course, Sandy never once spoke to him or looked at him for the rest of high school . . .

Except that night at Mr. Jingo's County Fair, a year later.

He'd slept with a few girls since. He'd lost his virginity to Cassie Tillman, who now waitressed at The Skylark and always offered him a small smile when he came in. That, however, had been a drunken, fumbling affair at someone's graduation after-party out at old Bassler House, a dim encounter neither of them much remembered, nor wanted to.

He was twenty-two years old. In decent health. Theoretically, his whole life still lay ahead of him, but he felt like he'd hit a peak when Sandy dry-humped him to orgasm at a junior high dance. And it didn't matter that she became the fodder of boisterous locker room talk over the years. Regardless of her reputation, the night he danced with her became crystallized in Bobby's mind as the best night of his life. A peak he'd never surmount. This truth rung slightly hollow in his gut, and was, in its own way, distinctly pathetic.

After graduation he tried not to think about Sandy. Mostly, he'd been successful. She hadn't been college material herself (had returned home after a semester at Herkimer Community College because of some vague trouble with a professor) and they didn't exactly travel in the same social circles. He hadn't thought of her for a while.

Until she'd started seeing Tommy Grummel.

It was 6:15. Fifteen minutes to close. Not only hadn't Bobby cleared his station soon enough to leave early, it seemed like everyone in Webb County brought in their scrap metal over the last forty-five minutes. Half an hour ago The Pit had been empty, its scrap pushed into the compactor at the back, the metals hauled off to storage. But now it was near half full again and Old Man Greene was being a pisser, making Bobby comb through The Pit until the last minute, threatening to make him stay late if he came across anything worth salvaging.

Bobby swore under his breath as he picked his way through mounds of scrap metal. Everything from junked bicycles, barrels filled with tin cans and other debris, old rusty tool boxes, old metal desks, washing machines and driers. You name it; it had been dumped over the last half-hour. Bobby hoped no one brought in any more lawnmowers or snow-blowers with aluminum engine blocks he'd have to drag out of the twisted piles of tangled, rusted and jagged metal.

In his frustration and haste, Bobby passed over the heaps of rusted metal, conducting only a cursory search. If he missed something good—a traffic sign, a tangle of copper piping accidentally thrown out with construction debris or another aluminum engine block—and Greene found out, there'd be hell to pay. He probably wouldn't fire Bobby but he'd definitely make him work The Pit for an extra month, to "teach him a lesson."

Something glinted off to his left.

Through a tangle of rusted metal pipes.

Bobby stepped over three crushed garbage cans. Tottered on one foot, then gingerly began climbing past what looked like the remains of an old metal swing-set. He cursed under his breath the whole time.

"Smelly old bastard," he rasped, "love to see *you* work The Pit, you arthritic son of bitch. Probably fall and break your neck, then find some way to blame it on one of us assholes . . . "

Bobby's rant trailed off as his right foot caught on a steel beam hidden in the rusted jumble. He hopped on his left foot until he stepped on a pile of rusted chain. The links slid under his heel, toppling him backward. With a shout, arms wheeling, he fell sideways; sure he would impale himself on some jagged piece of metal as punishment for his slander against the scrap metal god of Clifton Heights . . .

Luckily his hands slammed onto the top of a metal office desk instead. The rest of his body hit the desk's side. Pain flared in his hip, drawing hot curses from him, but even in his anger he realized how fortunate he was to have escaped serious injury. The old desk was solid. Banged his hip good. He'd be bruised to hell in the morning, but that beat getting cut by rusted metal.

He rested for a second on the edge of the upturned

desk, panting. "That's it," he rasped. "Fuck it. I'm done. Greene don't like it, he can kiss my skinny white ass."

To punctuate his point, Bobby slapped the side of the desk. It banged, shivered, and one of its drawers slid open, spilling its contents everywhere. Whoever owned the desk last hadn't emptied it before dumping it. Random office supplies—papers, boxes of staples, paper clips, tacks, loose pens and pencils—clattered onto the ground.

With a *thump* and rattle, a small wooden box fell out amid the clutter.

Bobby stared at the box. All sound around him faded. The compactor grinding, the crane banging metal cubes onto flatbed trucks, the indeterminate jumble of voices drifting from the main warehouse. All of it faded into a soft hissing white noise as he stared at the wooden box on the ground.

It was *wooden*. It didn't belong. This was a metal salvage facility. Of course non-metal things turned up here occasionally. Bicycles and lawnmowers with rubber tires, metal folding chairs with cushions, metal-frame futons with mattresses. But this polished, dark wooden box looked incongruous surrounded by piles of bent and twisted scrap metal. Not caring at all if anyone noticed, Bobby knelt and . . .

reverently?

. . . picked up the box. He sat back on the edge of the metal desk, settling himself at a comfortable angle, and examined it.

The top and sides were smooth and polished to a high gleam. This looked exotic to Bobby, considering he spent his days grappling with rusty, oil stained metal. He delicately turned the box over, absurdly worried about breaking it. It sprouted four impossibly frail-looking legs at each corner. No markings of any kind on the lid, which was secured by a simple metal clasp. Without thinking twice, Bobby slipped the catch and flipped the lid open.

Lush wine-colored felt lined the interior. On the felt rested what looked like three brass coins.

Two thoughts jumbled through his head. First: *Damn. These look valuable. Old Man Greene'll piss himself over this.*

Second: *Fuck the old bastard. Keep 'em yourself.*

Bobby picked up one of the coins. Though it looked thin, not much bigger than a quarter, it felt twice the weight. He opened his hand, settling the coin in his palm and hefted it again, examining it more closely.

Definitely copper or brass or something similar. Heavy for its size. And it looked *old*, with a strange design etched into its center, what appeared to be three question marks spiraling around a dot . . .

Bobby tilted his hand. The sun glinted off the coin. The etching looked like it was glowing. The thought occurred that maybe these coins were valuable enough to get him some sorely needed cash.

He decided in an instant.

He tipped the box, dumping the other two coins into

his palm. Looking around guiltily, he stuffed them into his jeans front pocket, tossed the box over his right shoulder and left The Pit, heading to clock out. Fuck Old Man Greene, anyway.

He had a fair to attend.

The last time Bobby actually talked to Sandy Clem was at Mr. Jingo's County Fair the summer after his freshman year. He'd been returning from the fairgrounds restrooms. When he passed the grandstands where everyone crowded on Friday night for the annual tractor pulls, he'd heard what sounded like someone quietly sobbing somewhere under the empty grandstands.

Someone crying.

A girl.

Bobby stopped and listened, conflicted. What to do? In a way, it was every adolescent boy's fantasy: comfort the girl hurt by her asshole ex-boyfriend, get into her good graces and her heart. Maybe there'd be some hand-holding, which might lead to kissing. Because she'd be so grateful for the comfort and all.

At the same time, Bobby knew even if girls didn't find him disgusting they certainly didn't think he was attractive. More than likely, if his imagined scenario played out the crying girl would probably rebuff him with curses, maybe even turn her boyfriend or ex-boyfriend on him for kicks. He'd seen it happen to guys like him too often.

Besides, if the girl was crying about her boyfriend, it didn't necessarily mean they'd broken up. Even if some dumbass *had* been a jerk to her, cheated on her or even hit her, it didn't mean they'd called it quits. In that case, it'd look like he was horning in (not far from the truth), which would put him in dutch with said dumbass boyfriend no matter how much of an asshole he'd been to the girl in question.

So he stood there at the grandstand's edge, wrestling with his anxieties, his hormones and sympathy. That sob sounded so wretched. So lost and forlorn. He stood there listening until he couldn't take it any longer. Something basic and *human* twisted inside at the sound of this unknown girl crying, washing away juvenile dreams of kissing and making out, also sweeping away his fears of vengeful boyfriends.

"Fuck it," he muttered.

Bobby glanced along the fairway. It was late and the crowds at this end of the fairway were thinning out. No one would see him if he ducked under the grandstands.

He stepped forward but hesitated, halted once again by worries of a psycho boyfriend or ex-boyfriend who might take offense at his advances. More than likely the whole thing wasn't worth it. More than likely, whoever was crying would tell him to piss off, and if the girl's boyfriend or ex-boyfriend or whatever heard about it, Bobby would probably earn nothing but a black eye for his troubles.

But there was her sobbing, again.

Like her heart was breaking.

Bobby had only ever heard someone cry so wrenchingly once: the night Dad left Mom and him for parts unknown. He'd been five at the time and mostly unmoved by his father's departure. Johnny Lee never hit him or treated him cruelly. He'd just acted as if Bobby didn't exist. Johnny Lee never wanted a wife or a kid in the first place, and though he'd only been five years old, Bobby completely understood what his father meant when he'd overheard him telling his mother Bobby was nothing but a "fuckin accident.' He'd never meant to have Bobby at all or get married to Bobby's mother, Mary. Johnny didn't hate his son and wife. He just didn't give a shit about them.

Still, Mary sobbed as if the world had ended the night Johnny Lee never came home from the lumber mill. Years later Bobby would realize his mother cried more because she feared an uncertain future on her own and less because her remote husband left. At the time, however, all he knew—as Mary held him, sobbing into his shoulder—was Daddy was gone and Mommy's heart was broken.

Now someone was crying like Mom the night Johnny Lee had left, only softer, somewhere under the fairgrounds grandstand.

Bobby glanced around again. He was alone, no one looking his way. He breathed deep and ducked around the corner, underneath the grandstand.

There, not ten feet away sat Sandy Clem, her back against the grandstand's rear wall, knees drawn to her chest, face buried in her folded arms, shoulders quivering with each quiet sob.

Bobby placed a hand against the rough plywood wall, took one step toward Sandy and then froze, paralyzed by uncertainty and, yes . . .

Fear.

But not fear of an avenging boyfriend or of Sandy's potential rejection. Back then Bobby was still ignorant of Sandy's growing reputation. What happened at the junior high dance the year before was (in his mind) *his* fault for being a spaz with crazy hormones. He hadn't blamed Sandy at all for ditching him because who *would* want to hang out with a loser who'd got so excited grinding with a girl that he'd messed his pants? That'd gross out anybody. It grossed *him* out, for sure. He was lucky she hadn't slapped him and then told the whole world what happened.

What he *really* feared as he stood there over the quietly sobbing girl whom he loved more than anything, was scaring her away again. She sounded so sad and alone. He'd no idea what he could do or say but he desperately didn't want to screw up. Making out, stealing a kiss or holding her hand was suddenly the furthest thing from his mind. He wanted to do something—anything—to make Sandy stop crying.

So he swallowed (tasting something acidic in the back of his throat), inched a step closer and whispered, "S-sandy?"

Nothing.

She only continued crying. Face in her arms, shoulders quaking. Bobby mustered something vaguely resembling courage, cleared his throat and said in a slightly louder voice, "Sandy? You okay?"

Sandy stiffened. Her snobs and sniffles instantly ceased. She raised her head slowly, cheeks and forehead flushed, nose red, eyes watering. She sneered, her sharp tone cutting to the bone, "Whatthe*HEll*youwant?"

Caught flat-footed, mouth hanging open, Bobby's mind scrambled, because *shit*. He was doing exactly what he'd been afraid of doing. Pissing her off. She was going to run away all over again.

He opened his mouth.

Closed it. Licked dry and cracked lips and stared wordlessly, tongue useless as his mind spun.

Sandy narrowed her eyes and cocked her head. "Take a fucking picture. It'll last longer, numb nuts. What the HELL's wrong with you, anyway?"

Her sarcastic ire made him squirm, but also unlocked

his tongue. "I . . . uh. Heard you crying. Are you . . . you okay?"

She snorted, closed her eyes and pinched her nose, rubbing it between her forefinger and thumb. "Yeah, genius. I'm fucking *fabulous*. Why else would I be hiding under the bleachers crying like a goddamn baby?"

Though she was presumably aiming her anger at him, it made him feel oddly better. The Sandy Clem he knew (though superficially) didn't cry. He'd rather hear her call him "Numb Nuts" all day long than hear her cry again.

"Uh. Oh." He swallowed and managed to say, before realizing he only had two bucks left in his pocket, "Do . . . do you want anything? Like a soda, or pizza or . . . something?"

Shit.

Two bucks.

That'll buy a whole lot of nothing.

Dumbass.

Sandy wiped her eyes with the back of her hand and looked at him sideways, not exactly smiling, not exactly sneering, either. "Geez. Aren't you all romantic and shit. You hoping for a piece of this? Buy the girl a Coke, give her a shoulder to cry on, maybe she'll let you tag second base?"

Bobby's mouth opened and closed but he couldn't speak. He didn't know what was worse. Her jaded tone . . . or that maybe she wasn't *exactly* wrong.

His guilt must not have showed in his expression, however, because her sneer faded. She waved the comment away. "Ah, forget it. I was busting you. I'm not . . . well, I'm kinda fucked up right now. Don't mean to be bitchy."

Intense relief spread through him. In reality, Sandy's diction was clipped, peppered with obscenities, but if anyone asked him what her voice sounded like at that moment he would've compared it to the loveliest music on the face of the Earth.

He offered a weak smile. "S'okay. I figured." He paused, the gears sticking in his mind, caught between backing away and leaving . . .

coward

. . . or leaping from a cliff without knowing if he could actually fly. Before he could chicken out, he opted for the cliff and plunged off its edge with, "Do you . . . wanna talk? I mean. I'm a good listener. Won't say anything. I'll sit here and listen. I won't tell anybody anything, swear to God."

She stared at him for a moment, her face blank, eyes deep and thoughtful. Then she asked, "Who the hell are you, anyway? I know you from somewhere . . . don't I?"

Bobby's cheeks flushed. Of course he wanted her to remember him, because if she'd forgotten, he'd meant nothing to her. Though he didn't expect to mean *everything*, he'd like to have meant something. But if she remembered him and the dance, she'd most likely remember . . .

He coughed and cleared his throat. "Bobby. My name's Bobby. We . . . uh . . . we danced a few times at the junior high dance last year."

She tipped her head, smiling slightly, eyes glimmering in recognition. "Okay. Yeah. Think I remember, now. You . . . "

Her eyes widened.

Bobby's stomach dropped.

"Yeah," she said slowly, "I *definitely* remember you, because . . . "

And Bobby felt ready to call it quits, right then and there. Anything to avoid her making fun of him. He stepped back, hands raised, stuttering, "I'm s-sorry. I . . . I didn't mean to bother you. I'll go, I won't say anything . . . "

Sandy's face suddenly beamed with concern, eyes soft and sympathetic. "No, it's okay. Honest." She leaned out and grabbed his hand, stopping him with a reassuring touch. She smiled, looking much more like the night he'd asked her to dance. "It's okay," she whispered. "It happens. It's cool. That's not why I didn't come back, honest."

"Really?"

"Really." She sniffed and deftly pulled out a pack of cigarettes and a lighter from her jeans pocket. "One of my girlfriends wanted to sneak outside for a smoke. We made it out but they caught us trying to sneak back in and booted us. *Couldn't* get back in, so I didn't ditch you, I promise."

Bobby nodded, remembering how he'd searched the gymnasium and the cafeteria for the rest of the night and hadn't found her. Of course, he hadn't asked around (didn't want to look like a total dork) but he'd looked and hadn't seen her, so her story made sense.

Of course, it didn't explain why she'd never talked to him afterward, walking by in the halls at school without a glance. But young love and lust were stupid and blind, and it was fair to say he suffered from both. "Oh, okay. That makes sense, I guess."

With an impressive adult expertise (to him, anyway), Sandy took a cigarette from the package with her lips. Murmuring around the cigarette, she held the pack out to Bobby and asked, "Smoke?"

Bobby never had, but he found himself instinctively taking one, holding it delicately between his thumb and forefinger. Before she could light her own, however, he gathered enough courage to blurt, "Honestly? I've never smoked before."

Sandy peered at him, cigarette dangling from her bright red lips. A slow smile spread. Oddly enough, it looked as if this information pleased her. "Never smoked before, huh? Well. Looks like I get to give you something *else* new."

"Why do people smoke, anyway? I mean, you always see these TV ads saying how dangerous smoking is, with lung cancer and all that, and . . . " He stopped, worried he was rambling, spewing his guts everywhere, and maybe he would somehow offend her in his babbling.

Sandy shrugged, lit her cigarette, inhaled, and then let the smoke trickle out her nose, making her look older than fourteen. "Why do people smoke? You get used to it and get a nice buzz. Kinda like booze and pot, but not as heavy. Chills you out. Relaxes *me*, anyway."

She held the lighter out to him. "Wanna try?"

Bobby thought for a moment, thinking of all the old slides they showed in health class of black lungs full of tar and shit, but in the end, he sat forward and stuck the cigarette between his lips, like he'd seen all the other big kids do, and Johnny Lee before he'd split. "Sure," he said with a weak shrug, "why not?"

Sandy leaned forward and flicked the lighter. "Here's what you do. Breathe in a little when I light it but don't breathe too deep or-"

Too late, soon as the lighter touched the end of the cigarette Bobby took in what he thought was a deep, manly breath. Stinging smoke hit the back of his throat.

He breathed it all in.

And exploded with a burst of coughing that bent him double, bringing tears to his eyes. His stomach lurched. For a second he was sure he'd puke all the food he'd eaten right then and there.

A hand thumped his back. "Whoa. Dude. Relax. Small breaths. Small breaths."

A wave of vertigo passed through him. For one

humiliating moment he thought he might pass out. He forced himself to breath slower, however, and his coughing fit gradually passed.

He straightened, glanced at Sandy, saw her smiling in amusement but not malice . . . and oddly enough, felt no embarrassment. He wiped his teary eyes, opened his mouth to speak, but found his throat still raw. He coughed less forcefully, swallowed and wheezed, "Holy. Shit."

She grinned. Her eyes glinted the brightest blue he'd ever seen. "S'all right," she said, clapping his shoulder with her cigarette hand. "That happens, too. Trust me. Go slow. I'll show you how to do it."

For the next half hour, she did exactly that.

Bone-weary, Bobby pulled his rattling Isuzu into the Quickmart on Haverton, a few miles before the fairgrounds. After paying the electric bill and buying groceries, he'd enough for maybe a Pepsi and a snack before hitting the fair. That should hold him over until he ate the usual fair food—Italian sausage, fries, and a beer or two—a few hours from now.

He parked his truck, wincing at the way it shut off with a metallic rattle. Just one more broken thing he could barely afford to fix.

Bobby shook his head, pushing those thoughts away as he entered the Quickmart. He grabbed a Pepsi and after several minutes of half-hearted debate, a pack of Twinkies.

At the cashier, he presented his purchases and started digging in his pocket while the cashier (a bored looking high school kid with red hair and an acne-scarred face) scanned his items. Bobby pulled out a handful of quarters.

He had a thing about quarters. Only carried them, no nickles or dimes.

He figured the price of the Pepsi and Twinkies would be two dollars and thirty cents. The Pepsi $1.75 plus the deposit tax, and the Twinkies fifty cents. Unconsciously he counted out ten quarters. He laid them on the counter as the kid—whose badge read RUSS GIVENS—droned, "That'll be four bucks."

Bobby scowled. "Four bucks? Aren't the Pepsis still on sale?"

Russ Givens shook his head and shrugged, as if commiserating with Bobby's plight. Yes, indeed, it was a crime Pepsis were no longer on sale. "Manager took 'em off sale this morning. Sorry."

Four bucks would put him over his budget for the evening. No way he'd be able to afford the fair and a meal. If that wasn't the most depressing realization of his life, Bobby didn't know what was.

Filled with a mild desperation making him feel very small (because who was *that* desperate to keep an annual trip to a ramshackle county fair?), he pushed forward the pile of change he'd deposited on the counter. "C'mon, man. Do me a solid. Maybe extend the sale for one more Pepsi. Whaddya say?"

Russ Givens frowned, shaking his head at the pile of change before him . . .

And stopped.

A soft look of surprise spread over his features. He glanced at Bobby, offered an oddly preoccupied smile and shrugged. "Sure. Why not? One more half-price sale."

A rare sense of well-being filled Bobby. Hell. Something was going his way for once. He grinned and saluted the now smiling Russ Givens with his Pepsi. "Thanks, man."

THROUGH A MIRROR, DARKLY

He turned and left the Quickmart, his melancholy ruminations momentarily assuaged by this minor triumph.

Twenty minutes later, fortified by his Pepsi and Twinkies, Bobby stepped onto the fairway of Mr. Jingo's County Fair. The smells washed over him, bringing waves of nostalgia. Some of his warmest childhood memories were of afternoons and nights spent at Mr. Jingo's.

The sugary smell of cotton candy and fried dough. The oil-fried scent of blooming onions. Hot dogs, hamburgers, and Italian sausage. The tang of garlic knots and pizza. Instant association conjured memories of riding the Ferris Wheel high into the sky, letting gravity press him back into the mildly uncomfortable cushions of the Zero G, the dizzying spins of the Tilt-A-Whirl and the slashes of The Scrambler, and last but not least: The Flying Bobs. The ride promising whiplash to the thundering bass of whatever new rock song was dominating the airwaves.

But it was the carousel, as always, which grabbed his attention and drew him off the fairway. He threaded his way through the kiddie rides and the usual games. The Hot-Shot, with its subtly too-small hoop. The Balloon Shoot-Out, at which patrons tried to pop slightly under-inflated balloons with dulled darts. And of course, the ever-popular Duckie Pond, a kiddie pool filled with rubber duckies. The only object was to hook a ducky with a three-pronged hook on a pole. Of course, the prizes ranged from plastic cars whose tires fell off within the first ten minutes of use to gelatin plastic squids that, when thrown against a wall, oozed to the floor. They usually held one's interest for two minutes.

Bobby passed all of these to stand before the carousel.

The only other place Sandy Clem had ever talked to him after that junior high dance. Here, they'd traveled around for what felt like hours, their hands bridging more than the distance between their enamel-chipped stallions. Bobby remembered that night as if it had happened yesterday, the tinny carousel music printed on his brain.

This was why he loved the fair so much. Why he always found a way to attend every year, whatever shape his finances were in. He wanted—no, he *needed*—to walk along the fairway crowded with vendors and game booths. He needed to gaze at the rides in their cracked-paint and rust-creaking wonder. He *needed* to stand before the carousel and remember the last time Sandy Clem had ever acknowledged his presence here on Earth.

It was a like a memory of heaven which felt like a slice of hell. The last night he'd held hands with Sandy Clem.

***

After twenty minutes spent tentatively learning how to inhale from his cigarette, Sandy suggested they walk around. They'd snuffed out their cigarettes and slipped out from under the grandstands back onto the fairway. Luckily it was late. Hardly anyone was around their end of the fair. No one noticed them.

As they drifted along the fairway toward the food vendors, the games and the rides, Sandy chatted incessantly about anything and everything. School and how it sucked. Cheerleading and how much she loved the flipping, jumping and catching part but how she hated the other bitches on the team. Some party she'd been at last week where someone dropped *acid* of all things, and how she was totally down with drinking, cigarettes and the occasional joint, but how acid was *fucked up*. How her guidance counselor wanted her to attend college because she could do complex math in her head but the idea of sitting in *any* class after high school was enough to make her puke. All she wanted to do was attend cosmetology school. Also, how her cousin waitressed at The Golden Kitty and made great tips because of her big tits. She was thinking she'd give dancing a try on Amateur Night.

And on and on.

It was enough to make Bobby's head spin. He didn't bother answering or trying conversation topics of his own. He let Sandy prattle on, nodding in all the right places, offering what he thought were appropriate facial expression and accompanying interjections, like "No shit?" and "Fuckin' A!"

Which was fine by Bobby. He hated talking and being the center of attention. Simply walking next to her was good enough. He listened to her, felt relaxed, at ease, but most importantly, he felt . . .

Wanted.

Because he *listened*.

Bobby didn't know much of anything and knew less about girls, but Sandy chattered away like someone who hadn't been allowed to talk for months. She acted as if she'd had all these thoughts and feelings stored inside forever but no one to tell them to, and now she was spewing out everything at once. It made Bobby feel special, though some part of him realized *his* presence was merely chance. He'd just happened along when he did.

But he didn't care.

He'd take it.

Halfway down the fairway Sandy emitted a little-girl squeal. She grabbed Bobby's hand (the pressure of her hand squeezing his felt like heaven), and dragged him off the fairway, past vendors and rides to the carousel at the far end of the fair.

She skidded them to a halt.

Staring, transfixed. Watching the carousel go around while she squeezed Bobby's hand so tight her fingernails dug into the back of his hand. It hurt a little bit.

It also felt wonderful.

Sandy was breathing heavy as she watched the carousel's revolutions. A half-smile creased her face, as if she were dreaming or seeing something far away. After several seconds of watching the rising and falling horses go by, she said in a breathless whisper. "You ever wish you could go away? Somewhere far away, I mean. Where no one would ever find you."

Bobby glanced from the carousel to Sandy and back again, unsure of the connection between the ride and what she'd said . . . though he realized with a start he'd often felt the same way. Most poignantly the Monday after that junior high dance a year ago, when Sandy passed him in the halls without a glance.

He swallowed. "Yeah. Guess I do."

In a flash, connections fired in Bobby's head. He abruptly realized they'd never actually talked about what had driven Sandy under the grandstands crying in the first place. He instinctively understood (in a way new for him) that Sandy was telling him now. Sort of.

Still staring at the revolving carousel, Sandy asked, "Do you like going home at night, Bobby? To your house? And your mom."

The question startled him, but when he thought about it, he realized home was okay. Though she nagged him about chores and schoolwork occasionally, he and Mom got along fine. Home was safe. Home was . . . well, home. If life or school sucked, or if he was reeling from rejection . . .

like last year, after that dance

. . . he could always go home, where everything became okay. In fact, the question made him realize how much he'd taken home for granted.

"Yeah. Home's okay. Mom's a mom, y'know? She bugs me about cleaning my room and doing my homework, makes me do chores and stuff, but she's cool."

Scowling, her brows furrowed, Sandy spat with a sudden vehemence, "I *hate* it. Wish I could torch the place, with that motherfucker inside . . . "

Sandy squeezed his hand again, hard.

Her fingernails cutting angry crescents into the back of his hand.

He endured it without a single word, because so many things became painfully clear. Bobby knew who that "motherfucker" was. The one whom Sandy hoped would be in her house when she torched it.

Her father.

The storm on Sandy's face passed as instantly as it came. Her brow smoothed out. She smiled, though it looked a little hard and forced around the corners. "See those painted murals, all around the carousel?"

Bobby reluctantly looked away from Sandy to the murals all around the carousel's stationary center. Alternated with mirrors were different countryside scenes. A yellow sunlit path winding through a forest. A pond in the middle of a clearing. Crumbled, rustic looking steps leading to a stately old manor. A bubbling creek in another forest, and a field of yellow wildflowers. When Sandy began speaking again, Bobby found he couldn't pull his gaze away from the vistas spinning before him.

"When I was a little girl, when . . . when my *father* would take me on the carousel, I'd sit and stare at those paintings. I'd pretend I could go there, if I stared hard enough. That everything around me—*him*—would disappear. And *I'd* disappear into the picture and run far away forever. When he . . . when he stopped taking me on the carousel, I'd ride it myself for hours, wishing the same thing. That I could disappear into whichever painting I stared at the hardest, go away from here and *him* and never come back, ever."

She fell silent.

They both stared at the carousel as it slowed.

Waiting their turn.

—◦◦—

Bobby barely restrained a yelp when a huge hand clamped onto his shoulder and Tommy Greely's bass voice rumbled, "Hey, Bobby. Made it, huh?"

Reluctantly tearing himself away from memories of the carousel and Sandy, Bobby flickered a weak smile as he turned and faced Tommy . . .

And a twenty-two year old Sandy Clem.

Who looked every bit as beautiful today. In fact, the only thing about Sandy not improved with age?

Her eyes.

Nestled in the crook of Tommy's muscled and rippling arms, her head resting on his massive shoulder, Sandy Clem was an enticing vision of womanhood. She'd filled out slightly in the hips and thighs, her breasts heavier but high and firm. Her blond hair cascaded over rounded, firm shoulders. Her lips glowed a blazing red as always . . .

But her eyes.

Bobby hadn't seen her much since they'd both graduated high school four years ago, but he could tell a light was gone from her eyes. In his memories of smoking under the grandstands and riding the carousel, her blue eyes snapped with a vitality he remembered envying. Back then, Sandy Clem had been *hot*, but she'd also been someone *not* to fuck with.

The young woman cuddling with Tommy Greely now offered Bobby a vacant smile, her pale blue eyes dull and listless. Something had died inside Sandy since Bobby last saw her, and for some reason he didn't quite understand, that knowledge hurt him much worse than her rejection.

Bobby swallowed. "Yeah, just got here. Not in time for free admission, though. Sucks, but whaddya gonna do?"

Tommy grinned and clapped Bobby's shoulder again. "No worries. We'll head over to the beer tent; douse our troubles with cheap local swill." As an afterthought, Tommy nodded toward him. "Sandy . . . you know Bobby, right?"

Sandy's smile was empty. His heart sinking a little, Bobby realized she was probably stoned. "Yeah, think so," she muttered. "Didn't I see you around school?"

Bobby nodded and then, compelled by an urge he didn't understand, he said in an amazingly steady voice, "We danced for a few songs at the All Saints junior high dance. And we rode the carousel together here a year later."

And there it was.

A little light shining in her eyes, reminding Bobby of who she used to be. "Yeah. I remember. Didn't I teach you how to smoke, or something? Under the grandstands one night?"

Bobby's cheeks warmed but curiously enough, it wasn't an altogether unpleasant sensation. "Kinda. Never smoked again, though. Mom smelled it on me when I got home and wailed the hell out of me."

This was only partly true. Mom *had* raised hell. But by the time he'd gotten home Bobby decided he'd never smoke again for one simple reason: he'd never spend another night like that with Sandy. If he couldn't be with her again, he'd never smoke again, either.

Sandy grinned weakly. "Not me. Hooked. A pack a week. A bitch. What can you do?"

Some of Sandy's veneer cracked. Bobby noticed a hardness around her mouth. Slight wrinkles there and at the corners of her eyes. Also, her skin, on closer examination, looked worn. Tough. Not leathery, like some of the bar whores he'd seen at The Stumble Inn every weekend . . .

But close.

She was on her way.

Tommy chuckled, interrupting the moment. "All right, kids. What say we play catch-up over at the beer tent? I'm getting hungry *and* thirsty."

Sandy tittered. A lusterless "ha, ha, I don't care whatever" kind of sound. Bobby nodded weakly, happy to fall in step with the couple on the far side of Tommy, where he didn't have to see the pale and cracked vision of what Sandy Clem had become.

Everything started out fine. After waiting in line, they sat at a table with their food, he and Tommy eating Italian sausages and chips, Sandy occasionally picking at a basket of fries. A frothy pitcher of Utica Club Ale completed their spread. The whole time Tommy rambled about work and how he and "the boys" saw some "crazy shit" at The Golden

Kitty last weekend when one of the "patrons" got tossed out for getting too grabby.

Bobby ate, drank and nodded along wordlessly. He tried to ignore Sandy, sitting with her shoulders slumped, picking at her fries while she started at nothing. Not able to stand her near catatonia any longer, Bobby eventually excused himself to the counter for more napkins.

Somehow in that time Sandy and Tommy got into a heated discussion of how they should spend the rest of their evening. From what Bobby could gather when he rejoined them, Sandy wanted to walk through the horse stables while Tommy wanted to watch the tractor pulls like he did every year. When Bobby sat, he noticed their first pitcher of Utica Club was already gone and a second one sat next to it, which wasn't helping the conversation any.

"C'mon, Sand. You can check out the horses 'n shit while I watch a few pulls. When you're done, you come over to the grandstands. I'll sit in the first row so I won't be hard to find."

Sandy scowled, pouting like a five year old. It dismayed Bobby how much her petulance disgusted him. This was not the Sandy Clem he'd fallen in love with years ago.

"But *Tommy*," she whined, "I *hate* tractor pulls. Smoke and dust gets in my eyes. Especially in the front row."

Tommy smiled.

Eyes glittering, cheeks flushed. If Bobby had known what Tommy was going to say he would've rushed to stop him, but there was simply no warning, no way he could've ever predicted Tommy slurring . . .

"Well, aren't *you* a Daddy's Girl. Don't wanna get your Sunday dress all dirty for Daddy?"

Time stopped.

All sound died.

For a moment, Sandy's face froze, wooden and

expressionless. And then Bobby saw it, flickering in her blue eyes, lighting them in a way he hadn't seen all night.

The old fire. The old burn. The Sandy Clem *no one* fucked with.

Tommy (even in his drunken state) must've sensed he'd crossed a line somehow because his smile faded slightly, but before he could say a word Sandy's arm cranked and she slapped him upside the face with an open hand hard enough to jerk Tommy's head around. Its impact sounded like a mini-thunderclap against the chatter in the beer tent.

"Asshole!"

She spun and ran away. Tommy sat, eyes wide with disbelief. He stared after her for several seconds shook his head, looked at Bobby and mumbled, "What the *fuck* was that?"

Bobby knew, of course.

Her Dad.

Tommy's joke about her being a "Daddy's Girl." And it trembled on the edge of his tongue. Tommy had always been a good friend to him. Always looking out for him, helping him at work, like today. If Tommy knew how he'd unknowingly set Sandy off, it would help a lot in smoothing things over when he found her.

Bobby opened his mouth, ready to tell him.

Shrugged, shook his head and muttered, "I have no idea."

They spent the rest of the evening searching for Sandy. Along the fairway, on the rides, in the horse stables, at the craft vendors, back at the beer tent.

But she wasn't anywhere to be found. She'd most likely

ditched the fair and either walked home to her trailer in the Commons or called Yellow Cab on her cell.

By the time the fair was ready to close, Tommy lost his patience. At first he'd been worried about Sandy (good guy that he was) especially considering he'd no idea what pissed her off. But an hour into their search the situation began to rub him raw. He hadn't done anything. At least, far as he knew. Sandy had never gotten pissed at his teasing before. Why now? He'd paid for her way into the fair, paid for dinner . . . what the hell was her problem, anyway?

Through it all Bobby remained silent, nodding and shaking his head in all the right places. Guilt stung him a little inside, but he kept his mouth shut. Tommy was a good friend, but he didn't deserve someone like Sandy. He *didn't.*

Because only Bobby knew about Sandy and her dad, though he didn't know anything for *sure*, having only pieced things together over the years. But *he'd* been the one to sit with her under the grandstands. *He'd* been the one to ride the carousel with her, eight years ago one warm August night.

He was the one who knew where she was probably hiding.

After he and Tommy parted ways at the fair's exit, Tommy shaking his head and mumbling something along the lines of, "Women, ungrateful bitches all of em," Bobby walked as fast as he could to the grandstands. Without bothering to check if anyone was watching, he ducked around under it.

He didn't find Sandy there. Only a matted place in the weeds and several stubbed out cigarettes. Marlboro Menthols, from the looks of them.

The ride home was uneventful and numbing. He felt washed out, with a little headache, but luckily he hadn't guzzled beer like Tommy and Sandy. It was ten. He needed to wake by six for work. He'd get a decent night of sleep and feel a lot better than Tommy would, for sure.

Sharp dismay filled him however, when he emptied his pockets onto the battered dresser and remembered those strange coins he'd found at work today. He only had two left. What happened to the third?

And it hit him.

The Pepsi and Twinkies he'd bought at the Quickmart. He'd been in a hurry, sticking his hand into his pocket, grabbing a handful of what he'd thought were quarters. Those weird coins were the same size. He must've snagged one of them along with the other quarters, giving it to the clerk at the Quickmart.

"Sunnuva*bitch*. Really?" He tossed the coins, his wallet and his TracPhone onto the dresser, stuck both his hands into his pockets, rooting around in vain. Nothing but lint. How much of an idiot was he? He comes across something at work which might be valuable, but he's so wrapped up in stupid little things like the fair and Sandy Clem he gives one of the fucking things away?

Bobby sighed and ran a hand through his hair. Maybe he could go back to the clerk tomorrow, see if he'd accidentally swapped one of those weird coins for a quarter. Hell, maybe he'd dropped it tonight at the fair. Who knew?

He turned, opened the top drawer of his dresser and swept the two coins inside. He covered them with his boxers and shut the drawer. He didn't own a lock-box, but no one would want to break into a rat-box apartment like this. The coins should be safe enough hidden in his drawer. At least he'd know where they were and wouldn't lose them tomorrow . . .

Like he lost everything else.

His dad as a kid. Every game he ever played on the playground or in gym. So many other things.

And Sandy Clem, above them all.

God. What the hell is wrong with you? After all this time, get it into your head: Sandy will never be yours. Ever. Not when she can have any guy she wants. Guys like Tommy.

Bobby shook his head. He'd lectured himself about Sandy so many times over the years. Usually a small voice countered those lectures, claiming only *he* knew the real Sandy Clem. But tonight it fell silent. Suddenly exhausted, he undressed and crawled into bed, hoping for dreams of Sandy and riding the carousel with her forever.

※

That's not what he got.

※

With a jerk, Bobby awoke, momentarily confused and disoriented. Where was he? Had he heard a noise? Music? Tinny carousel music, wafting from a wheezy calliope..?

He pushed himself upright and sat back against the bed's headboard, trembling and sweaty. He felt woozy and slightly feverish. He pressed the heels of his palms into his eyes and rubbed them, trying to remember . . .

a lake

with black shores dotted by glittering yellow rocks

*under a black sky with blacker stars gaping like holes
or mouths puckering around two bloated, yellow moons
sick with disease, shining over*
    something by the lake
    *a carousel with yellow horses all spinning around
its calliope warbling*
    *and Sandy riding the carousel, smiling, happy
free*
Bobby shook his head. He thumped his forehead with
his palm, trying to clear the scattered and fucking *scary*
shit out of his head. Figured, his luck. He'd wanted to
dream of *him* riding with Sandy on the carousel but instead
got a nightmare of Sandy on a carousel in some weird
fucked up place like an alien planet or something.

And yet.

She'd looked calm. Peaceful.

Happy.

Hadn't she?

He shook his head again, rubbing the back of his neck.
God. Maybe he'd drank more beer at the fair than he'd
thought. He bent forward, rubbed his face, kneading his
forehead with his fingertips. He cracked his neck and
glanced at the ghostly red numerals of the battered clock
radio on his dresser.

Five AM. If he hopped to it, he could stop at the
Quickmart on the way into work, see if maybe they still had
that coin he'd accidentally given them.

He flicked the bedside lamp on and got out of bed,
dismissing the stupid idea about the black stars in his
dream looking like the markings on the coins. Stupid.
Totally and completely stupid.

But that didn't make him feel any better.

A different cashier was working at the Quickmart that morning. There was already a line of early morning commuters buying their wake-up jolts of caffeine and over-warmed sausage-egg and cheese sandwiches, so Bobby browsed lamely through the store and left.

At work, Bobby made good progress on some of the items at his station leftover from last night: several hubcaps with tin rings attached to them, aluminum road signs and a weed-eater engine block he made quick work of. Work consumed him and before he knew it, his lunch-break rolled around.

Business in The Pit slowed after his lunch, so he worked at the redeemable can and bottle counting station for a few hours. All he did was take a patron's bag of cans and dump them onto a conveyor belt which ran them under a sensor, counting them. This knocked off several peacefully numb hours.

Bobby didn't see Tommy all day. When he asked around on his afternoon break someone mentioned Tommy called in sick, which made sense. Tommy put away a lot of beer last night. While he was usually "that guy" who could drink everyone under the table and report bright and alert to work the next day, Tommy had mentioned something to Bobby about heading to The Stumble Inn after the fair to "see if Sandy's knocking around there."

Which more than likely meant Tommy went there to drown his "sorrows" (whatever they were). If he met someone pretty and interesting along the way? Tommy was a stand-up guy who treated all the guys at work good. He'd never treated any of his girlfriends bad far as Bobby knew.

But the girls loved Tommy. He drew them in like flies to sap. If he hadn't found Sandy and sorted things out and he encountered a pretty young thing last night? Bobby Lee could guess how *that* encounter had ended.

Of course, twinges of guilt twisted his gut all through the day. At any time last night he could've shared what he *thought* he knew about Sandy and her dad, which would explain her reaction to Tommy's joke. But he hadn't. He'd kept it to himself.

Why?

Not because he *wanted* to scuttle the relationship between Sandy and Tommy, surely? It wasn't like *he* actually had a chance with her. And he wouldn't do it to spite Tommy, who'd been nothing but a friend since he'd first started working at Greene's.

The only answer was the memories of smoking under the grandstand and them riding their faded enamel horses around through the night on the carousel.

And how only he knew Sandy's greatest wish.

———

Standing before the carousel, Sandy gripped his hand so tight her nails bit into his skin. Bobby dug into his pocket with his free hand, suddenly convinced he'd somehow lost his last four tickets and his last chance of spending time with Sandy. However, after several panicky moments of rooting around in his pocket past assorted change, his lucky rabbit's foot, some marbles and a few shiny chunks of mica from the railroad tracks, he pulled out his final four battered tickets.

Sandy had hers. When the carousel stopped, after everyone else disembarked, the ride's conductor (a dark-skinned man with jet-black hair and a blank expression) announced last call. Bobby and Sandy paid their fare, scrambled aboard and mounted two horses near the inside of the carousel.

It was all the same to Bobby. He didn't care which horse they rode, but Sandy knew right away which one she wanted, as if she'd ridden it countless times before. A brilliant white stallion with a blue mane and tail, a color combination which only looked natural on a carousel stallion.

They mounted their horses and settled in, still holding hands across the expanse separating them, other hands grasping the poles spearing their horses. They said nothing, panting from their run across the fairgrounds, smiling foolishly at each other.

With a wheezing creak and groan, the carousel shifted forward. The calliope's tune blared into life. Slowly, achingly so, they moved forward, slowly, slowly, then slightly faster . . .

Though it was surely his imagination, Bobby thought the bored engineer was cranking the speed higher than usual for this last ride, just for them. They flew around the carousel, hands clasped together over the dizzying space between them. Sandy didn't look at him the whole ride. She stared at the spinning panorama of different countryside vistas mounted on the carousel's center column.

He didn't care.

Because somehow deep inside Bobby understood no one could ever totally have Sandy Clem. But he desperately wished (in the naive way of childhood) he could help make her dream come true. He wished to somehow send her into the magical realm of the murals she loved so much. He wished to somehow help her escape and find peace.

And he kept wishing as they rode around until, as all rides eventually do . . .

Theirs ended.

◦◦◦

When Bobby entered the Quickmart after work he saw the same scowling attendant who'd worked last night, Russ Givens. The one who'd "cut him a break" by giving him a Pepsi for half off after the sale. The guy Bobby must've mistakenly given that weird coin to.

Feeling oddly bold and confrontational—as if the guy had stolen the coin—Bobby approached the counter after the only other customer left. He said without preamble, "Hey. You were working last night. Think I gave you an old coin by accident, instead of a quarter. It's a family heirloom," he lied glibly (sounding more self-assured than he felt), "kinda sentimental. Used to belong to an old uncle."

The cashier's scowl deepened, threatening to swallow his face. He peered at Bobby suspiciously. "Yeah, I worked last night. But I sure as hell don't remember you. And I don't remember seeing this coin you're taking about, neither."

A strange annoyance filled Bobby. He actually felt a little pissed. "I came in last night. Wanted a Pepsi and a pack of Twinkies, but only had enough cash if the Pepsi was still half off, which it wasn't. I said, 'Can't you cut me a break?' and gave you the money. You looked at the cash, sorta blinked, said, 'What the hell?' and gave it to me half off. You saying you didn't? You didn't see that weird coin, figure it was worth something, so you let me have the Pepsi half off so I wouldn't remember slipping it to you?"

Givens leaned across the counter, hands placed flat on its surface, eyes bright. "Listen," he said in a tight voice, "*I DON'T. KNOW. YOU.* Ain't never seen you before. And I'd never cut anyone a break. Old Man Kretzmer ever found

202

out I'd be fired on my ass in a heartbeat. I ain't seen you and I ain't seen any coin, so beat it. There's a line forming behind you."

Bobby glanced over his shoulder. Sure enough, four people were standing behind him, each one looking slightly more impatient. An odd sort of weariness washed over him, sweeping away the strange resolve gripping him only a moment before.

"Sure. Uh. Sorry, I . . . "

Bobby snapped his mouth shut and beat a hasty retreat from the Quickmart, his cheeks burning.

In his apartment Bobby stood before his dresser, holding the remaining two coins in his palm. He tilted them, peering at them from all sides. Though it was probably a trick of the light, the spiraling question marks on the yellow coins seemed to shiver . . .

like black stars against a blacker sky

. . . and move.

What were they? Where did they come from? And what did they do?

He frowned.

An odd question. What did they *do*? They didn't do *anything*. They were trinkets he'd found in a box left in an old desk junked at Greene's Scrap Metal Salvage.

That's all.

not true

What did they . . . DO?

I wanted a Pepsi for half-price, Bobby Lee thought, feeling numb. *I wanted it for half price. I gave the cashier one of these coins by accident, thinking it was a quarter, and though the sale was over . . .*

The cashier gave him the Pepsi for half-price and was now pretending he didn't remember doing it.

But no.

Bobby remembered the way the cashier's eyes flashed, the annoyed-almost-angry but also confused scowl. He *hadn't* remembered giving Bobby a Pepsi for half-price.

He held the coins up closer.

What did they *DO*?

He stared at them for several minutes. Blinked slowly and swallowed. Images flashed in his head, of . . .

something by the lake

a carousel with yellow horses all spinning around

and Sandy riding the carousel, smiling, happy

free

Like a man dreaming, Bobby slowly stuffed both coins into his pocket, turned and left his apartment.

Bobby Lee blinked, momentarily confused. Feeling as if he'd been instantly transported from his apartment to here, he found himself standing outside Mr. Jingo's County Fair. He clutched one of those strange coins and briskly approached the ticket booth. A nondescript elderly man offered him a vague smile. "Help you?"

Bobby smiled shakily in return. Swallowing, hoping the ticket taker didn't notice his nerves, he forced a steady hand to extend one of the coins and say as evenly as possible, "I'd like an all-night pass, please."

The ticket taker accepted the coin. Lay it in his palm, regarding it for several seconds. Then he smiled vaguely, slid it aside and said, "Can do. Your hand?"

Bobby somehow kept his hand still. The ticket taker pulled out one of those orange, all-night plastic wristbands, affixed it around his wrist and said, "Have a nice evening, sir. Enjoy the fair."

Bobby nodded stupidly and wandered away from the ticket booth and into the fair.

Bobby didn't find Sandy in her hiding spot under the grandstands. Nor did he find any fresh evidence of her recent presence. From there, he wandered through the fair, past rides, food and craft vendors, game booths, the beer tent, through the horse stables and the 4H barn housing this year's blue ribbon rabbits, goats, pigs, and jersey cows. He walked for hours, circling the fair, hands stuffed into his pockets, staring into the middle distance, seeing hardly anything around him.

He felt vaguely aware of adults, teenagers and children casting him uneasy glances. On some level he didn't blame them. A scruffy, grubby guy (if only because he'd come straight from work) wandering around the county fair with a far-away look in his eyes was creepy enough to unsettle anyone, even *him* on a normal day.

But today wasn't normal.

Not at all.

Besides, two throbbing questions pulsed simultaneously in his head, pushing aside all other concerns. First, where was Sandy? He knew she was here. Something in his gut pulled at him—like a sort of radar—telling him she was here *somewhere*. Though it sounded crazy, he thought she was aimlessly looping through the fair one step ahead of him. Like in every place he'd checked, she'd moved on only moments before. And second?

those coins

what did they do?

He'd turned it around in his head the entire time he wandered through the fair. The coins *did* something. He'd accidentally given one to the cashier at the Quickmart and got exactly what he'd asked for: a half-price Pepsi, despite the recent sale being over. And he'd presented a coin to the vendor selling tickets out front, asked for an all-night pass and got it. And, he felt sure if he returned to the front gate and asked the attendant about it, the old guy wouldn't remember Bobby any more than the Quickmart cashier.

the coins
they give you what you want

Ridiculous.

Stupid.

Impossible.

He kept telling himself so while he wandered the fair until he found Sandy near closing time at the one place he knew she'd eventually be.

Standing before the carousel.

He approached her silently, realizing *he* hadn't found her. She'd simply ceased leading him on and had been waiting for him here.

He stepped next to her, alarmed at her slack features and distant gaze as she watched the carousel revolve. She didn't register his presence with any facial expression, but started speaking before he could say a word.

"My father died last year. Fucking bastard. Lung cancer. He spent his last few days at the Assisted Living Home, puking blood and chunks of his lungs."

Bobby opened his mouth but couldn't say anything.

Sandy's bitter tone washed away some of the dream-like veil covering his mind, but still fragments of a surreal compulsion floated around in his head . . .

the coins
what do they do?
I asked for something
the coins gave it to me
what do they do?

. . . making it hard for him to think of anything meaningful to say. All he could do was mutter, "I'm . . . I'm sorry, Sandy."

She snorted. It wasn't a pleasant or humorous sound. She looked at him, a cruel smile carving across her features, eroding her beauty and turning her face into a thin, lined mask. "Y'know, the sunnuvabitch called me a month before he kicked. To let me know he was sick. He was dying. He wanted to *see* me. To put things to *rest*. Motherfucker wanted me to let him off the hook so he could die in peace."

She snorted again, looking back to the carousel. "Fucking hung up on his ass. He called a few times after but I had caller ID and never answered. The last time, though . . . I answered, deciding to blast him, but . . . "

She cleared her throat.

Coughed.

Turned further away from Bobby so he couldn't see her face. In a rough voice, she rasped, "It wasn't him, though. It was the Home. Telling me he'd died in his sleep. Congestive heart failure."

She did an abrupt about-face, glaring at him. Not angry at *him*, he somehow understood, but more angry with herself. "Y'know, you'd figure I'd be *happy* his ass was dead, right? After what he'd done. How he'd . . . you'd think

I woulda danced a motherfucking Irish jig. But I didn't. You know what I did instead?"

Again, not giving him time to answer, she turned away and muttered, her voice thick with emotion, "I cried. Should've been laughing but instead I bawled like a little girl."

She shook her head, trembling loose two tears from her eyes, over her cheeks. "I'll never be free," she whispered, staring at the spinning carousel. "Never. Can't hate the bastard like I should and I just . . . can't . . . get away, I can't . . . "

She snapped her mouth shut, wrapped her arms around herself and shivered, falling silent.

The carousel slowed, its ride coming to an end.

A sudden desperation surged inside Bobby, opening his mouth and tumbling out the words he'd never before possessed the courage to say.

"Do . . . do you remember why you liked the carousel? You told me, the last time we hung out. You liked the murals. Said you used to dream you could slip into the murals and never come back, ever. If only you wanted it bad enough."

Sandy snort-laughed. "Yeah. Hell of a dream. Typical kid fantasy-shit, right?"

the coins
what do they do?
I asked for something
they gave it to me

He stuck his hand into his pocket, slowly withdrew the last of those weird coins he'd found. He opened his palm and examined it, thinking how that strange yellow pattern looked exactly like the black stars of his dream, thinking also of Sandy riding a yellow horse on a yellow carousel, looking content, happy . . .

At peace.

free

He closed the coin in his hand, squeezing it. Then looked at Sandy, thinking of the one thing he wanted most for her.

"Y'know," he whispered, "maybe dreams aren't so stupid. Not if we want them bad enough."

"Yeah." She shuffled her feet, her voice sounding strange and distant. "Sure. If only I wanted it bad enough. If only."

They stood still for several seconds.

The gatekeeper of the carousel barked last call. Several stragglers heeded. When the gate clanked shut and the carousel's ancient calliope wheezed to life, Bobby caught a glimpse of Sandy riding a chipped enamel white stallion with a blue mane and tail. She wasn't looking at him. She was gazing at the murals of different woodland and countryside scenes, spinning around the carousel's center.

Bobby squeezed the coin tight in his hand. He wished for something harder than he'd ever wished for before. Staring at the carousel, at Sandy Clem riding her chipped enamel stallion around, a stallion that looked, for a moment . . .

Bright yellow.

When the ride ended, Bobby squeezed his now empty hand into a fist. He turned and walked away, knowing in his heart things couldn't continue as they had. He wouldn't return to work tomorrow. He *couldn't*. And he couldn't stay in Clifton Heights any longer, either.

He needed to find his own mural, his own road. He needed to leave Clifton Heights behind to find it . . . like Sandy.

As he walked away from the carousel, he overheard a

little girl saying to her mother: "Did you see the lady in all the pictures, Mommy? The one walking on those paths? She looked so *real*. Like she was a real person. How'd they do that, Mommy? How they'd make her look so *real*?"

Something loosened inside Bobby Lee, flying free.

AND I WATERED IT, WITH TEARS

1.

HE SITS IN his idling truck, staring into the rain-streaked night, feeling the engine's throb in the seats. Rain hisses against the cab's roof while wipers smear water across glass with sliding *thunks*.

He presses his iPhone against his ear.

Listens.

Sighs "Goodbye." Hangs up, drops the iPhone onto the passenger seat, sits back and closes his eyes, feeling the engine's throb.

———∾∾———

"Andrew. I signed the papers this morning."

"Rachel . . . please. Let's keep trying. Just a little longer . . . "

"It's been a year, Andrew. We tried. And I'm tired. I can't do this anymore."

"Rachel . . . "

"The papers. Sign them. Don't drag this out. Please."

———∾∾———

Thursday
5:55 PM

Standing at the end of a line which hadn't moved for thirty minutes, Andrew McCormick pulled his iPhone from his pocket, slid his thumb across its touch-sensitive screen and groaned softly at the time.

KEVIN LUCIA

5:55 PM

The New York State Electric & Gas payment center closed at 6:00 PM. His apartment's electric bill was scheduled for termination at 8:00 AM tomorrow. But work started at 7:30 PM and he wouldn't get a break until eleven. By then his electric would be three hours terminated, and he was so overdue they'd demanded cash. No payment-by-phone or electronic checks. Worst of all, he didn't have near the amount past due. Only fifty bucks to spare until next Friday. Hopefully, that'd be enough to buy him some time.

If he'd kept current, he could've paid the damn thing over the phone or online. From home, work . . . his iPhone, even. There was an APP for that. There was an APP for everything, these days. Of course, if he'd managed to keep his teaching job and hadn't quit after . . .

No.

Don't.

He glanced around and saw nothing but dull gray cement walls. Tile floors. A small waiting area offering a few chairs, a bench, and a coffee table scattered with magazines. Fluorescent lights hummed above while bland pop muzak played over tinny speakers, barely covering the sound of trickling, gurgling water . . .

The rain outside, of course.

Not water rushing around him, sweeping him into darkness.

Just the rain.

He shivered slightly and squeezed his free hand into a tight fist, fingernails marking painful crescents into his palm. It was just the rain.

On the wall next to the receptionist's window (which appeared intolerably far away) hung a bulletin board. Its offerings ranged from a community calendar, a bake sale announcement, several handbills for local musicians . . .

And a row of "Missing Persons" posters.

His belly grew tight. Because of *course*, there wouldn't be one for Patrick, would there? Because nobody had listened to him, nobody believed.

Not even Rachel.

He closed his eyes and instantly felt disoriented as water rushed and gurgled around him, dragging him into the darkness. He massaged the middle of his forehead, where a dull pulse throbbed.

Well.

That certainly didn't help.

But as he rubbed, the throb eased. The gurgling water (surely just rain hitting the roof) faded. So maybe he'd avoided a migraine, this time.

Thank God for small favors.

You know what'd be another small favor? This line moving sometime before closing.

Andrew opened his eyes and glanced again at his iPhone.

5:58 PM

The line hadn't budged an inch.

"Damn," he muttered.

"I know, right?" This from a black man standing in line before him. "Like we ain't got somewhere to fucking be." He scowled at Andrew over his shoulder. "This is some lame-ass bullshit, right here."

Andrew sighed, stuck his hands and iPhone back into his pockets. He rolled his sore shoulders, cracked a stiff neck and said, "I hear you."

"It's like . . . damn," the black man gestured at the young woman in front, "folks got places to be, right? I mean, I get it. Been there, done that, pleading my case, just like she is. We all been there, right?"

Andrew nodded. Who hadn't? Paying bills on time was a dim fantasy these days.

"But when a line to China starts forming behind you . . . show some courtesy. That's all I'm saying."

Andrew grunted, wondering how often a line had formed behind *him* this past year, since . . .

No.

To distract himself he said, "I always mean to pay my bill online, but I've never quite got my checking account balanced enough. Don't ever know what's cleared and what hasn't. I . . . lost my old job and the new one doesn't pay as well. And I was never good at finances. My wife took care of those things."

The black man's face sobered. "Shit, man. I'm sorry. She pass?"

"No. We separated a year ago."

"Damn. Still sorry."

He waved and lied. "No worries."

"Anyways, I ain't never messed round with online shit. Identity theft and all." The black man grinned. "Was always afraid I'd pay a bill online, then get charged from BigHoes.com or something. So not only would I be out cash but in trouble with the old lady over porn charges ain't even mine. Course, I ain't gotta worry about that no more. Me and her ain't speaking. So guess I could scope all the porn I want, right?" He shook his head. "But porn sure ain't better 'n my lady, y'know? I'd rather have her."

"Oh. I'm sorry. You aren't . . . "

The black man waved, dismissing it as no big deal . . .

though Andrew somehow sensed it was. "Naw. Not married. Don't know if we'll get back together, man. Some shit just ain't worth it, y'know? Get tired of trying after a while."

we tried

I'm tired

can't do this anymore

"Yeah," Andrew agreed, forcing a light tone, pushing back the darkness inside, ignoring the way rain pattered against the front doors, trickling down the glass. "I suppose we all get tired of trying eventually." He paused. "You always pay in person?"

The black man nodded. "Yeah, in cash, too. There's something reassuring about it, y'know? Solid. Handing the electric company cold cash, paying the bill for sure instead of worrying a check might bounce. Bill's due Saturday and I was thinking I could pay this quick 'n easy on the way home. Course, this joint usually empty after work, but no. Figures. Not today. Helluva day at work and instead of going home and kicking my feet up, I drive through this fucking monsoon outside to stand in line forever, maybe for nothing cause they close on my ass. Cause missy there won't stop her yapping."

As if to underscore his complaint, thunder growled and the rain fell harder, gurgling and rushing against the windows and the front doors. The black man nodded at the ceiling. "See? Gonna be like Noah 'n damn Ark driving home in this shit."

Andrew ignored the rain rushing against the building and examined the black man's attire more closely. Plain, gray button-down shirt—'Deyquan' embroidered over the left breast—and uniform-gray pants. Feet shod in black work boots, similar to his own. "Work for the County?"

"Yeah. Whatever they want me doing, right? Garbage

detail, litter in the parks and playgrounds, trimming bushes 'n hedges along sidewalks, patching asphalt and clearing deadfall off roads in summer, shoveling and plowing come winter." Another big grin. "That's me, brother. Jack of all trades. And *this* Jack is tired as shit, man. How about you?"

He shrugged, tired of telling the same story, but with no energy to lie. "Used to teach high school English. Clifton Heights High. Lost my job. Now I'm working at The Can Man."

"Can'n bottle place on Route 434?"

He nodded. "The same. Not a bad place. And we're running a special." He managed a limp grin. "Six and half cents a can."

Deyquan smiled. "Hell. I oughta pay y'all a visit. You get commission for referrals 'n shit?"

He actually smiled. "Unfortunately not."

"Why'd you lose your teaching gig? District budget cuts? That's all you read in the papers these days."

"Something like that," he managed. Nodding at the front of the line, "What's the hold-up?"

Deyquan shrugged. "Dunno. Ain't been listening, y'know? Same ole thing. 'Can't pay my bill, single Mom, need electric or social services'll take my kid.' Shit like that."

Deyquan sighed, shaking his head. "I get it. Life fucking sucks sometimes. I know. Grew up in Philly before I came up here to play ball at Webb Community. Momma raised me and my brothers and sisters—all five of us—by herself." He gave Andrew a pointed look. "Sad. Some people just can't do it on their own, y'know? I mean, don't wanna judge, got no idea what shit she's going through, but damn. Just wanna get home an . . . "

"Please!"

Glass rattled against its metal frame, punctuating the sobbed exclamation. Startled, Andrew saw the young woman who'd been holding up the line pressing her hand against the receptionist's window, where she must've slapped it.

The receptionist—a stout, middle-aged woman—glared through the glass. "Ma'am. Last time. Please leave, now, or I'm calling the police."

The woman wore faded but clean jeans and a limp, tired spring jacket, which hung off her thin frame. Her stringy mouse-brown hair dangled in a limp ponytail. Her bony, trembling hand pressed against the glass. "Please," she whispered, tears shimmering in her voice.

Perhaps the receptionist's features softened around the eyes and mouth. Perhaps not. Regardless, she spoke in gentler tones, now. "I'm sorry, Miss Tillman. There's nothing I can do. You need to call Collections."

The woman's shoulders quivered.

Her hand slid off the glass.

She turned away and rushed past them, one hand clutching a worn brown purse, the other wiping tears from her angular face. Several jerking strides lurched her away from them and through the ladies room door.

"Damn," Deyquan muttered, shaking his head. "Now I kinda feel like shit, y'know?"

Andrew nodded but said nothing, a dim unease gnawing his insides as water continued to sluice down the front doors.

6:05 PM

Deyquan was getting the receipt for his payment (thanking

God, the Man Jesus and the Holy Fucking Ghost the receptionist stayed open long enough for him to pay) when a woman screamed from nearby.

"What the fuck?" He looked over his shoulder at the White Guy he'd been talking to a few minutes ago. "Who the fuck is . . . "

A door slammed open from the Ladies Room and out stumbled the woman who'd paid her bill before him. Middle-aged, medium height, average build, average everything. Soccer Mom Queen. Only now she sounded more like a Scream Queen in a B-movie fright-flick, leaning against the open Ladies Room door, wheezing.

He stepped toward her. "Hey! You okay?"

Soccer Mom swallowed. "Uh. She's . . . " She coughed and ran a trembling hand through plain, average brown hair. "I n-needed to use the . . . "

Her eyes widened.

She coughed again. Dug into her pocketbook, pulled out a green inhaler, stuck it into her mouth and triggered off a blast, sucking on it like a wino sucks on a forty ounce of Big Bear.

She swallowed, removed the inhaler and gasped, "My God. She's dead! I think. God, I think she killed herself!"

An image.

Of the girl who'd slapped the receptionist's window.

Please!

Shit.

He approached her. "What'd she do? Chug some pills, shit like that?"

Soccer Mom shook her head violently, panting, trying to catch her breath. Confusion and fear competed for control of her face. "No. I . . . think she . . . God. Drowned herself?"

Wait.

What?

Drowned herself?

What. The. Fuck?

"Yo, Miss Receptionist," he tossed over his shoulder. "Call 911!" He slapped White Guy's shoulder. "C'mon, chief. Let's check this out."

He trotted toward the Ladies Room without waiting for an answer. He nodded at Soccer Mom. "We got this. Maybe go over to Miss Receptionist, there. 911 folks'll probably want details."

Soccer Mom nodded, rushing off. The lingering terror in her eyes twisted Deyquan's guts. What the hell could've scared her so bad? Yeah, dead body, bad mojo. Maybe the girl cut her wrists and bled all over the place and . . .

But Soccer Mom said . . .

I think she drowned herself

An icy sensation prickled along his spine, making him wish he'd gone straight home today.

6:10 PM

Deyquan passed through the small foyer and stepped into the restroom. Looked ordinary as shit. White tile floor. Pale green concrete walls. Row of white stalls along one wall, white porcelain sinks and mirrors on the other. Only strange thing? Sounded like someone left a faucet running . . .

drowned herself

He rounded the corner.

Stopped and stared, a cold tension blossoming in his guts. White Guy (who'd apparently decided to Man Up) rasped at Deyquan's shoulder, "My God."

drowned herself

The young woman who only fifteen minutes before had been pleading her case with Miss Receptionist hung by her head and neck from a sink.

Her face, jammed into the sink.

Arms dangling limply at her sides.

Knees bent but hovering a few inches above the floor, not quite touching. Toes dragging on tile. The faucet was on, and the sink—clogged with the girl's face—overflowing onto the floor.

Deyquan peered at the neck's odd angle. It was probably broken. He stepped closer, but White Guy grabbed his arm. "Crime scene," he muttered, "shouldn't touch anything."

Deyquan nodded. "Makes sense. Shit. This brother ain't messing with no crime scene, that's for damn sure."

He turned and followed White Guy out of the bathroom. "Hell, yeah. One thing a brother knows is stay the fuck away from crime scenes. This one time my cousin Marcus saw a drive-by back in Philly, and he was stupid enough to—"

"Something's happening."

Deyquan and White Guy stopped. In the restroom's doorway stood Miss Receptionist, face blank and unreadable.

But her eyes danced.

Wide and bright, pupils jittering.

Deyquan's irrational fear grew. "No fucking shit. Lady just killed herself in y'all's bathroom. I'd say something's happening' all right."

A tight head shake. "No. Something *else*. Our phones. They don't work. Cells either. Damn Internet won't connect. And the doors . . . "

"What about the doors?" White Guy said, sounding more afraid than Miss Receptionist.

Miss Receptionist grimaced. Gathering the courage, maybe. She rasped, "Locked or something. Can't open them. Keys don't work. Windows won't open either. And I tried to break the glass in both a door and window with a hammer from the utility closet . . . but the glass wouldn't break. Hammer kept bouncing right off. Not a scratch."

"Wait," Deyquan said, "are you saying' we're . . . "

Miss Receptionist nodded so hard Deyquan thought her head might pop off. "Yes. We're stuck in here.

"We're trapped."

2.

He opens his eyes and blinks, wondering how long he's been dozing. It's still raining. Still dark, impossible to tell what time it is by looking outside. He straightens, runs a hand through his hair and glances at the truck's clock radio.

Late.

Getting late.

He needs to go. But he can't until he does something first, what it is he can't remember . . .

Wait.

Something in his pocket.

He put something into his jacket pocket before leaving for work this morning. Can't remember what . . .

that's happened a lot lately

. . . so he reaches into his pocket, fumbles around and pulls out a brown, cylindrical, plastic bottle with a white cap. His meds, of course. For the headaches and other things.

What other things?

Icy shock ripples through him.

Because he can't remember.

———∞———

"Counseling. I'll start counseling again, I promise. I'll call Dr. Martin . . . "

"No. God, Andrew. It's too late. I mean yes, go to counseling for you. Please. But it's too late for us. It's too late."

"Please, Rachel. Whatever it is I'm doing, I'll stop. I'll stop, I promise."

"Dammit, Andrew. Listen to yourself! It's not anything you're doing, it's . . . "

"But . . . I don't understand. I don't . . . "

———∞———

Thursday
6:20 PM

Andrew watched, feeling helpless as Deyquan swung the metal folding chair at the glass front doors. It bounced off with a loud thwack. He cursed and swung again and again, getting the same result, the glass trembling under each blow but not breaking or cracking. Not under hammers, an old pipe they'd found in a utility closet or now a metal folding chair from the waiting area.

"Sonnuva . . . "

Deyquan swung again, striking the glass hard enough to jar the chair from his grip. It clattered to the floor.

Deyquan cursed.

Kicked the chair against the glass door.

And then silence.

Punctuated by Deyquan's rasps. He stood, hands on hips, glaring. "What the fuck?" Shaking his head. "What.

The. FUCK? This is . . . shit." He waved at the glass doors. "I dunno."

Andrew tried his iPhone again. Any number. Home. School. Rachel's. He got nothing.

They stood behind Deyquan. To Andrew's right stood the receptionist, hands clasped around her cell, which apparently got no service, either. To his left was the middle-aged woman who'd discovered the body in the Ladies Room, clutching her Blackberry in one hand, her inhaler in the other, eyes wide and bright and frightened.

Of course she'd have an inhaler like Patrick's.

Of course.

Next to her slouched a sour-faced young man in his early twenties, hands stuffed into his pockets. He was tall and thin. Longish black hair curled to his shoulders, he wore a scruffy black beard and was decently dressed in tan slacks and a white, untucked polo shirt.

"Okay," Deyquan muttered, shaken but covering well, "this here doesn't make any sense."

"Still can't get a signal," Andrew said. "Can anyone . . . "

The receptionist hugged herself, not appearing so formidable now. "Landline's down. No dial tone. Tried my TracPhone, nothing. Tried the Internet Portal for the County and State Police, but couldn't get online. Hell, tried faxing something. No connection."

"Maybe . . . uh . . . maybe . . . "

Everyone looked at the young guy, who stared at the unbroken glass doors. "Maybe . . . it's like . . . a terrorist thing?"

Silence.

The kid continued, undaunted. "Yeah. Like, maybe . . . this is a terrorist attack? Y'know. They sneak in here, shut down the county's electric, cut us off from help. Take over Clifton Heights and . . . "

Deyquan scowled. "Shit. *Really*? Terrorists? Yeah, cause we such strategic targets out here in North Bumb-Fuck. This is just a customer service office, man. Ain't no generators to shut off. Dumbass." He waved at the unbreakable glass. "That ain't no terrorist shit."

He shook his head at the receptionist. "Where the hell you get him? He's a damn idiot."

She blinked and muttered, "Temp help. BOCES work program."

The kid frowned. "Hey. Not cool."

"This isn't happening," the middle-aged woman whispered. "I'm dreaming."

Deyquan shook his head. "Naw. This ain't no dream. Can't explain the glass . . . but this ain't no dream."

He paused and looked around, a somber expression settling on his face. "Think it's something else."

A chill crawled over Andrew's shoulders. The rain outside poured harder, water gurgling and trickling down the glass doors. Water from the *rain* of course.

Nothing else.

"What do you mean?"

Deyquan shrugged and looked away, as if he didn't want to meet Andrew's gaze. "Dunno, man. It's just . . . dunno." He waved the question off. "Let's go sit over in the waiting area." To the receptionist, "Anyone else here?"

She shook her head. "No. Only Kyle and me. We were closing for the night, when . . . "

Deyquan nodded. "All right. Let's see what's what. Cause . . . "

Deyquan looked at Andrew, now.

His expression unreadable.

"Dunno about you all, but I'm thinking' no way in hell that girl killed herself. Which means whoever killed her is probably still in here somewhere. Waiting on us to make the next move."

Andrew could only nod slowly.

And ignore, best as he could, the rain trickling down the glass doors.

6:30 PM

They sat in the waiting area, which consisted of several plastic and metal folding chairs, a cushioned bench pressed against the wall between the bathrooms, and a plain coffee table strewn with old magazines, coloring books and TV Guides.

Deyquan looked at everyone in turn before speaking. The receptionist (named Sue) and Soccer Mom (named Judy, but what the hell, he liked Soccer Mom better) sat next to each other on the bench, backs against the wall, hands clasped in their laps. Every now and then, Soccer Mom took a hit from her inhaler. The kid—Kyle—sprawled on one of the plastic chairs to his left. Andrew sat to the right, where Deyquan could see him.

Good thing.

Because the guy made Deyquan nervous. Not sure why. He acted too jittery. Andrew was standing behind him in line the whole time so he couldn't have . . .

But still.

"Okay," he leaned forward, elbows on knees. "Here's the deal: Dead girl in the bathroom, face stuffed in the sink. Drowned maybe, though how the hell it happened, got no idea. Phones don't work. No fax or 'Net. No email. Doors and windows won't open, and somehow . . . " he swallowed.

"Somehow the glass in them won't break. Even when hit by a damn chair. And this is regular glass, right? Not special safety glass?"

Sue shook her head. She and Soccer Mom looked dazed. Kyle sat there, blinking. Andrew, next to him?

It felt like he was waiting.

But for what?

Deyquan continued. "So I don't know what to say about the glass. I mean . . . shit. But something else is grinding my gears. Don't think that girl offed herself. Knees weren't touchin' the floor. So how the hell she keep herself steady? And who can make themselves drown in a damn sink?"

"Murdered," Sue whispered, staring off over Deyquan's shoulder. "You think someone . . . murdered her?"

He shrugged. "Yeah. And unless someone slipped out in the ten minutes it took to kill her . . . and I don't see how he could . . . he's still here, somewhere. Trapped with us."

"You're assuming a male," Andrew said. "Why?"

Deyquan shrugged. "Dunno. Makes the most sense." He nodded at Sue and Soccer Mom. "No offense to you all, but if this ain't suicide, had to be a guy. I mean, girl must've fought back. Kicking and swinging. Take some power to hold her down. Only one of you looks strong enough for that," he gestured at Sue, "and hell, we know you didn't do it. You was taking everyone's cash at your window."

He paused, rubbed his neck, kneading muscles tight from a hard day's work. "There's another problem. Girl was in there for maybe fifteen minutes. How the hell someone sneak past us, kill her, sneak out again? I mean, it don't . . . "

"Why?"

Everyone looked at Soccer Mom, who still appeared dazed. "Why kill anyone? For what reason? Who would sneak in here . . . "

She wheezed, took another hit from her inhaler, exhaled slowly and continued. "During a storm like this and drown someone?"

Kyle sneered. "Terrorists. Obviously."

Deyquan waved Kyle off, peering at Andrew. Did he flinch a little at *drown*? "Telling ya, it ain't terrorists. What you think this is, fucking Red Dawn with Patrick Swayze and shit? Don't you read the newspapers? Don't need a reason to do crazy shit these days. Last month, newspaper says some redneck stuffed a guy in his wood-chipper 'cause he didn't like the guy's dog barking' all day. Shit."

"No one came in," Sue stated flatly. "Positive. Four people in line, including that girl . . . Lizzy Tillman's her name . . . and everyone else in the office gone for the day, so . . ."

"Wait!"

Soccer Mom looked up. "What about her little boy? My God, I forgot . . . in all the panic . . . God, he must be so scared, must've run off and hid in here somewhere . . ."

Deyquan frowned. "Don't remember no little boy, lady."

Soccer Mom leaned forward, her face suddenly flushed. "You didn't see him? I did. After I paid my bill, I called my husband. Was talking and saw the boy out of the corner of my eye, sitting on this bench. Figured he was her son. She kept talking about social services taking her child, so I thought . . ."

Sue shook her head. "No. That was Lizzy Tillman. Lives in the Commons Trailer Park. She's got a little *girl*. No boy."

Soccer Mom's eyes narrowed. "I'm sure of it. Saw the little boy sitting on this bench. Noticed how strangely dressed he was."

"What do you mean?"

Deyquan noticed an odd tightness in Andrew's voice.

"Well, he looked dressed for swimming," Soccer Mom answered slowly. "Wore bright, multi-colored Hawaiian shorts and a rubberized, long-sleeved top, like what swimmers wear. His hair looked damp, and he wore rubber swim shoes. Both my kids have those."

Deyquan grunted. Damn if Soccer Mom didn't act sure. But he hadn't seen shit. "Didn't see no kid, lady." He glanced at Sue and Kyle. "You guys?"

Kyle—still looking pissed—shook his head. "Was out back, entering payments into the databases."

Sue, however, looked unsure. "Can't say. Was focused on closing out transactions. Didn't see a little boy, but I wasn't looking, either."

"I saw him. I did. But he was gone when I finished, so I thought maybe he'd gone to the bathroom."

Deyquan looked at Andrew, who was staring off, eyes unfocused. "Hey. Andrew." He looked at Deyquan, blinking, as if struggling to wake. "You see this kid?"

Andrew shook his head. "No. I . . . I didn't."

Sue grunted, as if giving in. "Security cameras. Under normal circumstances I'm not supposed to show the footage to anyone."

Deyquan grinned. "Lady, this shit's far from normal. And when we get out of this, if your bosses fire you for showing us security footage? Fuck em."

Sue stood and quickly moved toward the office door, next to the receptionist's window, as if relieved to be doing something. Everyone fell in step behind her.

Andrew stood slowly.

Waiting for them all—including Deyquan—to pass, while he shuffled after them. As if, Deyquan thought, he didn't want to watch the footage.

As if afraid of what he'd see.

6:50 PM

They stood in a closet-sized security room past the front offices, away from any windows, which fortunately diminished the sound of the rain trickling against the glass. Andrew could relax somewhat, though he swore the ceiling was leaking water into a dark, shadowed corner somewhere.

The ceiling, leaking.

That was all.

Leaking.

Sue sat before an old steel desk. On it, a slightly out of date computer monitor, keyboard and mouse. On the floor next to the desk stood the computer tower itself. Next to it, two larger black towers—servers, Andrew recognized.

"There's cameras at the main entrance and employee entrance and exit." Sue clicked an icon on the screen. "Also one above the waiting area. It's digital. Streams continuously to those servers on the floor. Can be recalled any time."

A command box appeared on the computer's screen. Sue clicked an option, splitting the screen into four different perspectives. The upper left and right windows showed the rain-soaked employee entrance and exits, the lower left showed the main entrance and front parking lot, the lower right the now empty waiting area. "I can enter a time and date through the past week and play it right here."

She looked over her shoulder at them, her face wooden. "So. When?"

Judy checked her Blackberry's call history. "I was

talking to Barry around . . . five of six. That's when I saw him. While on the phone."

"How long was your call?"

Judy tapped her Blackberry. "Ten minutes."

Sue raised her eyebrows. "So you glimpsed a boy no one else saw in a ten minute window?

Judy glared at her. "I *saw* him."

Sue shrugged. "We'll see." She turned back to the computer.

"This is stupid." Kyle crossed his arms, scowling. "C'mon. A boy no one saw except you? Really? No one else saw this kid and you're carrying on like-"

Judy's eyes flashed, her mouth hardening at the corners. The way she turned on Kyle, Andrew thought he'd have to physically restrain her from scratching the kid's eyes out.

"I saw him," Judy insisted. "What the hell do you know? You weren't out there when-"

"Hey, now. Relax," Deyquan cautioned. "Don't need no war in here. Let's chill the fuck out."

"Whatever," Kyle muttered, digging into his left front pocket, pulling out a rumpled pack of Marlboro Menthols and a lighter.

"I'm asthmatic," Judy snapped with a tight smile, holding up her green inhaler.

Kyle threw his hands into the air, turned and slouched out the door.

"Go out front, Kyle," Sue called, "Don't want the office smelling like smoke tomorrow."

"Whatever."

The door to the waiting area opened and slammed shut.

Andrew glanced at Judy, trying not to paste Rachel's face over hers and barely succeeding.

"You okay?"

She nodded, her expression pleading. "I saw him. Swear."

"Well," Sue clicked 'PLAY,' "let's see."

7:00 PM

Kyle sauntered out into the empty waiting room, his shoes squeaking eerily against the silence. Intermittent lightning flickered through the glass doors, throwing ghosts on the floor. Rain hissed outside.

He pulled out a cigarette, stuffed the pack back into his pocket, lit the cigarette and stuffed the lighter back into his pocket. He puffed deeply, inhaling the menthol smoke, which buzzed against the back of his throat.

Stupid motherfuckers.

All of them.

Especially Deyquan, ragging on his terrorist theory. Like he knew any better. Such bullshit. Seriously. A girl dead in the bathroom, drowned in a fucking sink. Who did that? Not your average psycho-serial killer. That was straight-up, hardcore assassin shit. Like stabbing someone's brain through their eye with a pen. Or strangling them with piano wire. He should know. He played Assassin's Creed and Call of Duty and Splinter Cell, 24-7. He'd seen all the Jason Bourne movies, too.

He took another drag and held in the smoke. He needed to relax. While those numb nuts were crowded in a closet like goddamn fish in a barrel obsessing over a ghost boy, some government-trained merciless motherfucking assassin was hiding in the shadows, waiting to pick them off one by one for love of country or God or Allah or the Flying Fucking Spaghetti Monster.

But he wasn't having any of it.

Because he was a goddamn American. And if the rest of those idiots couldn't see the danger?

Fuck them.

He'd save his own ass.

The American way.

With a deep drag on his cigarette he approached the front, but instead of grabbing the chair and renewing the assault on those weird glass doors that wouldn't break . . .

dead giveaway for a secret government installation, any dumbass could see that

. . . he shrugged, muttered, "What the hell?" and shoved the door's metal push-bar.

It clicked.

And the door swung open.

7:15 PM

Sue maximized the lower-right perspective to full screen. She clicked 'PLAY' and the video began of the line at the receptionist's window. Andrew stood behind Deyquan. Their heads moved as they talked. In front of them Soccer Mom chatted on her Blackberry. Out of sight, at the receptionist's window under the camera's angle, was where Tillman would've been.

For several minutes nothing happened, the bench between the restrooms empty.

Deyquan glanced at Andrew. Dude's face was pulled tight, eyes jittery. He was a fucking nervous mess.

Why?

What the hell did this guy know?

"There she goes," Sue muttered.

Deyquan looked back to see Tillman lurching away

from Sue's window toward the Ladies Room. She disappeared inside.

Seconds passed. Minutes.

Nothing.

Just Soccer Mom paying her bill. He and Andrew quiet now, standing there, staring nowhere . . .

The video flickered.

Horizontal lines running across the screen.

"The hell?" Sue batted the monitor. "Keep telling management we need a new PC with more memory, but do they listen to me? No . . . "

The video flickered again, dissolving into pixilated static, then resolving into Soccer Mom standing in the waiting area, talking angrily into her Blackberry . . .

And a little boy sitting on the bench between the restrooms.

Deyquan shivered.

Because though he knew it was impossible, he couldn't shake the feeling of the little boy staring into the camera.

At them.

7:20 PM

The door opened.

Kyle stood there, smoking and staring into the rainy night, listening to the downpour hissing against the gravel parking lot. Puddles were spreading. Thunder rolled in the distance. Lightning flashed pale waves across the ground. Cold air whipped and snapped past the door, chilling Kyle, raising goose-flesh and an involuntary shudder. He hunched his shoulders against the icy blast.

"Damn," he whispered. Pale-blue smoke puffed from his cigarette. "*Damn*," he repeated, more forcibly. He could get the hell out of here if he wanted.

Ditch this fucking joint.

Leave those losers behind to figure shit out while he got his ass home. If he bailed now, he could be on his couch tossing back brews in ten minutes.

He took a deep drag.

Flicked his cigarette out into the rain-slicked night.

Stuck his hand into his pocket, feeling his car keys. His white little Ford Escort sat at the parking lot's edge, near an old elm tree. All he needed to do was run through the rain for three minutes, tops. He'd get soaked . . .

But he didn't give a shit.

He wanted out of this place right-the-fuck-now and he didn't care how. So he stepped farther out the door, pushing it open wider. Wind drove cold needles into his exposed skin. Cold rain splattered his brow and cheeks. His car sat there, bathed in moonlight, waiting.

For him.

"Fuck this." He shoved the door open and plunged into the rain, dashing to his car. The rain pelted his head and shoulders and back, instantly soaking him to the skin. He splashed through water-filled ruts along the rolling, uneven parking lot. It was cold. Damn, it was cold.

But whatever. There his car sat, a few feet away. He was soaked, but soon he'd be inside, heater cranked and radio pumping, driving home and . . .

Lightning flashed across the sky, casting the parking lot into stark relief. Thunder growled. Startled by both the lightning and thunder Kyle stumbled on a rut. He toppled forward, arms flailing, hands grasping at air. As he plunged headfirst into a pool of muddy rainwater he thought he saw the shape of a small boy standing between him and his car.

Then his eyes and nose and mouth filled with muddy water.

7:30 PM

"Holy shit," Deyquan breathed, staring at the little boy. He was sitting on the bench between the restrooms, indeed looking dressed for a swim.

"Told you."

"My . . . God," Andrew gasped.

One look at Andrew's blanched face, his wide and glittering eyes and Deyquan grabbed his shoulder. "What? You know something we don't?"

Andrew shook his head, never taking his eyes from the computer screen. "No . . . I . . . "

"Look."

Sue pointed, finger trembling slightly as the boy stood and stared straight at the camera.

At them.

Like he knew they were watching.

And with sharp military precision, he pivoted to his right. Took two brisk steps and pushed into the Ladies Room while Soccer Mom chatted on her Blackberry, Deyquan paid his bill and Andrew stood behind him, staring at the floor, hands in pockets, shoulders sagging.

The video flickered again.

Twisting, distorting, dissolving into static, then snapping back to the inside of the Ladies Room. Lizzy Tillman stood over a sink, shoulders heaving as she cried silently.

An eerie quiet descended, pregnant with expectation until Deyquan rasped, "Didn't say there were cameras in the bathrooms."

Sue stared at the computer screen, motionless, features carved from stone. "That's because there *aren't*."

Deyquan's belly filled with ice as the little boy walked into the restroom, stopped and stared at the crying Lizzy Tillman.

7:30 PM

"Shit!"

Kyle lurched from the puddle he'd fallen into. He wiped frantically at his eyes, spitting out foul water. The rain beat harder, pelting his back and head with stinging drops. He was completely soaked now. Soaked and royally pissed.

"Dammit!" He slapped the water, sending a muddy-brown spray. He hated water. Hated it. Ever since he was ten years old, when he and his brother Danny were screwing around barefoot on the end of the family dock at Clifton Lake. They'd been wrestling when Danny (several years older, taller and stronger) pushed him off the dock's edge. Whether on purpose or by accident, Kyle never knew.

He'd fallen in backwards. While the shock of hitting cold water was unpleasant, what happened after was worse: his feet plunging to the bottom, sinking into the pond's soft mud past his ankles to his mid-calves. The water only came to his chest . . .

But the mud.

Oozing between his toes.

Sucking on his ankles and calves, like it was alive and eating him.

When his father and brother pulled him onto the dock, mud and slime caked him knees to toes. In the mud, things were crawling. Thin worms. Bugs. Water-mud-things, small and hardly worth noticing, except they were slithering around on his mud-slicked skin . . .

He shivered.

Slapped the puddle again, which was quickly spreading and deepening in the unrelenting rain.

Fuck this.

He needed to get in his car. Would soak the seats to hell but he didn't care. Blast the heat and the radio and . . .

He put a hand into the pool to push off . . . and felt it sink into soft, squishing mud . . .

which didn't make sense, the parking lot was gravel

. . . squishing mud pulling him *down.*

"What the . . . "

A sliver of panic sliced through his guts as he yanked his hand. It held fast.

Something yanked back, pulling his hand and then arm deeper into the soft mud to his elbow. "Shit!" He yanked and pulled, only serving to mire his arm deeper.

A desperate frenzy gripped him.

Not thinking, he stuck his other hand into the water to find some solid ground for leverage . . .

It sank into the mud, also.

Then he felt it. Mud rising around his knees, feet and ankles. Slipping into his shoes and between his toes, coating his shins and calves.

Something yanked him farther into the water and mud, sucking eagerly, pulling his face within inches of the water.

He cursed and gasped and shouted but didn't scream.

Not until he felt the things slithering along his mud-slicked skin . . .

3.

He stares for several minutes at the pill bottle, nudges it around with his thumb so he can read the prescription, to make sure. Which is silly, because this is *his* prescription. What else could it be? Whose could it be?

Still.

He's been so uncertain lately, about things he thought he knew but apparently didn't, things he should've known but apparently did not. Or worse, had forgotten.

Better safe than sorry.

He thumbs the bottle over. The label reads: McCormick, Andrew. Risperdal. Dr. Martin. That all looks right . . .

Something else feels wrong, though. In the bottle's heft. He closes his hand around it, makes a fist and shakes it.

No rattle.

Nothing.

Empty. The bottle's empty. For how long? He opens his hand, turns the bottle over with trembling fingers, desperately searching for the refill date.

And he stops.

Reads the date silently. To convince himself, because this is . . .

Impossible

. . . highly unlikely. Improbable, but there it is.

A week ago.

His meds ran out a week ago. And he hasn't refilled them. Why? Why hasn't he..?

It comes in a bright flash of painful memory, like a spike driven through his forehead . . .

like one of his migraines

. . . when his prescription ran out a week ago he decided to wean himself off them without consulting Dr. Martin or Rachael. He's been so tired lately. Groggy and unfocused. Oversleeping, coming to work late. So when his prescription ran out . . .

He'd let it.

And forgotten about it.

Something cold stirs his guts, making him faintly sick as sweat beads his forehead. Because what else has he forgotten?

What else?

"I don't understand. Maybe I should, but I don't. Tell me what I'm doing and I'll change, I'll . . . "

"No! Goddammit, you DON'T get it! Can you stop being you? Can you change your face? No, you can't."

"Rachel . . . "

"Every time I look at you. Get it? Whenever I see your face, it hurts. Over and over and over. I can't do it anymore. I'm sorry."

"You're sorry? He was taken from ME, Rachel. From me! He was TAKEN! And none of you believe . . . "

"NO! No more of this! You've got to face it, Andrew, let it out and deal with it: NO ONE TOOK HIM! You LOST him, Andrew! YOU LET HIM GO! And I can't LOOK at you anymore because of it, dammit!"

**Thursday
7:30 PM**

Andrew's chest tightened, a greasy nausea swirling in his gut as the little boy stepped closer to Lizzy Tillman. Voices screamed in his head: *Stop this! It's impossible! It can't be.*

But it was.

In eerie silence Lizzy Tillman straightened, looked around, as if sensing the boy's approach. But as she glanced left, then right, Andrew realized though *they* could see the boy inching closer . . .

She couldn't.

As she turned the sink's faucet on, stuck her hands under the water (dammit if he couldn't hear the water trickling over her hands, against the porcelain), she froze, gazing into the mirror over the sink, entranced by something only she could see.

The voices in Andrew's head kept screaming and the water from the faucet kept trickling into the sink, though the video feed made no sound . . .

For a moment Deyquan forgot they were watching recorded footage, tempted to yell at Lizzy Tillman: *Get the fuck out! Run! Freaky-ass kid's getting closer! Get your ass out of there, now..!*

The video flickered.

Rippling with static.

The mirror's glass melted and formed liquid hands—the best Deyquan could describe it—which grabbed the sides of Lizzy Tillman's head, yanked her forward . . .

And slammed her face into the mirror.

Over and over.

Her hands flailed, fingers sliding off the sink's smooth porcelain edges, feet kicking and toes skidding on tile.

Next to Deyquan, Soccer Mom gasped and triggered her inhaler. Andrew muttered, "Oh God . . . "

While Sue sat and stared.

As those hands slammed Lizzy's face into the mirror once more, hard enough to jerk her whole body, and then shoved her head face-first down into the sink. The faucet knobs spun, water gushing.

Over her head.

Into the sink.

Filling it past her face to her ears as she grabbed at the sink's edges weakly, arms and legs growing sluggish. Her struggles dissolved into sporadic twitching.

As those hands held her face down.

And the water filled the sink to overflowing.

7:35 PM

The video flickered, dissolving into static, then resolving into the waiting room. Soccer Mom still talked on her Blackberry, Deyquan still paying his bill, hidden by the camera angle.

Andrew stood center focus.

Shoulders slumped, hands in his pockets.

"Stop it," Deyquan rasped. His throat felt raw, like he'd swallowed glass. He coughed and said more clearly, "Pause it, stop it . . . something."

Sue—still staring—clicked 'PAUSE.'

Something thumped.

Deyquan glanced over his shoulder and saw Soccer Mom backed against the wall, her eyes wide and bright and wet. Hitching and gasping, she stuck her inhaler into her mouth and triggered another blast.

Deyquan turned and gestured at the screen. "What . . . what the *fuck*?"

A slow, mesmerized head-shake. "I . . . don't know. We don't have cameras in the bathrooms."

He pointed at the screen. "Bullshit! An . . . fuck! What the hell was that shit with the mirror..?"

He closed his eyes.

Rubbed his forehead with his fingertips. "No, no.

Bullshit. Gotta have cameras in the bathroom. Just didn't know it is all and you clicked on it by accident. And what the *fuck* was up with that mirror?"

"I'm telling you," Sue's voice rose, "there's no cameras in the-"

"No way. Fucking gotta be-"

"Hey!"

Sue turned, eyes bright and angry. "I've worked here for twenty years. There's no. Goddamn. Cameras. IN THE BATHROOMS!"

Deyquan waved. "Okay, okay. Just . . . rewind it. Gotta see it again, figure this shit out."

"Oh God," whispered Soccer Mom, voice small and childlike, still wheezing. "Please, don't."

He waved her off. "Don't watch it then. We gotta . . . figure this shit out . . . "

"God, please, no."

Sue's face stiffened.

She nodded, turned and clicked 'PLAY,' starting the video over from before. But they saw no boy. During Lizzy's flight to the bathroom, still no boy. No point of view change, either. No scene of Lizzy's gruesome death in the bathroom.

Only the waiting room.

Soccer Mom on her Blackberry, looking angry. Deyquan paying his bill out of sight. Andrew standing slump-shouldered, hands in pockets. When Sue clicked 'PAUSE,' the video-Andrew glanced up.

Staring into the camera.

At them.

And something clicked in Deyquan's head. Not the whole puzzle, but one piece.

Hell.

A motherfuckering *big* piece.

But he wasn't saying anything yet. "All right. Fuck the cops and crime scenes and shit. Any gloves round here? I'm looking at the body." He turned and slapped Andrew's shoulder. "And you're coming with me."

7:45 PM

Judy Cavanaugh cowered in the corner of the small security office. She hugged herself, wheezing, her throat dry and tight. She clutched her inhaler like a talisman to ward off evil. She told herself this was all a bad dream.

Not believing it, at all.

She bit her tongue to keep from screaming. Because if this wasn't a dream . . . what had she just seen? A girl killing herself in a public restroom—drowning herself—was bizarre enough, but Judy had stood behind Lizzy Tillman in line. She'd heard the desperation cracking in her voice as she pleaded to have her electricity turned back on before social services took her child away. So maybe the girl *had* been desperate and distraught enough to . . .

but what about those hands coming from the mirror?

And the phones?

Well, it was storming out. Badly. Wind, rain and lightning. No cell phones, Internet or fax, so maybe a line or tower had blown down somewhere . . .

then why did they still have electricity?

. . . but the doors and windows, all locked? And the glass? Why wouldn't it break? Maybe Kyle's wacky terrorist idea wasn't so wacky . . .

where is he, anyway?

. . . and she'd been so sure she'd seen a little boy and the footage had proved her right. But the other things the video had shown.

In the bathroom.

Where there apparently weren't any cameras.

God. What did it mean, what was it . . .

Yet here she was.

In this small and shrinking ratbox security room, unable to catch her breath despite using her inhaler, while Deyquan and whatshisname went out and played CSI and Sue sitting there and scrolling through the footage, searching for a camera angle that didn't exist . . .

She gasped, wheezing thinly, her throat closing again, chest tightening like an iron hand was crushing them.

Panic filled her, thrumming along her nerves. Her heart thudded against her chest. She gasped, getting no air, which spiked her panic higher, making it harder to breathe. She stuck her inhaler's nozzle into her mouth, triggering a blast.

Nothing.

She triggered again, sucking as deeply as she could, triggering the inhaler over and over.

Only to get nothing.

She realized a numbing truth.

Empty.

Her inhaler was empty. All her replacement charges were in her purse out in the waiting area, which might as well be hundreds of miles away with her lungs spasming so uselessly. But she needed them. *Now.*

She didn't bother saying anything to Sue. Dykey old bitch was still entranced by the security footage, searching the video feeds, mumbling "Gotta be here, gotta be here" over and over. Judy instead stumbled out the security office's door and lurched toward the waiting area, the edges of her vision blurring with each tortured, futile gasp.

7:50 PM

Sue Cranston—customer service receptionist for the Clifton Heights NYSEG office for the last twenty years—barely registered Judy's rasping exit. She dimly remembered Judy telling Kyle . . .

where is he, anyway?

. . . she was asthmatic and sure enough, all her wheezing and hacking sounded like an asthma attack. And under normal circumstances . . .

this shit's far from normal

. . . she would've helped the poor girl, but right now Sue was on a mission to find a non-existent bathroom video feed which had apparently disappeared . . .

if it existed at all

. . . because she'd decided Deyquan must be right. Though she'd reviewed security footage numerous times, physically checked all the cameras and had never seen a camera in the bathrooms, had never been told by her bosses cameras were installed there, there *must* be a camera in there, because how else could she explain what had happened? Explain how the camera over the waiting room suddenly began transmitting video from the ladies bathroom without a corresponding camera?

Impossible.

As impossible as a little boy sitting on the bench, largely ignored by everyone . . .

what about the mirror and those hands?

. . . as impossible as him disappearing off the footage. And how could the whole bathroom scene . . .

and the mirror's hands

. . . get recorded through a camera they didn't have, then get erased? She must have accessed a camera in the bathroom she didn't know of—maybe one recently installed—and she must have accidentally deleted the footage or erased it somehow when she'd restarted the video stream.

Cameras that didn't exist but did.

Footage there one minute, gone the next.

Ridiculous as it seemed, it all sounded like some of Kyle's more paranoid ramblings. Which made her wonder as she clicked the mouse and once again advanced through video of the waiting room (seeing no little boy, no bathroom footage) where the *hell* was Kyle?

She bit the inside of her cheek, worry twisting her guts. Hated to admit it but she felt something for that stupid-ass kid. Kyle had only worked here for a few months and mostly he was like the rest of his generation: lazy, self-centered and cynical without the life-experience.

But he'd grown on her.

God help her, he'd grown on her these past few months. Snarky as hell, like her. Kind of an asshole, but his dirty jokes made her smile. She was fairly sure Kyle didn't like people much, like her, too.

And hey.

She might be a stodgy old maid at forty but Kyle's sneering insouciance touched something deep inside thought long dead. Kyle was like a Bargain Right "James Dean." Far from the real article but close enough to raise wisps of memory.

She sighed while looking through the video feed again, knowing how everyone saw her. Short and solid but not fat, broad with thick arms, flat chested with tree-trunk legs. She hated long hair—loathed messing with it—so she'd always worn it short. A buzz-cut, these days, because at her age a bob-cut no longer made her look sprightly and winsome, just ridiculous.

So she knew what she looked like.

Could see it in the ghostly reflection on the computer screen: her squarish head and jaw. Butch-cut hair graying at the temples. Hard, steel-gray eyes.

A dyke.

Lesbo.

And she knew her co-workers—probably even Kyle—thought so. She was one of the 'guys.' Living alone with several cats and a special "friend."

But it wasn't so. She'd once been thinner. Attractive to boys in a tomboyish way. But time and hard living had thickened her body and heart, stealing her lithe youth and replacing it with a chunky, asexual middle-age, turning her brisk sass into a half-snarling sulkiness.

Lesbo.

Dyke.

Butch.

But the reality couldn't be further from the truth. That was *really* why she liked Kyle, despite his lazy ass. Because in a way he reminded her of the kinds of guys she used to run with. Riding shotgun-wild nights along winding asphalt trails under the moon, doing things in back seats only whispered about during Sunday school.

Before she'd turned into this.

So there it was.

She liked Kyle. Liked trading good-natured insults with him. Liked ragging difficult customers behind their backs and ripping their clueless administrators. She even enjoyed sharing crack-pot conspiracy theories with him, though he believed them more than she did. She just liked to listen to him rant while they took smoke breaks out front . . .

The video flickered.

Rippling with static, like before.

"Whoa." She sat back, lifting her hands. Maybe she'd found the missing footage-

The screen dissolved into static.

Then resolved into the rain-drenched front parking lot, from the camera over the main entrance.

She sighed and shook her head. Camera A out front. Maybe the system was buggy, jumping through all the feeds randomly. But she needed to find that missing footage—

Her thoughts ground to a halt.

She frowned.

Leaned closer to the monitor, squinting at the parking lot (which looked like it was flooding into a goddamn lake) and saw a crumpled form out there.

She gasped.

As the video footage zoomed in at a dizzying rate, which she knew was impossible, because their security cameras didn't have pan or zoom functions . . .

Her mouth dropped open.

As she leaned closer, an icy fist squeezed her lungs. Her heart pounded. The humped pile in the parking lot looked like someone on their hands and knees praying, face-down in the water . . .

Face-down.

In the water.

She covered her mouth. "Oh . . . God."

Something inside her broke. She blinked, fought back a wetness in her eyes, because it couldn't be him, the doors were locked and the glass wouldn't break so how could Kyle be out there, lying face-down in the brown lake flooding the parking lot, oh God, did he drown? In the parking lot, did he drown because muddy-brown hands (like those impossible quicksilver hands from the mirror) grabbed his head and pulled him into the water? *Oh my fucking . . .*

She stopped.

A desperate thrill pulsing through her.

Because the body was moving.

Twitching, shivering.

The body lying face-down in the water shuddered all over. Bucked, straightened, lurched upright and turned.

Walking toward the camera.

Toward her.

7:55 PM

Deyquan eased around the corner into the ladies bathroom, stepping carefully. The floor was flooded from the faucets still gushing over Lizzy Tillman's head. His heart pounded as he led Andrew to her body. *Stupid*, a part of him yammered, *this is fucking stupid. Brother messing with a crime scene. How stupid can you be?*

Another voice deep inside knew different. This wasn't a crime scene. This was something else. And by the time the police did get here, Deyquan knew—with an increasingly sick clarity—they'd be far past petty shit like corruption of a crime scene.

Far past.

Still, he wore rubber gloves snatched from a cleaning closet. Because he wasn't *that* fucking stupid.

Several more squelching steps later they stood next to Lizzy Tillman. Deyquan still couldn't see her face, but the swirling water's pinkish tinge told him enough.

He glanced to his left. Andrew didn't blink. Just stared at Tillman, face slack, eyes wide, mouth open slightly.

Deyquan turned the faucets off.

The gurgling flow vanished, leaving a faint trickle of water leaking over the sink's edge to the floor. Silence filled the room. Desperate to crack it, afraid it might suffocate him, Deyquan rasped, "So . . . okay. Yeah. Guess I'll . . . "

He gestured at the back of Lizzy Tillman's head, which he noticed with a certain sick grimness didn't bob or float in the water-filled sink but was firmly lodged. What that meant about the condition of her face, he didn't want to consider.

But he'd see for sure in a minute, wouldn't he?

He breathed deeply.

Grabbed Lizzy's damp, limp ponytail.

Braced his other hand on the sink's edge, the wet porcelain slippery through the thin rubber of his glove. He pulled.

Lizzy's head wouldn't move. It remained stuck in the sink.

"Sunnuvabitch," Deyquan muttered. He yanked, hard.

Pulling Lizzy's head out of the sink with a sharp, wet plop, flipping her ruined face into view.

And wishing he hadn't.

Because her face was a hammered mess. Nose crushed back into her face. Brow and cheekbones shattered. Her face a sagging mess of torn flesh.

Deyquan stared, his mouth working silently. He swallowed bile, looked at Andrew, whose face was a sickly shade of gray. Eyes wide as dinner plates. Mouth wide, upper lip twitching . . .

Andrew gagged.

Splashed across the flooded floor and puked against the wall.

Deyquan slowly eased what remained of Lizzy Tillman's face back into the sink. Her squashed face fit neatly back into the sink, like an interlocking piece of a child's building-block set. Like a goddamn human Lego.

"Damn," he whispered, stepping slowly away. He

stripped the rubber gloves and dropped them, not caring at all about crime scenes, now. "Damn. I mean . . . shit. What the fuck is . . ."

A great, intestinal heaving interrupted him.

A gurgling, burping, retching.

Liquid splashed. Deyquan looked over his shoulder, a weakly sarcastic comment on his lips, but it died when he saw Andrew leaning on his forehead against the wall, panting softly.

Not puking.

As those horrible, abdominal retching sounds continued. As if someone were puking their guts out.

In the waiting area.

8:55 PM

Judy stumbled out into the waiting area, throat closing tightly, lungs aching and shivering and trembling, sucking on nothing. Black spots peppered her vision, head and heart pounding in time. But she saw it.

Her purse, sitting next to the bench, where she'd left it.

She stumbled toward it, reaching, as if she could magically call the inhaler cartridges from her purse to her hand by thinking, wishing, wanting.

She managed two more steps before the floor tilted.

Her legs folded beneath her and she fell, hands slapping cold tile, catching her short of smashing her forehead. Her inhaler clattered onto the floor and spun out of reach as she rolled onto her side and curled into a fetal ball. She lay there, shivering, gasping, clawing at a throat refusing to open, drowning on the dead air trapped in her lungs.

Her vision darkened more.

The tips of her fingers and toes grew cold.

Panic thrummed inside. She couldn't die. Not like this, not without telling her bastard husband she knew about trampy little Mandy at the office, knew he hadn't been staying late this past month working on the Feinstein account, he'd been working on Mandy. She knew and she couldn't die because then she'd never be able to stick it to him where it hurt, hire the best divorce lawyer in the Utica-Rome area and take him for all he was worth and if she died like this who would make the kids breakfast, pack their lunches, take them to school and get them after, cook dinner, do the laundry, wash and fold and stitch their clothes, plant the garden and can vegetables and buy groceries, balance the checkbook so she could organize the PTA's next bake sale and coach her youngest daughter's Junior Miss softball team to another league championship . . .

Something clenched and twisted inside.

Judy Cavanaugh pulled in her arms and legs. Managed to roll onto her hands and knees and inch toward her too-distant purse. She'd never make it but she wouldn't go without a fight, goddamn it . . .

Rubber squeaked against tile.

Swim shoes stepped into view.

Weakly, she looked up, drooling, not caring. All she saw was a shadowed, child-sized silhouette standing above her. A boy, who extended his hand.

Offering her an inhaler.

Judy didn't hesitate; logic, reason and caution powerless in the face of her terror. With new-found strength, she snatched the inhaler (which, oddly enough was blue, while hers was pale green) but she didn't waste another second thinking about that. She rolled over onto her back, stuck it into her mouth and triggered a blast.

Eyes snapping wide as she got nothing but water.

Foul, dank, gushing from the inhaler into her mouth as she reflexively breathed, gagging and choking, as the water continued to flow.

Somehow she rolled to her knees, pulling at the inhaler, but it wouldn't come out. It kept forcing water into her, which triggered her gag reflex. She heaved, bucked, guts cramping as she vomited but it had nowhere to go . . .

Water spurt from her nostrils. Her head, heart and lungs thundered. With one last yank, she pulled the inhaler from her mouth, following it with a projectile stream of bile and the partially digested remains of what she'd eaten for lunch . . .

And water.

Streams of it.

Gushing endlessly from her mouth, her life ebbing with its flow. Water, tasting of dank mildew and blood.

4.

His hand closes around the prescription bottle, making a fist. The hard plastic digs into his palm, pushing the confusion away with pain.

The meds have made his thoughts sluggish, made him forget things, and he doesn't want that anymore, because Rachel's right. He's got to let it out. Face it, deal with the truth, whatever it might be, because the thing growing inside has gotten too big. He can't keep it inside anymore.

Time to let it out.

He closes his eyes, squeezes his fist tight and whispers, "But I'm afraid of what will happen next."

There is no answer, save the hissing rain, so he opens his eyes. With his free hand, he jabs the automatic window controls on his door's armrest, rolls down the passenger-side window and without hesitation tosses the bottle away.

The night and the rain swallow it, instantly, silently.

He leans back.

Closes his eyes and waits for a sign, some feeling of peace and resolution, to tell him he's done the right thing, and the end is near.

It doesn't come.

He sighs, straightens and opens his eyes. Looks out his window, into the dark night rain and wonders: If he lets it out . . . what will he find? What will it be? What is he so scared of?

He can't wait any longer.

So he turns the key, kills the engine and reaches for the door.

"So what do you want, then? There's got to be something I can do."

"Yes there is. Go away."

"What? Rachael, how can you be so . . . "

"No Andrew. I mean it. No more calls or emails. No texts, no letters, no Facebook messages. No more lawyers. Sign the papers and go away. It's the only way we can move on."

"If that's what you want."

"It is. More importantly, it's what I need. And whether you believe it or not, it's what you need, too."

"All right. Fine. I'll . . . go away."

"Thank you, Andrew. And I'm sorry. Goodbye."

He sighs, "Goodbye." Hangs up, drops the iPhone onto the passenger seat, sits back and closes his eyes, feeling the engine's throb.

━━━━◆━━━━

9:10 PM

For the first time Deyquan couldn't move, could only stare while Andrew knelt by Soccer Mom, who lay face-down in a large pool of water.

Andrew extended a tentative hand toward her. Maybe to grab her hair, pull back her head, show her face. But Deyquan hoped the hell not. He'd already survived seeing the Tillman girl's face. That had been enough.

"D . . . don't." He coughed. Ashamed at the way his voice wavered, he forced a rougher tone. "Fuck it. She's fucking dead. Just fucking leave her."

Andrew nodded.

Rocked back onto his heels, looked at Soccer Mom's outstretched hand and what lay a few inches from it, on the floor.

A blue asthma inhaler.

Andrew sucked in a hissing breath. "What . . . ? No. Impossible."

As Andrew picked up the inhaler with trembling hands, Deyquan looked away, rubbing his forehead with the heel of his palm, trying to stifle a pounding throb behind his eyes.

Fuck this shit. Can't take no more. People dying, fucking windows won't break and spooky-ass video recordings erasing themselves . . .

"Shit," he chuckled, on the edge of hysteria. "All cause I wanted to pay my goddamn bill early. Fuck it, man. Next time, let the fucker go to collections."

Lightning flashed outside, flickering through the glass front doors.

"Damn," Deyquan whispered, rubbing his forehead harder. Didn't want to go to those doors. Didn't want to see what was out there, because he was through, dammit. Fucking over it.

Lightning flashed again.

Illuminating a humped, prostrate form.

Like someone lying on their face, praying to goddamn Mecca. And, half-aware and mumbling to himself, Deyquan stumbled toward the doors.

9:15 PM

Andrew gently cradled the blue inhaler, dimly considering how Judy must have sucked on it before dying. Rain outside crashed against the building, rushing in torrents, gurgling against the windows, as the world splintered around him.

Because this was impossible, finding this blue inhaler. Impossible, like everything else happening tonight. Lizzy Tillman, killed by something . . .

hands that came from the mirror

. . . and the phones not working, doors not opening, glass not breaking, the rain rushing and trickling and gurgling like something pulling him down, the impossible little boy no one remembered seeing in the video footage, impossible, because he looked so much like . . .

can't be, can't be

. . . impossible, because if he remembered right, Judy waved a green inhaler at Kyle . . .

where was he, anyway?

. . . impossible because Andrew didn't have any of these blue inhalers, anymore; he'd thrown them out months ago . . .

"No," he rasped, turning the inhaler over with

trembling fingers, feeling the cool plastic. "It's impossible. Can't be-"

He didn't have time to form another thought. Two hands grabbed fistfuls of his jacket, yanked him to his feet, and a fist slammed into his jaw, throwing him backward.

9:20 PM

Deyquan stumbled to the glass front doors. He jiggled the push-bar, knowing it wouldn't open but trying anyway. He grunted when the door wouldn't budge, as expected, and placed his hand flat against the cool glass. Glass that wouldn't break, even under a pipe and a metal folding chair.

Lightning flashed overhead, casting ghostly shadows and moonglow shapes across the now flooded parking lot. Throwing the body into stark relief, lying face-down in the water. Lightning flashed again. The body's white polo shirt glowed in the night.

Kyle.

Kid wasn't praying to Mecca or anything else out there in the rain, face-down in the flooded parking lot.

Dead.

He was dead.

Along with Soccer Mom behind him and the Tillman girl, drowned by something . . .

by hands that grew from a mirror

. . . in the ladies bathroom.

Dead. All dead.

Drowned.

And Andrew, acting nervous all night long, like he knew something. Then . . . the puzzle piece to it all. A big motherfucking puzzle piece. The way Andrew stared into the video camera, looking so much like the mysterious, disappearing little boy.

Especially in the eyes.

"Damn," Deyquan whispered, thumping the glass with his flattened hand. "Damn."

Sudden anger pulsed through him; a certainty Andrew was holding something back. His anger mixed with fear, however, a kind of fear he'd never felt before, because he'd been right. This shit wasn't a terrorist plot or some other nonsense. This shit was something else.

Something *worse*.

He spun.

Quick strides carried him across the floor. He was on Andrew before the guy could react. Grabbing his jacket, yanking him to his feet. Before he was consciously aware of doing so Deyquan hauled back and punched Andrew's jaw, sending him onto his ass, hands flailing, face registering not only shock and dismay . . .

But guilt, too.

Because somewhere deep inside . . . he knew. Motherfucker knew what was happening, knew why Deyquan punched him, or at least suspected, which only made Deyquan angrier.

"Okay," he forced through his teeth. "I . . . I've fucking had it. Can't explain this shit, no way. Ain't gonna try, no more. But you fucking know something. Dontcha? Have known this whole fucking time, but ain't said a word. Well, I'm done. Gonna talk, right the fuck now."

Andrew's pale face crumpled, eyes wide and miserable, gasping like a fish dying on shore, starving for breath in open air. "I . . . oh, God. I don't . . . "

"For starters," Deyquan pushed on, ignoring Andrew's stammers, "who's the boy? You know him, don't you? Saw it in your eyes, first time we watched the video. And don't be bullshitting me. Not now."

Andrew shook his head in short, jerky sweeps. "N . . . no. God. It's impossible. Can't be him, c-can't be . . . "

"Who the FUCK is it? Tell me or I'll . . . "

"My son! Goddamn it, I . . . I think it's my son."

Deyquan nodded. He'd first noticed how similar they looked when Andrew gazed into the camera in the recording of them standing in line. But that didn't explain anything else. "Your son? But what . . . "

"No, no, no. It's impossible. Can't be him," Andrew insisted. "It can't be him."

"Why?"

"It's . . . it can't be . . . "

Annoyance pricked at Deyquan, threatening to reignite his anger. "C'mon, man. Don't be holding shit out on me . . . "

Andrew shook his head, closed his eyes. "It's impossible, dammit, he's gone, he's . . . "

———•~~•———

" . . . scared, Andrew. Can't you see? Look at him. He's shaking like a leaf."

Andrew tried not to bristle at the peevishness in Rachel's voice, tried instead to focus on the warm sun baking his skin, on the laughter and joyful screams of children enjoying rides, on the canned eighties and nineties pop music blaring over the park's loudspeakers. It had been a good day and he wasn't going to let Rachel's paranoia spoil it like always.

He gripped Patrick's thin and shivering shoulders (shivering because he was wet, *NOT* because he was scared) and squeezed playfully. "Naw. You're not scared.

Right sport? Fact, you've been brave today. Going on all these rides for the first time."

Patrick nodded eagerly. Smile tentative at first, but quickly exploding into a big grin. "Yeah! Sure have. Thanks to you, Dad."

Andrew felt not only pride for his son but also an unaccustomed sense of satisfaction, of a job well done, confirmation that maybe he wasn't such a bad parent, after all.

Because raising Patrick with his severe asthma hadn't been easy. Often a chore. A burden, Andrew shamefully thought, in his darker moments. Andrew grew up an average, healthy, robust kid. Adventurous, outdoorsy, he'd romped through the woods, all of Adirondack Park his playground, working summers with local farmers and lumberjacks, playing three sports a year in high school.

It had taken a long time for him to accept Pat's ailment. He wasn't and never could be the same kid Andrew was, which made today special, because he'd been trying so hard to encourage Patrick to *live*. Take moderate risks, be adventurous, be a boy, to romp and play in the woods, climb trees, fall and scrape his knees, run his bike off homemade jumps, mess around in the creek out past Mr. Drake's hay fields, spending every day all summer cooking to a golden brown under the sun.

Instead of hiding inside.

Instead of cowering in his air-conditioned room behind his iPad, books and comic books, instead of always jamming that goddamn blue inhaler into his mouth, triggering it off at the slightest provocation; whenever he got slightly winded, fatigued, upset, scared or worried. Instead of shying away from anything potentially interesting, active or even remotely physical.

So today was a triumph. A planned one, which made Andrew feel even better. An excursion to Old Forge's huge water park, Enchanted Forest. An attempt he'd concocted with the approval of their family pediatrician (and Rachel's grudging approval) to encourage Patrick to be adventurous, physical, and active.

And they'd done it.

They'd triumphed over the Ferris Wheel, the Tilt-A-Whirl, the bumper cars; screamed through the Flying Bobs and then for their grand finale, conquered the kiddie water slides.

Now they were going for the gold.

Black River Falls. A twisting, enclosed, serpentine water slide with a 250-foot total drop, from start to finish. He'd first conquered this bad boy himself when he was ten. Now it was his son's turn, and in the heat of today's little triumphs, Andrew felt sure they were ready for the challenge.

He thought—hell no, he knew—Patrick was loving this. Could be imagining it but he thought Patrick stood straighter, walked quicker, smiled wider with each ride they bested. His confidence was growing, bit by bit. He'd only needed his inhaler once today, because of his excitement after the Flying Bobs.

He was ready for this. So ready. Andrew knew it and loved seeing his son emerging from his cocoon, acting alive for once. If only Rachel could understand, see the sparkle in their son's eyes.

But a small sliver of doubt rippled through him. Because maybe Rachel was right. Patrick was a people-pleaser, after all. He hated disappointing folks, especially his parents, always willing to do his best for them. Maybe Black River Falls was too much for him. Maybe he was scared but was putting on a good show for his parents, for *him*, especially.

He squeezed Patrick's shoulders again. "Y'know, it's been a heckuva day, Pat. A great one, and I'm proud. Don't need to ride this one, if you don't want to. Got nothing to prove to me, pal."

Patrick glanced over Andrew's shoulder.

At Black River Falls looming above.

His wide grin flickering, ever so slightly. Did a shadow pass across his face? It evaporated soon as Andrew saw it, and Patrick looked at him again, eyes sparkling. "Naw, Dad. I'm game. Let's do it."

Andrew smiled, feeling delighted at his son's courage. He patted Patrick's cheek and said, "That's my boy."

~~~

Patrick acted brave and exuberant all the way to the top, eagerly staring at Black River Falls' winding twists and turns. Even when the attendant said he couldn't take his beloved inhaler with him (no external devices of any kind allowed on the ride) Patrick maintained a determined expression.

Unlike Rachel, when Andrew handed her the inhaler. Face carefully composed, she gave Andrew a look he couldn't quite decipher as the inhaler passed from his hand to hers. A look of resignation.

But they'd be fine. They'd batted a thousand today.

They'd be fine.

Even as Rachel turned her back on them and slowly descended the water-slide's steps with an eerie (and not a little overly-dramatic) air of finality.

They'd be fine.

Even as they settled onto the bright neon inner tube floating in the ride's loading pool, he thought: *we'll be fine*. As water rushed down the tube, the tide tugging at their ankles, rocking the inner tube: *we'll be fine*. As Patrick's thin hands clutched the handles, Andrew sitting behind him. As the ride's mouth gaped before them, pitch black and depthless, the water gurgling around them: *we'll be fine*.

"All set?"

For a moment, as the black entrance loomed bigger with each second, as Patrick's shaking form leaned back into him, Andrew felt it. His own shiver of trepidation, uncertainty.

Of fear.

He quashed this tremulous sensation instantly, resentful of Rachel's paranoia. He girded himself, stoked those flames of adventure high and shouted: "Ready!"

The attendant pushed them forward.

Barely nudging them.

For a brief second Andrew saw himself stick his foot out, snag the tube's edge and halt their progress. He saw himself apologizing to the still bored attendant and leading a grateful and relieved (but gamely protesting) Patrick back to Rachel, who would also act relieved and happy for once, proud of the decision he'd made.

The moment passed.

Water gurgling and rushing around them as they shot forward, the tube's blackness swallowing them whole.

Instantly, Andrew knew he'd made a mistake. He was wrong.

Horribly wrong.

Because he hadn't counted on such total darkness. Such spinning disorientation. Such confusion as he tried to hold onto the tube's handles and Patrick as they fell.

As water in absolute darkness rushed and gurgled all around.

Patrick screamed.

Andrew opened his mouth to shout something encouraging . . . but the tube banked. They slalomed sideways, high into a steep curve, then plunged downward at an impossible angle.

Water slammed into his face.

Cutting off any encouragement he could offer. Choking him as they hit another hump, swerving as water gurgled and pulled them into the darkness . . . gurgling and laughing at them.

At *him*.

As they slid into another sharp, downward curve, jostled and rocked . . .

. . . and Patrick screamed again.

High, shrill, inarticulate.

Another thump and a rolling, sliding sound, as Andrew's fingers suddenly held nothing but air and Patrick's screams faded ahead of him, Andrew screaming also as he fell through the darkness forever.

9:45 PM

Deyquan stared at Andrew. He didn't have any kids of his own, but *shit*. Would have to be a fucking robot not to feel bad after that story.

Andrew put his face into his hands and sobbed (oddly enough, crying as badly as if the accident had just happened), unable to continue. But Deyquan didn't need him to. Kid with bad asthma slips out of his dad's hands on a big ass water slide. Kid who probably wasn't much of a swimmer to begin with, and . . .

Then it hit him. Kid drowned, all alone.

Like that Tillman girl.

Kyle and Soccer Mom, also.

266

He rubbed the bridge of his nose between his thumb and forefinger. Cleared his throat and forced himself to speak. "So. Your kid—damn, I know this is a shitty question—but your kid drowned." Andrew wiped his eyes, looking confused for a moment (like he wanted to say 'no, that's not true') but he nodded. "A little over a year ago," he rasped.

"Right. Shit. Your kid drowns, then a year later, three people trapped in a NYSEG office during a crazy-ass storm drown. With all this other freaky shit like unbreakable windows going on. And that was your kid in the video. Wasn't it? Dressed like he was going to a water park?"

Andrew nodded, face twisting with confusion and pain. "Yes, but I don't understand . . . it's impossible . . . "

"Fuck that noise, man. Crazy shit's happening, people dying, and something's trapped us here . . . "

Deyquan trailed off, remembering. By the look of realization dawning on Andrew's face, he'd realized it, too. "Shit. Sue. Those other folks all died alone, and now she's . . . *fuck*."

He turned and sprinted toward the offices, not caring if Andrew followed . . . except, if everyone had died alone and Andrew didn't follow him . . .

One of them was next.

10:00 PM

They stopped several feet short of the security office, at the pool of water slowly spreading down the hall from the now-dark room, a dark room lit by intermittent, arcing sparks flickering eerily here and there, over Sue's slumped form and her chair and the floor. The servers sparking. And from here, though Deyquan couldn't tell for sure, it looked like

Sue's head was buried in the computer monitor's screen, as if something had smashed her face into it.

He grabbed Andrew's elbow, holding him back. "Shit. Don't wanna mess with . . . pretty sure she's gone." Andrew nodded weakly. Lips trembling, nothing coming out. Deyquan pulled at Andrew's elbow, tugging him back to the waiting area.

10:15 PM

They stood at the glass front doors, looking out into the parking lot (preferring Kyle's more distant body than the drowned Soccer Mom behind them), which was flooded several feet by now. At least from here, they couldn't see Kyle's face.

Deyquan shook his head, feeling tired, old and defeated. "So. This all done by a ghost or something? Your kid . . . he doing all this?"

Andrew shook his head, looking lost. "I . . . don't know. I . . ."

"So, what? You been hearing shit at home? Strange noises at night, crying in the basement and shit, stuff getting moved around when you walk out of rooms?"

Andrew paused, again looking guilty and unsure, as if he still didn't believe all this was real. "After the . . . accident, I started suffering from severe migraines, and what the doctors called severe auditory hallucinations."

Deyquan frowned. "Ain't that basically hearing things, like I said? What'd you hear?"

"Water," Andrew whispered, staring into space, face slack, loose. "For a long time, I heard water. Rushing, gurgling, trickling . . . laughing. At me." He snorted. "Got so I couldn't turn on a goddamn faucet, let alone do the dishes, take a shower, water the garden. But I wouldn't admit to myself why I was hearing water all the time. I repressed it. Along with everything else."

Deyquan shook his head. Sighed, looking back out into the raining night, gaze studiously avoiding Kyle's body. "Don't make sense, it being your kid's ghost. Why us? No offense, but we had nothing to do with it."

"This isn't happening. Can't be. It's another hallucination, a dream, because I stopped my meds. A week ago, I stopped my meds, and I threw the empty bottle out the truck window before I came in here tonight . . . "

"Hey!" Deyquan grabbed Andrew's shoulder and shook him. "Don't start pulling the same shit as Soccer Mom. You was there. You *saw* the video. And, shit . . . remember when I said this wasn't a terrorist attack but something else? This shit is *something* else. And it's gotta do with your kid, somehow."

Andrew closed his eyes.

Lips trembling, and for a minute, Deyquan worried he'd pushed him too far. But then Andrew's face resolved, jaw firming, and he opened his eyes. "I know. Because it's my fault. I killed him."

Deyquan raised a hand, pity swelling inside. "Hold on. Easy, man. You didn't kill him. Was an accident, sounds like."

"I know. But I was selfish. Irresponsible. And I've been denying it for nearly a year. I retreated into . . . "

His voice broke, as if he was ready to cry again, but he held on and continued in a husky voice. "I retreated into a fantasy, telling myself Patrick was abducted at the water park, so I couldn't take responsibility for my mistake. A little boy wouldn't understand, I don't think. Especially the confused, angry spirit of a little boy. If that's what this is."

"Man, c'mon. Do I have to say it? I mean . . . I know you've seen the movie, right? 'They're here' and all that."

Andrew shrugged and shook his head, misery painting his face. But then his eyes grew thoughtful. "You're still alive. Why?"

Deyquan grunted. "Right. Cause I ain't been alone yet."

"Or . . . " Andrew paused. "Because you've been with *me* the entire time."

Deyquan blinked. "Shit. You're right. Since the beginning, when we was talking in line . . . "

And then, the puzzle piece. The big motherfucking one. "Hey. Maybe you don't remember . . . but on the video, when you looked into the camera . . . what the hell was you thinking about?"

Silence.

A strange expression . . . of fear? amazement? wonder? . . . settled over Andrew's face. "Oh. My. God."

He turned and looked at Deyquan, eyes bright and fearful. "I know," Andrew whispered, "I know what this is." He blinked several times. "At least, I think so. And it's not a ghost."

Deyquan frowned. "Ain't a ghost, then what the fuck is it?"

Andrew touched his pale, sweating forehead and combed a trembling hand through his hair. "I never accepted Patrick's death, convinced myself he'd been abducted, imagined him alive somewhere, and while the medications got rid of the hallucinations and headaches, it also helped suppress the truth. The less I hallucinated water rushing and drowning, the more I could pretend . . . "

Deyquan nodded slowly, a cold horror growing in his belly. "The more you could pretend it didn't happen. And like . . . maybe the headaches was the truth. Banging around your skull, trying to get out?"

Andrew nodded thoughtfully. "Maybe. And then I stopped taking my medication a week ago. Could hardly concentrate at work, couldn't wake up in the morning, so I stopped taking it. Before I came in here tonight I threw my last bottle out my truck window. Knew the meds were leaching out of my system, but I threw them out anyway, so when that lady came out of the bathroom, screaming 'she's dead, she's dead,' I thought . . . maybe it was . . . "

"A hallucination?"

"Yes." A swift nod. "Yes. Because I hadn't taken any meds in so long. But it was real. It was. And I wonder. If you keep something inside long enough . . . what happens? What do you grow, inside?"

Deyquan swallowed and tasted something bitter, like bile. "So . . . you been on meds for months, bottling up all the bad things—the headaches and hallucinations—also pretending your son was alive somewhere, not dead. And tonight, you walk in here, med free, and all those bad things come roaring back out cause they been stored up . . . "

"There's a poem," Andrew whispered. "By William Blake. 'The Poison Tree.' About nursing hidden anger. And of it, Blake says: 'I told it not; my wrath did grow.' So all these things inside me . . . have been growing? Into what, I wonder? And then the following couplet reads: 'And I watered it in tears, Night and morning, with my fears.'"

Andrew continued, "It's not my son's ghost or spirit or poltergeist, or whatever. It's something else. Something . . . I think . . . I created."

Deyquan nodded slowly. "Out of your fears and tears and anger and all. All the time, you watering it. Making it big and strong. And now you done with your meds, it's broke out into the real world."

KEVIN LUCIA

"And," Andrew continued, looking at something past Deyquan, "it's *here*."

Rubber soles squeaked on tile.

Deyquan turned.

———— ∽∽ ————

Andrew swallowed at the sight of the little boy stepping from the hall into the waiting area. A part of him wanted to crumple to his knees, fold himself into a weeping ruin, because this boy—this *thing*—standing before him was his son, to the last detail.

Black, straggly hair, still wet from the water park. Thin, slight build, looking younger than his seven years, and dressed the way he'd been the day he died. *Died*. Not taken. Not abducted. But died.

you lost him!

But the boy—the *thing*'s face.

Blank. Slack and empty, its eyes deep pools of swirling nothingness. No humanity glimmered there, no essence of any kind. This wasn't his son. More like a rough copy, an echo.

Or a projection.

i told it not
my wrath did grow

Not his son, or his son's spirit, either.

Andrew straightened, flexed his fingers and stood resolute, determined, because for the first time in a year, he knew what to do. Knew—and accepted—the truth.

But the cost.

Oh God, the cost. These people. Strangers who'd no stake in all of this, dead.

i told it not
my wrath did grow

272

And standing here before him . . . fantastically, impossibly . . . the figment of his wrath made real.

i watered it, in tears
night and morning, with my fears

And he'd watered it, given it sustenance from his fears and tears and repressed anger, until it become a blind raging thing, and when he'd stopped taking the medication . . .

it's broke out into the real world

This thing had trapped them here, killed all these people . . . and it was from *him*.

"You asked me what I was thinking when I looked at the security camera?"

Deyquan nodded, but said nothing, staring at the image of Andrew's wrath, fear and guilt given life. "Tonight I heard from Rachel. She signed the divorce papers. It's over. We got into an argument. Our last, I suppose. Of course she was trying, one last time, to make me see the truth. And I didn't listen . . . "

"C'mon, man," Deyquan murmured. "Shit's hard."

"At the end I asked her what she wanted me to do, if there was one thing she wanted me to do, one last thing, and she told me: Go away. The only way I could make things right was to go away. So . . . "

He looked into the boy's still, empty-abyss eyes.

Reached deep inside.

And sighed as the front doors behind them clicked open. Without looking, he murmured, "You should leave, Deyquan. Because, I think . . . Rachel's right. There is only one solution to all of this."

A strong grip on his elbow.

Deyquan shook him. "Bullshit. You can walk outta this thing with me. So those other folks died. Shit. People die all the time. Deal with your inner whatever, put it to rest . . .

and walk the hell outta here with me. We'll go home; get trashed . . . cry and shit, or whatever. Just don't . . . "

"Deyquan."

Andrew looked at Deyquan, warmed by the concern on his face, and felt himself smile for the first time in a while. "Thanks for trying. But going home and getting drunk and 'moving on' is not going to work. It's too big now. Too late. And it's my fault." He looked back into those depthless black eyes staring at him from the other side of nothing.

"Only one way to put things to rest, now."

go away

"Aw, shit. C'mon, man . . . "

"Go home, Deyquan," Andrew said, more forcibly. "Call your girl. Go home and for Christ's sake, call her. Understand?"

The grip on his elbow released. Though he kept staring at the little boy, he felt Deyquan's presence at his side linger for several more seconds, as if he were groping for one last word. "Shit. White people. Fucking lunatics, y'all are."

But there was no heat there.

Andrew smiled wider. "Don't I know it," he whispered.

"Fuck it. Take care, man. Wherever the hell you going."

Footsteps, moving away. The door opening, then closing with a slam and a click, ringing with finality.

Silence.

No rushing or gurgling water. Only silence.

Andrew took a step toward the thing that looked like his son. It didn't move. Just stood there, motionless, staring back at him with eyes as deep and black as the shadowed mouth of Black Falls River.

One last step.

Then he knelt.

Gently grasped the boy's shoulders. Did something spark in those dead eyes? A flash of recognition, perhaps?

He bent and pulled the slight, wet form close, wrapped his arms around it and closed his eyes.

And then he was falling.

Down a black, twisting, turning slide, water rushing all around, roaring, gurgling, sweeping him along a winding darkness, and not letting go.

Early Friday Morning

" . . . the damage caused by this rain and the resultant flooding has been devastating all along the Eastern Coast and inland. The death toll has reached into the hundreds so far, with untold thousands, perhaps millions of dollars in damage, both business and residential . . . "

Deyquan paced across his small studio apartment, phone pressed to his ear as it rang. The television blared in the background but his nerves were so fried he only heard snatches from it as the phone kept ringing.

"C'mon, baby. Pick up. Pick up the goddamn phone."

" . . . here are pictures from Vestal, New York, where the Wal-Mart in the Town Square Mall was flooded to the ceiling . . . in Pennsylvania, a house swept into the Susquehanna River, crashing against the underside of a bridge along Route 209 in York County . . . "

The phone, ringing.

Deyquan, pacing and muttering. "C'mon, Rosalie. Answer. The Fucking. Phone!"

" . . . and though the flooding here in Adirondack Park hasn't been nearly as severe, we have received our own bit of damage. Also some tragedy, as apparently—

according to Webb County Police and the Sheriff's Department of Clifton Heights—four local people drowned last night in the NYSEG customer service center off Old Barstow Road, which apparently flooded due to extreme run-off from Clifton Mountain. Authorities are not releasing their names at this time . . . "

Deyquan half-turned, facing the television, mouth hanging open, ready to protest loudly, because there'd been *five* when he'd escaped last night, not four. So what happened . . . ?

she told me: go away

The phone clicked on the other end.

And everything else became unimportant.

"Baby! Hey, it's me. Deyquan! You all right? No flooding over there..? No, wait . . . no. Listen. STOP. That's not why I called. Don't care about it, no more. Let's talk, baby. Please.

"Let's talk."

<hr/>

His truck fishtails, tires sliding on the rain-slicked road but he corrects his drift, gently steering into the slide. Slowly his truck recovers and continues forward under a black sky and black stars that pulse and swirl, strangely alive.

He blinks, confused because he doesn't remember starting the truck, pulling out of the parking lot, or turning onto this strange road. He doesn't recognize it, at all. Strange black trees—not Adirondack pines—reach for the sky on either side.

He doesn't know where he is or how he got here. Also doesn't remember exactly what happened to him and certainly doesn't remember ever traveling this winding, dark, tree-crowded road before.

He doesn't remember anything.

He looks down the road, which shimmers black under his headlights, framed by those strange trees, with a glowing yellow double-stripe cleaving the darkness ahead. There's a sign up ahead on the right, and though it looks like the kind seen all through the Adirondacks, he doesn't recognize the name printed on it in gold Copperplate font: *Carcosa.*

Carcosa.

He's never heard of it.

But that doesn't matter because he knows exactly where he's going, regardless of the name.

Home.

ARCANE DELIGHTS

I SLOWLY CLOSE the journal, settle it in my lap and gaze at its black leather-bound cover. I rub its pebbled surface lightly, thinking.

Only stories.

These are only stories. Fantastical stories. A little more fantastical than I usually prefer, though well-written, by someone with a much greater command of the craft than I yet possess. The vivid characterization, meticulous attention to detail and a surreal sense of *place* makes me *want* to believe these stories happened, but I know they *couldn't* have, and am ready to dismiss them as nothing more than fiction . . .

Except for Father Ward's story.

Father Ward, priest at All Saints church and headmaster at All Saints High. Casual childhood friend and more recently: my former boss.

The story depicting his return from military service overseas supposedly took place eight years ago, when I was still teaching at Seton Catholic in Binghamton, so I wasn't around when those events supposedly happened. And by the time I came to All Saints, most of my fellow teachers were newer like me. So during my tenure there I never heard any stories in the faculty room about Father Ward, Savior of a Young Boy Who Was Almost Killed by a Satanist. Also, though I chatted with Father Ward often about his service overseas and how it "tested his faith," a "test" he claims he didn't pass until he came home and faced his "demons" head on, he was never specific about the details.

What was his test, exactly? What "demons" did he face?

The problem I'm having is this: If I allow myself even the *slightest* bit of wiggle room for the veracity of Father Ward's story in this journal, the door is opened wide for all sorts of *other* things.

Like a child-devouring demon named Moloch or Baal. An odd yellow taxi and odder coins bearing a strange design popping up all over town. A ghostly boy maybe born of a man's deep pain and self-loathing. A strange place called Carcosa—with black skies and even blacker stars—where it seems lost people go when they've nowhere else. Someone or something named Hastur (a name which runs cold shivers down my spine even thinking it).

I slide my feet off the desk, stand, set the journal down and start going through the rest of the box's contents, mind whirling. The storm depicted in the journal's last story was the one which ruined Arcane Delights. Four people *did* die that night in the flooded NYSEG center on Barstow Road, though their names escape me at the moment.

Which is odd, isn't it? That I can't remember the names of the only casualties of that storm. Also, I played basketball with a Deyquan at Web Community College before I transferred to Binghamton University. He *had* grown up in Philadelphia. I have no idea what he's doing now. Whether he still lives locally, works for Webb County, or experienced a night of terror during a torrential downpour several years ago.

I have no intention of tracking him down to find out.

Also, my first year at All Saints I taught Vocational English for Seniors. Bobby Maskel was in it. An average student who could've done better if he'd applied himself. I also *remember* a Sandy Clem, a cheerleader. I didn't have her in any of my classes, however.

I have no intention of tracking them down, either.

THROUGH A MIRROR, DARKLY

And there's the minor connection to Cassie Tillman, my newly hired employee. According to the story in this journal, she knew Bobby Maskel. And this town is too small for Lizzie Tillman *not* to be related to Cassie. A cousin, perhaps? An aunt? And did Sandy Clem's father die of congestive heart failure during Cassie's tenure at the Assisted Living Home?

I have no intention of asking her any of these questions. Wouldn't be appropriate of me as her new employer, obviously.

Moving a small bundle of paperbacks—poetry collections, WB Yeats, Robert Frost, Walt Whitman—I notice a rectangular piece of paper the size of a postcard lying at the bottom of the box. I set the poetry collections aside and pick it up.

Of course, I *have* seen several Yellow Cabs patrolling the streets of Clifton Heights. But I've never ridden in one and I don't pay much attention to them. I don't plan on doing so anytime soon, nor am I contemplating a trip out to the old Shelby Road Cemetery or Bassler House, looking for strange symbols on doorknobs.

They're just stories.

That's all.

As I examine the paper rectangle, I *do* think about the power of stories. As a former English teacher, lover of books and fledgling writer myself, I know this truth intimately. I *believe* in the power of stories . . .

But I don't want to believe so much, right now. Maybe I'm even *afraid* to believe.

On the piece of paper two things are written. The first is a quote from *Through the Looking Glass*, by Lewis Carroll. I recognize it immediately.

"'The time has come,'" I whisper, "'to talk of many things.' "

The lines below are poetry, of an unfamiliar origin. But as I read it, a creeping chill coils around my spine, though I have no idea why.

"'The Thing, they whisper, wears a silken mask
Of yellow, whose queer folds appear to hide
A face not of this earth, though none dares ask
just what those features are, which bulge inside.'"

An ominous quiet descends as I trail off. An expectant quiet, as if the lines of the oddly haunting verse are an invocation to . . . something. Or *someone*. Though it's a ridiculous flight of fancy, I stare at the door leading out front, half-expecting someone to walk through at any moment.

A heartbeat passes.

The clock on the wall out front ticks, much louder than it should.

Nothing happens. As, of course, should be expected. What could happen, of course? This is just a scrap of poetry, and these are just stories.

Stories. That's all.

I'm not a coward.

I'm *not*.

Still, I fold the piece of paper and stick it back into the box.

Closing the door behind me and locking it, the early fall sun feels warm and friendly, helping to diminish the chills those crazy stories set loose in my bones. As a reader and writer I of course need solitude, but I also love being with my family. Right now, I want to be with them more than usual. The most haunting thing about those stories . . .

stories, only stories

. . . was the melancholy thread of loneliness running through them. I imagine it's because I've spent the last few hours alone (trying not to think about Dad's Alzheimer's), but I'm desperate to stave off an inexplicable loneliness that nips at my heels as I exit the store. I'm meeting Abby and the kids at The White Lake Inn for dinner. I don't want to waste another second. I want to be there with them, *now*.

Before I can cross the street to my parked car, however, a throaty rumble catches my attention. From up Main Street comes a school bus, of a much older make and model. And though it's only four-thirty and bright and sunny, when the bus passes . . .

I can't see who's driving.

Because it's pitch black, inside.

AUTHOR BIOGRAPHY:

Kevin Lucia is the Reviews Editor for Cemetery Dance Magazine. His short fiction has appeared in several anthologies, and he is the author *of Hiram Grange & The Chosen One*, the short story collection *Things Slip Through* and the novella duet *Devourer of Souls*. He's currently finishing his Creative Writing Masters Degree at Binghamton University, he teaches high school English and lives in Castle Creek, New York with his wife and children. Visit him at: www.kevinlucia.com or add him on Facebook at either www.facebook.com/kblucia or www.facebook.com/authorkevinlucia.

Other Crystal Lake Publishing Collections

Stuck on You and Other Prime Cuts by Jasper Bark

Samurai and Other Stories by William Meikle

Where You Live by Gary McMahon

Things Slip Through by Kevin Lucia

Tricks, Mischief and Mayhem by Daniel I. Russell

Connect with Crystal Lake Publishing

Website (be sure to sign up for our newsletter):
www.crystallakepub.com
Facebook:
www.facebook.com/Crystallakepublishing
Twitter:
https://twitter.com/crystallakepub

With unmatched success over the last two years, Crystal Lake Publishing is quickly becoming the go-to press for Dark Fiction authors and fans. We publish the highest quality Dark Fiction books and poetry collections, which include Horror, Sci-Fi, Fantasy, Thrillers, Suspense, Supernatural, and Noir.

Crystal Lake Publishing puts integrity, honor and respect at the forefront of our operations.

We strive for each book and outreach program that's launched to not only entertain and touch or comment on issues that affect our readers, but also to strengthen and support the Dark Fiction field and its authors.

Not only do we publish authors who are legends in the field and as hardworking as us, but we look for men and women who care about their readers and fellow human beings. We only publish the very best Dark Fiction, and look forward to launching many new careers.

We strive to know each and every one of our readers, while building personal relationships with our authors, reviewers, bloggers, pod-casters, bookstores and libraries.

Crystal Lake Publishing is and will always be a beacon of what passion and dedication, combined with overwhelming teamwork and respect, can accomplish: Unique fiction you can't find anywhere else.

We do not just publish books, we present you worlds within your world, doors within your mind, from talented authors who sacrifice so much for a moment of your time.

This is what we believe in. What we stand for. This will be our legacy.

Welcome to Crystal Lake Publishing.

We hope you enjoyed this title. If so, we'd be grateful if you could leave a review on your blog or any of the other websites and outlets open to book reviews. Reviews are like gold to writers and publishers, since word-of-mouth is and will always be the best way to market a great book. And remember to keep an eye out for more of our books.

THANK YOU FOR PURCHASING THIS BOOK

9 780994 662644